Satan's Devils MC - Next Generation Book #1

COPYRIGHT

Published 2019 by Trish Haill Associates

Copyright Manda Mellett

ISBN: 978-1-912288-54-0

Cover Design by Wicked Smart Designs

Edited and formatted by Maggie Kern at Ms.K Edits

Proof reading by Melanie Farrow at Professional Writing Services

All rights reserved. This book or any portion thereof may not be reproduced or used in any manner whatsoever without the express written permission of the author except for the use of brief quotations in a book reviews.

www.mandamellett.com

Disclaimer

This is a work of fiction. Names, characters, businesses, places, events and incidents are either the products of the author's imagination or used in a fictitious manner. Any resemblance to actual persons, living or dead, or actual events is purely coincidental.

Warning

This book is dark in places and contains content of a sexual, abusive and violent nature. It may not be suitable for persons under the age of 18.

CAST OF CHARACTERS

Officers

Wizard – President

Hawk – Vice President

Hound – Sergeant at Arms

Heart – Secretary

Dollar – Treasurer

Joker – Road Captain

Mouse – Computer Expert

Patched Members

Drummer (ex-Prez)

Wraith (ex-VP)

Peg (ex-Sergeant at Arms)

Blade (ex-enforcer)

Bullet

Lady

Jekyll

Marvel

Rock

Shooter
Truck
Drifter
Truck
Sharp
Roadkill

Prospects

Nathan
Butcher

Old Lady's and Children

Olivia (Hawk's)
Sam (Drummer's): Eli (Hawk) and Zane
Sophie (Wraith's): Olivia, Zoey, Eliza and Hilda
Tash (Blade's): Sabrina and Mason
Darcy (Peg's): Noah (Throttle) and Lisa
Marcia (Heart): Amy, Jacob, Isabel and Alexis
Maya (adopted daughter of Joker and Lady)
Mariana (Mouse): Yiska, Maria and Tanya
Becca (Rock's): Rose and Aidan
Ella (Slick's): Faith
Allie (Truck's): Hope
Carmen (Bullet's)
Sandy (Viper's)

Members who've moved on

Hyde – left the club
Dart – transferred
Beef – transferred
Road - transferred

Deceased Members

Adam

Buster

Tongue

Hank

Viper

Slick

Kidder

Shortass

SATAN'S DEVILS MC

PROLOGUE

Drew

[Drew aged 17, Amy aged 7]

"Hey, squirt. Fancy escaping this joint?"

Amy's little face snaps expectantly toward mine, her stillness suggesting she's holding her breath.

"I'm going to visit the Desert Museum. Wanna tag along?"

Slowly she gets to her feet, her eyes wide. She glances around as if to check that it really is her I'm addressing. When she sees there's no one else there, her eyes widen. "Go to the Desert Museum? With you?"

Fuck, but this little girl gets me in the feels. She's a delight to be around, cheerful, friendly and helpful. So much so I've noticed that Marcia depends on her a lot. With three-year-old twins and a baby just a year old, her stepmom is run ragged. While I expect she'd be horrified if I pointed it out, and it's certainly not my place to do so, Marcia takes advantage of

1

Amy's naturally sunny disposition. An 'Amy can you help me,' or 'Amy, Jacob's crying can you go see to him', or 'Amy, can you tidy the twins' toys up', has Amy leaving what she's doing and happily completing the task. She likes to help and seldom complains or refuses.

I'd first met her when my life changed dramatically two years back. Rather than living in a trailer, existing hand-to-mouth, often going hungry, my older sister and I had come to live among the bikers of the Satan's Devils Motorcycle club. When Mariana married Mouse, all changes were for the better. Important to a growing lad, different to all my years prior, my stomach was always full.

Mariana had looked after me since our mom was taken away when I was just nine, and she only fourteen, but apparently no one knew about the two kids who were left to fend for themselves.

I was born in the United States, conceived as a result of the rape which had caused Mom to flee her home country. Mariana was just four when she had been smuggled over the border. After Mom had been deported, we'd lived under the radar, terrified the same fate was on the horizon for my sister. When Mom had arrived back in Colombia, she'd been dead within months at the hands of our father.

Mariana's now well on the way to achieving her legal status, and that's all thanks to Mouse and his MC brothers. I owe them a debt I doubt I can ever repay.

That I wanted to make restitution was a bone of contention between myself and my sister. I want to prospect next year when I become eighteen, but she doesn't like the notion at all. To her, education is all important. We reached a compromise. Mouse is the technical guru of the MC, and I'd become fascinated with how he searches out information, finding it no matter how many layers it was buried. When he suggested I obtain a degree in computer science, just as he'd done himself, I saw a way to both satisfy Mariana's desire for me to continue my studies, and to pay back the club. I knew I'd eventually end up working with Mouse.

With everything happening, I'd had little time to get out and explore. We'd never had money to go to the local attractions and couldn't afford the school trips, so there are places I've always wanted to see. Now that I'm mobile with my own car, I can visit them myself, and as school's broken up for the summer, I've got some spare time.

"Yeah, squirt. I want to go and would like some company." And that's the honest truth, even if it's only that of a seven-year-old girl.

"She's been before," Heart, her father, says fondly. "She went with the school last year." His lips press together. "She loved it. We should have taken her again, but the twins and Alexis are quite a handful."

I appreciate that. The shit they have to get together before taking Jacob, Isabel and the baby out seems ridiculous, and a good reason they tend to stay on the compound.

"I want to go," Amy cries with excitement, then adds, obviously remembering the lessons drummed into her, "Thank you."

"Well alright then." It's good to bring some fun into her life.

"And get ice cream?"

"We'll see." I glance at Heart, he raises his chin.

Heart's face shows his love for her as he says, "You be good for Drew, Amy."

Amy tugs at my sleeve. "I want to see *all* the animals there. And play in the playhouse, oh, and can I hold a snake? Please, Drew?" Her little face framed by the gorgeous blond locks she got from Crystal, her birth mother, is lit with excitement.

A chuckle comes from my throat. "You want to be a pack-rat, do you? We'll see what we can do."

"You sure you're ready for this?" Heart grins at me. I give him a lift of my chin to show that I am, conveying in that one gesture that he can trust me with her.

"And the monster?" I'm stumped for a moment, but then remember the Gila monster, the venomous lizard which is native around here.

"Whatever you want, sweetheart."

With Amy chattering nonstop from the time we get into my car until we arrive at the Arizona Sonora Desert Museum, I know I made the right choice. Amy deserves some excitement, some dedicated time to her.

I admit to feeling like I'm back to being a kid myself as I let her lead me from exhibit to exhibit, sharing her delight in the animals and reptiles, seeing the wonder through her child's eyes.

"Can I have a pig?" she asks, as we pause at an enclosure.

"They're called javelinas," I correct her.

"Have what?"

"Javelinas," I repeat patiently.

"Well, can I have one? I'd look after it. Can you ask Daddy?"

I chuckle. "What do you think Grunt would make of that, Amy?"

"They could sleep together," she suggests with a stubborn expression. For a second I have an image of a wolfhound-cross and javelina snuggled up together, it makes me laugh. Something I've been doing a lot of today.

"They live outside, Amy, and they smell." I pinch my nose and grimace to make the point, and she sniffs the air.

"Ew," she exclaims as the smell hits her and she realises it's coming from something completely unsuitable to be a pet. Just like that she forgets about her unreasonable demand.

Our day is made complete by the consumption of ice cream. I had a cone myself. If I'm honest, this is the first time in my life I've felt completely free from everything my seventeen years had thrown at me.

So when I return home, Amy so tired she's dozing beside me, it's easy to think this won't be the last time, and we'll go on a few more outings in the future.

~

[Drew aged 19, Amy aged 9]

"That's right. Hold the reins…" I lean over the small pony and position her fingers and thumbs correctly, then I take a firm grip of the lead rein.

"Heels down," I remind her, and click my tongue to get Patch, the elderly eleven-hand pony whose temperament is ideal for teaching a child, plodding sedately forward.

She squeals, half in fear, half in delight, as Patch begins to move.

"How's she doing?" a loud voice calls.

"Look at me, Mouse!"

"I'm watching, sweetheart. You're looking good up there. Straighten your back and let go of the saddle horn now."

"Hey look at that. You're doing great." I encourage her when she bravely does what Mouse said.

Mouse, a great horse lover and rider, had taken over a ramshackle riding stable when the owner retired. That's where the three of us are currently living, and I've learned to find my way around a horse and while my skills are nowhere near Mouse's, I'm not a bad rider myself.

I thought Amy might enjoy meeting the horses and ponies and learning to ride, and I hadn't been wrong.

Two weeks later I'm proud as punch as she trots in a circle around me, and not long after that, she progresses to the more energetic palomino named Sunny who she soon comes to adore. She loves the experience so much she now wants to go to the stables all the time. I compromise, and we end up going weekly.

~

[Drew aged 24, Amy aged 14]

"*I* want to go." She stomps her foot.

"Amy, you can't."

"It's not fair. You're taking Sabrina to the movies, and I want to come too."

Not only do I now possess my Master's in Computer Science, I've completed my prospecting time for the club and have been patched in. With my up-to-date knowledge, Mouse has to admit occasionally, I can make programs behave which have been dancing circles around my brother-in-law, which has earned me a reputation as a computer wiz. It was no surprise really that my road name was settled on as Wizard.

To Amy, I'll always be the youth called Drew who took her out everywhere. Nowadays, she's the only person who calls me by my legal name. Old habits, it seems, are hard to break. I often wonder if it's a way to remind me of our past, before I joined the MC and have more on my plate than entertaining her.

It's hard to accept that our relationship is changing, she's no longer a cute little girl, but a teenager who thinks she's more mature than she is. She can no longer monopolise my free time, and this isn't the first occasion when I've had to turn her down.

How to explain to her that now I want to spend time with a girl, and, a thought I keep to myself, hopefully the night will end up with a good fuck. Of course, since I got my patch I've played with the whores, but am discreet, as we all are in front of the kids. I don't think she looks at me as a man with needs way beyond what she can fulfil.

I glance over at Heart, but he shrugs as if to say I'm on my own. In return, I glare.

Amy's still sweet and helpful, but she's at that age when she's not grown but not a child any longer. She's eyeing me now with narrowed eyes, and when she sees I'm not going to give in, she storms out of the clubhouse.

I heave a sigh, knowing I can't leave it like that, knowing she's upset, not sulking, I run after her.

"Hey, how about we go next week? You and me together, yeah?"

She's stopped so I nudge her. "Just you and me. Be more fun than having Sabrina there."

Her face alights like the sun reappearing from behind the clouds. "Really?"

"Really."

Her eyes brighten, and then she shouts, "I'm going on a date with Drew."

Well, fuck me. That's not what I meant. I go to correct her but find that I can't as she dances around in a circle waving her arms in the air. Love her like this, so innocent, long may she live a life without cares.

[Drew aged 27, Amy aged 17]

"Drew, can I have a word?" I look up to see Amy's father stomping toward me. Inwardly I groan, having every expectation I already know what he's going to say.

"Heart," I breathe out, resigned to this conversation.

He nods toward a table and pulls up a chair, I kick out the one opposite and sit down.

Heart takes a deep breath. "Wizard, you're a fucking good brother to have at my back. But there's ten years between you and Amy…"

"I know, Heart. Believe me, I fuckin' know." Christ, I've started avoiding her. Whenever I enter the clubroom, she's there making a beeline for me. I've noticed the way she hitches up those shorts, showing off long thighs and legs, even thrusting her boobs at me. "I do nothing to encourage her, if that's what you're thinking."

"I know, Wiz, but you and her? Not going to happen. Not in this lifetime. My nightmare is seeing her knocked up and throwing her life away."

I feel my back straightening. "You think I'd fucking do that to her? I'm twenty-seven, man, I'm not a perv who goes after seventeen-year-old girls." Fuck no. It's experienced women whom I prefer, and certainly ones in my age group. But deep down I know that I'm lying to myself and to Heart. Amy's grown from a child into a beautiful young woman and, damn it, I'm just a mortal man. Whoever has red blood running through their veins would find it hard to resist such temptation, but to take advantage would ruin the life she has set out in front of her.

He stares as if he doesn't quite believe me, and that hurts. Although he's right to be suspicious, I can't lose the trust of a brother, I've worked too hard to get where I am. I've been completely honest in what I've said to him, a man of my years doesn't have any business with a teenage girl.

Abruptly standing, he looms over me. "Don't care how the fuck you do it, but you nip it in the bud, Wizard. I'm sick to death of seeing her mooning around after you."

So am I. It gets old fast having to ignore her flirtation all the time, forcing myself not to respond. Whatever's in her head, it's not going to happen. My brow creases for a moment, hating to do anything to hurt her, but, however gently I've tried verbally to set things straight, nothing has worked.

After a moment I move from my chair, going to the bar where Heart is now drinking a beer.

"Look, the only way for her to get it into her head that I'm not interested is to show her. I've tried everything else I can think of, Heart."

He swings around, an eyebrow raised.

"Send her down to the clubhouse later on tonight, on one pretext or another. Up to you how you do that, Brother, but I'll take it from there."

Heart's far from stupid. "You'll let her see you with a whore?"

Sighing deeply, I nod. I don't want to do it for two reasons. One, I know Amy will be hurt, and the second is I prefer my fucking in private, even though the sweet butts don't care. Silky or any one of them would be all up for my cock, anytime, anywhere. It's not as if they haven't been fucked over the pool table many times before. Something's got to get it through to Amy that I'll never see her the way her teenage hormones want me to, to convince her I really am not into little girls.

Well, I've promised and the plan's put into motion, I can't stop this now, despite my misgivings that maybe I should have tried something gentler. Heart plays his part pretending they've run out of beer, and she enters the clubhouse to grab a few bottles just in time to see me thrusting my cock into the sweet butt.

Peering over my shoulder, I see her eyes widening in horror, then, already wiping tears from her eyes, she runs out.

I resist the impulse to run after her, and get off Silky, not into what I'm doing anymore.

~

[Drew coming up 28, Amy coming up 18]

Fuck. I can hear Heart's voice from here. He sounds angry. Walking into the clubhouse I see I was wrong. He's fucking furious.

"You are *not* going to Phoenix and that's final. You're staying here." His hand hits the table.

"They've got a great nursing program, Dad. Look at the curriculum," his daughter offers calmly.

"No."

Thank fuck. Don't want Amy or any of the kids for that matter moving off of the compound. Fuck knows what could happen to them out there.

Unseen by the disagreeing pair, I watch and listen to their altercation with interest, admiring that Amy's trying to approach this reasonably, rather than making it a shouting match. But for all her patiently spoken words, I think with a smile, there's no way she's going to come out the winner. Heart won't let her go. I smile to myself, *she's not going to get what she wants.* Heart's never going to allow her to move off of the compound and live over a hundred miles away where we're not on hand to provide assistance should she get into trouble.

Uh uh. No way.

~

[Drew aged 28, Amy aged 18]

"I'll fuckin' miss you. Anything, anything you need darlin', I'll be there. Anyone gives you any trouble, you let me know." Heart's eyes glisten.

Amy's leaving tomorrow, in the end getting her way, and has enrolled in a nursing program in Phoenix. She successfully wore her parents down, though it had taken some time to do it. Of course the threat that she'd just leave anyway persuaded them to give her independence. I know Heart's hoping she discovers her mistake. All her life she's been surrounded by friends and family, she'll be lost on her own. But she's intent on studying up in Phoenix.

Heart had even asked me to talk to her, but our relationship has soured, and she's only been cold with me since she'd seen me months back with the sweet butt. It had worked, she'd stopped flirting with me. I'd lost the girl who saw me as boyfriend material, which was a decided plus, but I'd also lost my friend, that fun-loving easy-going girl who I'd enjoyed spending time with.

"Hey, Amy, I've got a laptop for you, and here's a brand-new phone with everyone's numbers programmed in."

Hearing Mouse, I grin. Yes, we may have made certain both devices have the latest tracking software programmed into them.

She rolls her eyes as Heart continues rambling on about how he'll come get her if she just says the word. "Dad, I'll be fine. Mouse, thank you."

I fucking hate it. Slamming my beer on the bar, I walk out.

The next morning I wander down to the auto-shop where Amy's getting into Heart's car. Marcia's saying a tearful goodbye as she's not going with them, staying behind with their other kids. I suspect it's because she'll lose it if she went and had to leave Amy alone in a strange place.

Well, I've done what I can, it's up to her now. I've checked out every piece of information I could find about the dorms where she'll be staying and making sure her route to the university won't take her through any neighbourhoods she should avoid. I admit, I was looking for a security flaw or an inherent danger as an excuse that she shouldn't go there, but no, she'd chosen well. I had nothing to give Heart to use to challenge her.

While she's given warm hugs to everyone else, she hasn't said one word of goodbye to me, let alone let me hold her for one final time. It's up to me to make the approach. I walk to the passenger side of the car, place my hand on the roof and lean in through the open door, simply staring at her for a moment as I imprint the image of her on my mind. One final try to leave on good terms. "Goodbye, sweetheart. Remember you can always come home if you don't get along on your own."

She stares back, unsmiling. "I won't be back, *Wizard*," she says, prophetically, then determinedly turns to stare out of the front window.

I straighten my back and stand. Silently wishing her well, while conversely hoping she'll soon come running back, admitting she was wrong.

$\sim$

From then to now…

Amy never returns. Or not for anything other than short visits. In between her semesters, she volunteers at the hospitals *for experience* she says, but I don't think any of us are fooled. The compound is her home no longer and nothing here holds any particular attraction for her.

Me and her? Well, as the years pass, when she does come back, we gradually get into a better place, and can at least talk courteously to each other.

I concentrate on being the best member the MC has ever had, my hard work and dedication paying off when Drummer steps down as prez, and I move to the seat at the head of the table.

I'm Wizard, President of the Satan's Devils MC. The Tucson chapter isn't just a part of the club, it's the mother chapter. Not only did I have to earn the trust of the local brothers, but the respect of all the members, officers and presidents of all our charters. It had been an uphill struggle but I'd succeeded.

Amy? Well, she's made a new life in Phoenix. Like everyone, I was as proud as punch when she got her bachelors, then her masters, and has now become a registered nurse.

On the rare occasions she comes back home she appears happy, and while I prefer to think of her as the sweet little girl I took to the desert museum, she's that no more. Whether it's her profession, or just the natural progression of the years, there's a new earthiness about her and her manner when she jokes with my brothers suggests she's an innocent virgin no more.

CHAPTER ONE

Amy (Age 27)

"*How* are you feeling?" Xander looks at me sideways as he drives down the I-10 toward Tucson. We left Phoenix an hour and a half ago, so we're getting close.

Trouble is, the nearer we get, the more nervous I'm feeling.

"I'm not sure I can do this." I bite my lip.

"You don't need to." His face is tight. "We can still turn around and go home if you prefer."

I don't reply, while inside I want to jump at that option. Missing Christmas at the clubhouse would send out a message I don't want sent.

"Look, your dad's a good man from what you've told me about him, and your stepmom has always had your back. No one's going to hold what happened against you. Don't you think it would be a weight off your mind if you came clean and explained? What happened wasn't your fault, Amy." The last is a statement he's made time and again, but that's not how it feels to me, and not how my family would see it. On the other hand, if they do view it Xander's way, that reaction would have implications.

There are some things you can say to your father, and some things you can't. Especially when he's a member of a one-percenter club. "If I did, Xander, whatever part he thought I'd played, the outcome would be the same. He'd want to sort it out for me."

I think I hear him mumble, *nothing wrong with that.* But I might have misheard. I hope I have.

"Xander, I've only myself to blame—"

"No you have not," he rounds on me before flicking his eyes back to the highway. "Never think that."

I shrug. It was me who'd put myself in the position I had. It's time to change the subject, it's not as though we haven't been having this discussion for the past three months. "Thank you for coming with me. I'm sure you'd have preferred to have spent Christmas with your own family."

He reaches out his hand and rests it momentarily on my thigh. I feel the warmth which is removed before I can react. "You need me," he replies, simply. "They don't."

"I don't deserve you, Xander."

But he's silent and doesn't reply.

We come up to the turning. "Here." I point it out. "After that saguaro that looks like it's waving its arm." As a kid I always thought the ancient cactus was waving to welcome me home or say goodbye depending on whether I was coming or going. Somehow it had survived the wildfire that had swept down from the mountains, hell, it must be more than twenty years back. An event well remembered by my family, my twin brother and sister had been born in the midst of the flames and smoke. Baptised by fire as Dad often says.

He'd also add that it had given them their fiery composition, and he might have a point. I was the quiet one of the family, the obedient little girl. Jacob and Isabel, the complete opposite, had given Heart and Marcia more than one headache over the years. Hard to think they're twenty-one now, legally able to drink. *Where has the time gone?* Dad and Marcia had been luckier with Alexis, my younger sister, nineteen now. She, more like myself, is quiet and thoughtful, possessing no desire for rebellion.

But I had rebelled, I remind myself. Though the decision had been forced upon me, it had turned out to be one of the best moves I'd ever made until three months ago.

"This must be it, now." Xander's been driving slowly up the track that the brothers work hard to maintain, but still seems to attract potholes like a plague. I wince in sympathy for the suspension of his expensive car, but all credit to him, he doesn't say a thing.

"Show time," I say, softly, a rolling feeling in my gut as the gates of the compound come into sight. "Pull up. The prospect doesn't recognise us." Getting out of the car, I raise my hand and waggle my fingers, knowing we're expected, but I can't recall having seen the man who's on guard duty today before. But then, it's been a long time since I last returned.

With a chin lift and cautious stare, the prospect comes to the gate.

"I'm Amy."

He doesn't reply, just presses a button and the big gates slide back on their rails. He waves us to a halt as we enter the compound. When I open my window, he steps to the driver's side. "Cars have to park behind the auto-shop."

I nod. Nothing's changed since I've been gone, except a new man who doesn't understand I was born on the compound and lived here while I was growing up. I indicate where Xander should go, then wait while he gets our bags, and stands easily holding one in each of his strong hands. I know there's no point offering to carry my own.

It's surprisingly quiet as we walk the couple of hundred yards up to the clubhouse. Xander looks around him. "It's peaceful here," he observes. "I'm surprised you ever wanted to leave."

Sometimes, so am I. But I had ambitions and wanted to fulfil them, and I have—making a life for myself up in Phoenix. Of course, there was something else that had made it impossible to stay, but as the years have passed, I barely think of the reason anymore. When I do, it no longer seems important.

As we draw closer, I hear music flooding out from the clubhouse, and despite my misgivings at coming home, my lips curve as I hear the Christmas tunes I've heard every year since I was born. Christ, some of that music must be seventy years old now, but none of the more recent stuff can compete with the old favourites. If I'm not mistaken, I'll find Peg's in charge of the music tonight, and heaven help anyone who tries to take over the controls from him. Another sign things here don't change. It's me that's coming back different. *And broken.*

I pause on the veranda, Xander takes my hand. "Deep breath, Amy, that's right. Take another one. This *is* going to be fine."

I do as he suggests, sucking air deep down into my lungs then exhaling out, then, I do it again. Well before it's the truth, I tell him, "I'm ready."

He pushes the door open and stands back, allowing me to precede him inside.

"Showtime," I repeat under my breath.

When I burst in, a forced grin firmly in place on my face, everyone turns. Knowing what's expected I make straight for the Christmas tree. "Tell me you haven't done it yet?" I sound like a needy child.

"Of course not," Sophie, the old VP's wife rushes forward and is the first to give me a hug. "That's your job, Amy."

"Amy, baby." Up steps my dad, Heart. "Fuckin' glad to see you. Thought you weren't going to make it."

"Sorry, Dad, but it was work. We couldn't come until later today. I had a shift…"

"Well you're here now." He brushes away my excuses and beams as he kisses my forehead. I notice his age is showing, his once blond hair lightening and thinning at the temples, but he keeps it just as long as ever. His face might be creased, but it's still the familiar one of my dad. His eyes go to the man standing behind me and narrow slightly, as Sophie interrupts.

"Can we get this done first, then you can visit together? The kids are impatient to see the tree finished."

The kids, including Olivia, now the new VP Hawk's old lady, are all in their late teens or early to mid-twenties now. Though they might be grown, they're standing around eagerly, just as they do, and have done, every year since they could walk. I notice Zoey and Zane rolling their eyes, as if trying to exclude themselves from Sophie's definition. I suspect we'll all always stay kids in our parents' eyes.

Heart laughs, putting his arm around my stepmother as she eases her way past the assembled bikers and steps up alongside him. She shrugs off his touch to hug me tightly.

"You're home," she states, while her eyes give me a mother's appraisal. I smile brightly and genuinely when she adds, "So get on and do your job."

Twenty-two years ago, Dad had disappeared from the club. He'd returned with Marc by his side, and a snow globe Christmas ornament. It had been the first year we'd ever had a Christmas tree in the clubhouse—that was down to Sophie bringing her British traditions home. Seeing Dad's eyes glisten as normal on this occasion, I know there must be some significance in that ornament, but I'd never asked exactly what. Just that as a child it was me who placed it as the last decoration on that first ever Satan's Devils Christmas tree. From then on, adding the final fixing had always been down to me.

As I have in years past, I take the ornament out of my father's hands, and carefully place it front and centre. While everyone claps and cheers, the snow globe slowly turns in a breeze that I didn't realise was blowing, and I turn to see who's opened the door, but no one has entered. It must have been my imagination.

"Yeah! Happy Christmas, everyone!" Wizard, the prez, bellows out. "Welcome home, Amy, and welcome…?"

"Xander," I introduce him. Though I suspect Wiz already knows exactly who he is. They wouldn't let anyone on the compound without him being fully investigated first. "This is Wizard," I clarify to the man who's now by my side.

"The prez." Xander shakes his hand.

"And you're the heart surgeon." Wiz looks impressed.

Xander's not a man for boasting and simply dismisses his many years of training with a short, "It's just a job, man."

"Hey, big Sis." Jacob and Isabel approach, and it starts a procession of people all wanting to hug and greet me. The men stand back to let the girls approach first. There's Eliza, Hilda, Maya, and Hope, probably easier to say who's missing, and that would be Slick's family who live in Pueblo, Faith, her mother Ella, and Jayden. Slick had died a few years back.

After the kids, the old ladies approach, and then the men start to come over.

The tension which immediately assails me is relieved a little when Xander puts his hand to the middle of my back, and before they can complete their approach, clears his throat and addresses my dad.

"I understand there's a family meal later, can we get our bags dropped off and have a little time to freshen up? It's been a tiring day and a long journey."

Thank you, God. Or, rather, Xander.

"Sure. We've given you a suite, Amy, as everyone else is staying up at the house. Thought you'd like some space to yourselves."

That sounds great, a place where I can unwind and drop my act. "Thanks, Dad."

"Come on, we'll take you up." My stepmother's giving me a scrutiny I'm not sure I like, she might not be my blood mother who I can't even remember, but she's had an uncanny way of being able to read me since she came into my life when I was three—or was it four? Young enough, I barely recall a time she wasn't there. At her visual examination I start to wonder whether coming back for Christmas might have been a mistake. If Dad gets one whiff of what's bothering me, I know he'll go off half-cocked. *Half-cocked? Fully loaded more like.*

I realise being the daughter of a Satan's Devil carries its own complications. They're all protective men, one sniff of trouble and they want to head it off. *Am I that good an actress that I can fool everyone that nothing's wrong?* I have to be. I can't let them know. No one would be able to understand what had happened, and I don't need anyone else to point out that I'd brought it on myself.

It's a mild winter evening with just a slight chill in the air when Xander walks beside me following Dad and Marc past the blocs, each housing pairs of suites occupied by single brothers.

"You're doing great," Xander leans in, speaking quietly. "Just a few more minutes and you can relax."

"Do you think they can tell?" I whisper back.

"Of course not," he reassures me. Though I think that he's wrong. I'm more attuned to my family than he is.

"This is you." Dad comes to a halt. "You've got both suites to yourself. Choose whichever you want." He hands keys over to Xander, making me smile. Yup, that's Dad, thinking a mere female can't open a door.

I hadn't told Dad about bringing Xander until just a few days ago. He's clearly giving us options for different sleeping arrangements, we can use both rooms or just the one. I appreciate his thoughtfulness. I'd been vague about exactly who the man I was bringing with me was, and hadn't given details about our relationship.

"When you've gotten settled come back down," Marc tells me, eagerly. "We'll be eating in about an hour."

"Tell me it's one of Ma's recipes?" I beg.

"Of course." She smiles at me. "Would we ever use anything else?"

Life moves on. I might now be twenty-seven, but some things remain exactly the same. I suppose it's what makes the place home, everything's more familiar than not. It's just me who, this time, is different.

I swear Dad winks at Xander as he walks back down to the clubhouse, the second love of his life by his side.

Yeah right. Got that wrong Dad. And we've been given two suites. Suddenly I worry about the sleeping arrangements tonight.

Gentlemanly, Xander opens the main door, then indicates the two leading off to the left and the right. "Any preference?"

When I shake my head, knowing they'll both be identical, he opens one, and carries both bags inside. Putting them down by the door, he continues over to the patio doors that open onto a balcony with views over the mountain ranges surrounding the Tucson basin. He turns with bemusement in his eyes.

"Christmas at a biker compound, you said. You didn't think it was my thing, you told me. Hell, Amy. This could be a vacation resort."

Now we're alone, I can relax, enough to smile. "That's exactly what it was. It burned out, what, thirty-five years ago? The club bought it up and rebuilt. There's even a swimming pool though it's not warm enough to use now."

"This was where you grew up?" He knows full well it is, so I don't answer the rhetorical question. "Does everyone live in a suite like this?"

"The men without old ladies, yes. But there are several houses at the top of the compound built for families and couples. I lived in Heart's house up there. I expect Eli and Olivia will be building one for themselves now." The corners of my mouth turn down, and I place my hand to my forehead.

Proving how well he knows me, Xander steps closer, but keeping free of my personal space, keeping a comfortable distance between us. "Hey, there's someone out there for you, Amy. I promise you that."

I turn away before he can see the tear forming in my eye. But I should have known better. He never misses a thing.

"You will get through this. You *will* come out the other side." Using gentle fingers with a light pressure, he turns my chin so I face him again, and his dark brown eyes stare into mine. It's hard to break my gaze.

Of course he knows exactly when to push and when to retreat, as he lets his hand drop and his lips curve into a smile. "Why do you and Heart call her Marc, when the others call her Marcia?"

"There's a story about that." I smile, remembering how

Dad and Marc met. He literally wouldn't be alive if he hadn't met her, she'd saved his life more than once. "Marc needed a place to stay after her house was destroyed. Dad was out in California and rang Drummer, who was the prez then, asking to put Marc up in his old house. That's all the club knew. Can you imagine their surprise when a woman turned up, and a cop at that?" Now I chuckle. "They'd stocked Dad's house up with beer and condoms, thinking they were expecting a man."

He chuckles loudly. "What does she prefer to be called?"

"Marcia by the women, but she won't mind whichever name you use."

"Her house was destroyed, you say? What happened?"

I either never knew all the details or hadn't been told. Not unusual if it came under the heading of club business, so I give him the little I knew, while not admitting there's probably more to it. "There was a fire, it burned."

My answer satisfies him. Then he purses his lips for a moment, a sign he's thinking. "Is there anything I should or shouldn't do or say while I'm here? Any protocols? First time I've ever been near a one-percenter motorcycle club."

I give him the only instruction I've heard a thousand times during my life. "Just don't ask questions if you're told something comes under the heading of 'club business'. Oh and don't touch anyone's cut or bike without their permission. They're sacrosanct."

CHAPTER TWO

Heart

"Well she's home, Heart." Marc's hand finds mine as we walk back down to the clubhouse. "You can stop worrying now."

"Can I?" I ask her, my eyes looking unseeing into the distance. "She's not been home for months, and now she turns up with a guy we only heard of a few days ago."

"A guy with a good job and a great reputation. You know Wizard checked him out. An impeccable record, no trouble with the cops…"

I can't help it, I laugh. "You think that would worry us if he'd been arrested? Come on, babe."

She chuckles loudly. "I suppose it might even be a recommendation in your eyes." I get a hard nudge to my arm. "Look, you should be proud of how she's turned out. She's done so well for herself, going to college and becoming a registered nurse, studying hard for all her qualifications and has gotten a great job in Phoenix."

I'd rather she'd taken a position closer, but can't criticise her for wanting to live her own life. While I'd had misgivings when she stepped out on her own, she's thrived, and yes, I do have immense pride for her. As for how much she'd achieved, Marc deserves much of the credit. "You should be proud too, babe. You encouraged her." Not to move away, of course, but to follow her dreams and become a nurse.

"Not as much as Mariana."

Yeah, Mouse's wife, also in the same profession, hadn't hesitated to share her knowledge when she'd found my daughter was interested. Amy had become exactly what she wanted to be, and as I remember, something she'd shown an aptitude in from the start. "Huh, do you remember Amy playing doctors and nurses with the kids in the clubhouse?"

Marc giggles. "I remember having to undo bandages when she'd tied too tight a knot. It was the only time I saw her bossy with the kids."

Amy had been the oldest. Well there was Wizard of course, but he didn't really count. He was always too mature to be called a kid. But then, he'd lived a hard life until he came to us.

My lips thin. "I suppose she's playing doctors and nurses for real now with this Xander."

Another thump to my arm. "She's a grown woman now, Heart. Put that damn shotgun back in the cupboard."

"He hurts her, I'll still get it out," I warn as we near the clubhouse. I put my hand on her arm and stop her forward progress. "You know I've been worried, Amy hasn't been home for months. And there was something, a light in her eyes missing. It was more like she was putting on an act when she entered the club. Do you think everything's right between them?"

"If it's not, she's a big girl. She needs anything from us, all she has to do is ask. You can't keep fixing her life for her, Heart, she's not your little girl anymore. She's an adult, and has to be allowed to make her own mistakes, and rectify them when she does."

Marc's right. But it's hard. I suppose guilt drives some of my concern for her, unable to ever forget the time when I walked out and abandoned her when she was just three years old. Since then I've done everything I can for her. She might not need her dad anymore, but until the day I die, I'll be there for her.

She's an adult, though, and can make her own choices. I grin, I'd noticed she'd come back with yet another tattoo. Nothing wrong with that, just another sign she's not my little Amy anymore.

"Heart?" Now Marc stops me when I start walking again. "See how she is later. No pressure, but maybe you can have a word with her if she still doesn't seem right? She may just be tired. She said she'd come off shift and then had that journey."

I nod. "I'll be having a word with that boyfriend of hers too."

"Really, Heart?" Her eyebrows go to her hairline and back down. "Asking what his intentions are?"

I shrug, unrepentant, as I open the door and step back to let Marc proceed me. "Of course."

"Hey, Heart. Good to see Amy."

Inside the clubhouse, Drummer's standing with Hawk and Zane. I envy him. His oldest son's become the VP of the club, his younger is studying at the university in Tucson and still makes the compound his base. Of all the children of the surviving members, Amy's the only one who's moved away. So far, anyway.

"Yeah. Great to have her back," I answer him.

Drummer's eyes narrow. "She good?"

As always I value my ex-prez's opinion, same as I did

when he was in charge of the gavel in church. "What do you think?"

"She wasn't her normal self." It bothers me he'd also seen it. "Think it's got anything to do with this Xander?"

If it has, he won't be leaving the club. I've got a nice piece of ground with his name already on it up in the forest under Road's trial bike racing track. Road might have transferred out long ago, but that's how we still refer to our burial plot.

"Did it surprise you?"

"What? That he's a big, black fucker?" I shrug. "Don't give a damn as long as he treats Amy right." My eyes narrow. "And the jury's still out on that."

Wraith walks over to join us. He nods at Drummer and his sons. "Nothing much changes, does it? All my kids are helping out in the kitchen."

"Just like all good women should." Peg joins us, a subtle dig that despite trying for a son, Wraith ended up with four girls. "You running along to join them, Marcia?"

Drum and I bark joint laughs at the look on my woman's face.

Marc just winks at him. "Still can beat you on my rat bike, Peg. Don't go forgetting that when you want to prove who's got the bigger balls."

Now I'm chortling at Peg's expression. He's always hated anything that wasn't a Harley, but nowadays has to bite his tongue a lot more. Most of us have moved onto electric models and even mine's a foreign-made bike.

"Hey, men are wanted." I point out to the others. Joker and Lady, Rock, and Bullet have rolled up their shirt sleeves and are moving furniture around. It looks like they could do with some help.

As Marc does indeed disappear in the direction of the

kitchen, I step up and stand by a table. "Where do you want this, Sam?"

As Drummer's old lady organises tables being pulled together to try and fit everyone in sitting down, a marathon task of organisation if there ever was one, the men all step in to help lift and move while Sam sorts the logistics out. It's going to be a big affair tonight, everyone is here for Christmas, brothers, old ladies and all the children.

Amy and Xander appear when we're still in the midst of making some sort of order out of the confusion, and despite my misgivings I'm impressed when Xander immediately too sees what needs doing and starts to pitch in without being asked.

Having done my part, I raise my chin at Drummer and take a moment to have Amy by myself.

"Let's sit down for a minute." I lead her to a couch. "Seems ages since we've chewed the fat. How's life in Phoenix? Everything okay, sweetheart?"

I sit, but Amy doesn't. "Yeah, Dad. Peachy. Look, I better go help, I'm sure Sophie could do with extra hands in the kitchen…"

"With her own four daughters and everyone else, sweetie, there won't be any room in there. Come and talk to your old dad for a moment. It's been months since you've been home."

At last she does. "You're not old, you're only fifty."

I shrug off her observation. There's something in the way she wants to evade a conversation that's making me worried, and I want to get to the bottom of what it is. "Now, how's work going? Your apartment okay? You're not having any more trouble with your landlord?" It had taken ages for her to get some broken plumbing sorted, not so long after I'd had a word. "Has Xander moved in with you, or are you going to move in with him? Or getting somewhere new together?"

"Dad," her eyes roll, "it's early days as yet with Xander."

But she must be serious about him. "You've never brought a boyfriend home for Christmas before."

"He had nowhere else to go, I couldn't leave him alone."

But her eyes shift sideways in a—*I'm not telling the whole truth*—tell. I decide to leave that alone, for now, anyway. Especially when she goes on the offensive.

"You don't have a problem with him, do you, Dad?"

Not pretending to misunderstand her, I cringe at her accusing words, throwing back, "Fuck no. Red, brown, yellow, or fucking purple as long as he treats you right, sweetie. And does he?"

Now there's no looking away. "He does, Dad."

Perhaps their relationship is more significant than she's admitting, and that's the reason she's brought him here. To get my blessing? Is she nervous I won't approve? Well, let's see what the next couple of days hold. Apart from that lack of sparkle in her eyes, he's ticked every box so far. I hadn't missed how gentlemanly he's been to her.

I watch closely, carefully, as the evening continues. Tables set up, buffet style food is brought out. Tomorrow will be our Christmas dinner when we'll eat far too much and probably suffer for it after, so tonight it's tasty but fairly light.

With the whole MC family here, conversation doesn't falter, and the evening becomes raucous as everyone jokes and laughs. I notice Amy start to relax more as her head bows closer, and she giggles at something Maya's telling her.

Joker puts down a slice of pizza he was just about to bite into. "If you're telling her…" he starts warningly.

Lady puts his hand on his husband's arm. "Hey, your fault for leaving my Christmas present where she could find it."

Of course there's a lull in the conversation at that point.

"What the fuck was it, Maya? Don't keep it to yourself," barks Marvel.

"A pack…" she starts, then breaks off seeing her two fathers' eyes narrowed at her. She collapses in laughter.

Amy, showing a spirit that she hasn't up to now, giggles loudly. Maya's probably already told her.

Maya tries again, "A pack, a pack of assorted flavoured lubes."

"What the fuck's wrong with that?" Blade calls out, pulling Tash to him. "Where'd you get it, Joker?"

"Dad!" Mason and Sabrina, Blade and Tash's kids deride as one.

Wraith and Sophie's youngest at thirteen pipes up, her head shaking in confusion, "Flavoured lube? Doesn't lube go on a bike?"

Her question has the result of making Sophie go bright red. Wraith makes a show of covering Hilda's ears while everyone else cracks up.

Jeez. Just another night in the clubhouse. Not that we often have one where everyone's here together at the same time. I risk a sideways glance at Xander to see how the heart surgeon's taking it, but he's leaning casually back on his chair, grinning widely, his hand lazily draped over the back of Amy's seat. Not her, I notice. He seems to be acting politely, not touching her too personally in front of her parents.

Marc notices me watching the pair and leans in. "I suppose soon we'll have a third generation, when the kids start having kids of their own."

I look from Amy back to her. "Fuck no. I'm not ready to be a grandpa."

But I wasn't quiet enough. "Don't worry about me on that score, Dad." Amy's fast, *too fast?* to reassure me.

Has she and Xander decided not to have children? A pity

if so, Amy would make a great mom. *In time,* I add quickly to myself. She's not even thirty. But I look again at her carefully, Crystal and I were both younger than her when she'd come along. Another puzzle piece to ponder. Why's she so adamant she won't have kids?

Christmases have changed, I muse, looking around, regretting how time has passed. Now all our children are at least teenagers, no more stockings are placed under the tree, and the presents are no longer toys which need assembling when the kids are asleep. I knew better how to deal with Amy back then. I smile to myself, remembering her glee and delight when it was time to open stockings and find out what Santa had left.

Once all the food has been eaten, tables are cleared with everyone trying to lend a hand, making me think if less of us helped it would be done in half the time, but hey, tripping over each other is all part of Christmas in the clubhouse.

One of the kids, Peg's son, Noah, hell, he's Throttle now and the enforcer so kid isn't perhaps an appropriate term, but anyway, he puts on some music and the youngsters get up to dance. When a slow song comes on, Joker and Lady sway gently with Maya sandwiched between them, I dance with Amy, while Marc is in Jacob's arms, and Isabel and Alexis make fools of themselves. I notice Xander doesn't take the opportunity to have Amy in his arms, in fact when Wizard approaches her she turns him down, even Zane gets turned away. It slowly dawns on me as the evening progresses, the only man she's danced with has been me, her father.

There are other little things I notice, as the night goes on. Amy goes to the bar but Xander follows her over, a word to her and the prospect, and then she's turning with a glass of water in her hand which I'm certain she hadn't intended to order.

Once again I wonder if I'm reading too much into it, but have to speculate whether Xander is too controlling and taking over her life?

Don't like that thought. Not my independent and have-at-the-world little girl who left at eighteen to move alone to Phoenix.

It's close to midnight and the party is still going on. The lights on the Christmas tree twinkle, the room is filled with laughter and love, but the more I sneak glances at my oldest daughter, the more convinced I become that something isn't right.

A short while later, I watch her walking across the floor, heading in my direction. Xander's walking beside her, close, but not touching as he's been all along. Her head's down, her eyes meeting no ones, her lips aren't curved up. She looks like a clock that's wound down.

"We're heading up to the suite now," Xander speaks for them.

I stand, placing my finger under my daughter's chin, and raising it so I can see into her eyes. Like before, I notice there's no sparkle, no excitement, even though it's Christmas Eve. "You alright, sweetheart?"

"I'm just tired, Dad. My last shift was long and then the drive here…"

Plausible excuses. I decide to shelve my doubts until the morning, she looks tired and not up for further interrogation tonight. So leaning in, I kiss her on the cheek. "Goodnight, sweetie. I'll see you tomorrow." Then to Xander I tell him straight, "I'd appreciate a talk with you in the morning."

He sends me a chin lift. Guess he's been expecting that.

CHAPTER THREE

Xander

*A*ll evening I've been watching Amy, surreptitiously checking in with her, asking discreetly and quietly, "Are you doing okay?" It pains me to see the effort she's making just to keep talking, let alone smiling and laughing. As the night goes on, I see she's relying a little bit too much on alcohol, when she goes to get more, a word in her ear has her reconsidering. The last thing she needs is to lose that little control she has.

I know her father has been watching her with dawning suspicion, and a few of the other men of his generation have been casting her glances of concern and giving frowns in my direction, but mostly I believe she's getting away with the act she's putting on.

I wish I could take this pain from her, I hurt on her behalf. It irks me she can't even relax amongst her family. It seems there's now nowhere where she can let down her guard.

Of course I came here with her. She'd been worrying for weeks, trying to come up with an excuse why she couldn't go home for Christmas, battling with the knowledge of how much her absence would hurt her family and friends. The least I could do is make sure I was here to lend my support. I can balance her or whisk her away if it all gets too much.

I *know*, when no one else does, and she can't admit it.

I *understand* when no one else can.

It's blatantly obvious, trying to act as if everything's normal is taking its toll on her. Just after midnight, I suggest she's had enough. We've stayed long enough, no one will think anything of us departing. When her eyes find mine and she nods gratefully, I know I was right. Politely we take leave of her father. I'm not surprised to receive his threat, worded as a promise, to talk with me tomorrow. If Amy was mine, I'd be wary as well and wanting answers.

"Did I get away with it?" she asks as soon as we enter her suite.

"You did," I reassure her. Doubts that she didn't quite, which is why tomorrow I'll be facing Heart, I keep to myself.

"One more full day, then we'll go home." She sounds as if she can't wait for that moment.

Briefly I close my eyes. I hate that this time she should be enjoying with people who obviously love her is being so marred. She doesn't deserve this, whatever she thinks, but there's no point me telling her. I've tried over and over again to convince her, but she doesn't want to hear it let alone allow herself to believe.

"I'll go get ready." She picks up her bag and disappears into the bathroom.

Patting my pockets, I realise I must have left my phone on the table in the clubhouse. "Amy? Just going back down to get my phone. I'll be straight back."

"Okay."

"I'll be back in moments," I stress.

Christ, I wish I could do more for her, I muse as I stride

quickly down the slope, hating how nervous she is. I reach the clubhouse fast, and go in through the door, then come to an abrupt halt, my lips curving. It seems after our departure, the married men, women and youngsters all went to bed, and the single men have come out to play, out in the open, with women who are scantily clothed. One man's being sucked off, he looks up and gives me a satisfied and totally unashamed wave. Another is fucking a woman on the only available flat surface, the pool table.

A third woman, her top off, is leaning back against the man holding her, while another stands in front, his mouth noisily sucking her tits. Her head is thrown back in pleasure.

I grab my phone, and walk back out into the night, grinning. What I've just seen explains a lot about Amy and how she views sex.

When I return, I've either been as fast as I'd promised, or she's slow, but I'm in time to hear the shower cut off, the toilet flush, and then she comes out demurely dressed in pyjamas and a robe which she discards only as she slides into bed. I don't miss that she looks relieved I'm back.

Knowing how exhausted she is, I make short work of my own ablutions, and soon am lying on the opposite side. Her light's off, mine is still on. I flick the switch plunging the room into darkness.

"Thank you, Xander." She repeats the words she said earlier.

Gritting my teeth and fisting my hands at my sides, now she can't see, I'm at last able to react like I want to. "Goodnight, Amy."

I stay awake until her breathing evens and then follow her into sleep.

She awakes screaming.

"It's okay, it's okay." I make sure to keep my distance from her, comforting her with just my voice. "I'm here, it's me, Xander. You're alright, Amy. You're safe." I can feel her trembling, so violently it's shaking the bed. "Shush, you're safe."

Gradually her shudders begin to lessen. When I can't feel them anymore, I hear her say, "Safe?" Her voice sounds so small it tugs at my heart and hurts.

"Safe," I repeat, as firmly as I can.

"Talk to me," she pleads.

I settle back with my arms behind my head and think how to get her mind off her nightmare. "How does Christmas day work here?"

She's quiet for a moment. Her voice starts weak, but gets stronger as she explains what I should expect. "People exchange gifts in the morning, each family on their own. Then we all accumulate in the clubroom, there'll be gifts for the single men under the tree. Sam, Drummer's wife, usually arranges that. Most of the men and the lady's riding club will be going out on a run after all the presents are open. Dinner will be late afternoon, the normal beef and hams and turkeys."

"Turkey?"

I'm able to hear the fondness in her voice as she enlightens me. "Sophie's British, though her accent's starting to go now. She refuses to have Christmas without turkey and all the trimmings."

She yawns loudly. Wanting her to rest, I ask no more questions. It's not too long before the sound of her breathing changes, and she's asleep. I hope for her sake I'm not disturbed again, but sometimes her nightmares reoccur more than once each night.

I stir in the morning before her and go take a piss before returning to the bed. My moving must have disturbed her, as she's wiping sleep from her eyes when I return.

Still wearing the sweatpants and tee I wore to bed, I lean against the doorjamb leading into the bathroom. "Merry Christmas."

A weak smile, but in return she repeats, "Merry Christmas."

I know we don't have the relationship where we exchange gifts, but I couldn't resist buying something for her, something appropriate for a friend to give. Crossing the room, I reach over into the bag and retrieve the box wrapped in shiny gold paper. Returning to the bed, I hand it to her.

I hope she doesn't feel awkward receiving something from me, it's only a small trinket compared with what I could afford to purchase, but she gives an impish grin, reaches into her purse lying on the floor beside her, and brings out a small box which she passes to me.

Thank fuck I had something for her. It had been touch and go whether I'd buy anything at all.

"You first."

"No, you."

I grin. "Together," I compromise. But though I tear off the paper, I'm watching her as she opens the gift I've given to her. Silver, not gold, so it's not over the top, but it's a chain with a pendant.

"It's beautiful," she says.

"The charm is a Hamsa," I tell her. "At the top is the all-seeing eye. It has various meanings in different parts of the world, but represents inner strength, protection, and good luck. It's always supposed to warn the wearer of evil."

"Too late," she replies, with a tear in her eye.

Reaching out, I touch her hand lightly, knowing I don't want her crying today. "Never too late. You survived."

"Did I?"

"Yes," I say firmly. Then I start to open her gift to me. It's thoughtful, but as mine was, not over the top so its meaning can't be misconstrued. I might be a top surgeon, but when not operating, I wear an earring in one ear. She's given me a new silver stud in the shape of a skull.

"I love it," I tell her. And I do.

"Thought you'd like it as an act of rebellion."

"I'll wear it in staff meetings," I promise her. "It will go down well along with me saying I spent Christmas with an outlaw MC."

She giggles. It's a great sound and I have to force myself to refrain from kissing her. Picking up my bag, I indicate the bathroom. "Just going to get freshened up. Or do you…?"

"You go first. I'll doze for a while."

When I'm showered and dressed, I notice she's sitting up examining the necklace I bought her. I smile. Seems like I've chosen right.

"Want me to put it on for you?"

In reply, she lifts her hair, giving me access to her slender neck. I fasten the clasp for her, seeing it drape beautifully above the rise of her chest.

While she's in the bathroom getting ready, I replace the stud in my ear, grinning a little. It's hard to tell what it is unless you're up close.

"I was going to buy you a heart, but thought that would be a bit girly."

"It's perfect," I tell her. "It will remind me of this walk on the wild side." Not that I've seen anything worse than bikers getting drunk and noisy up to now, ah, mustn't forget seeing them in action late last night. I think it's best I don't let on what I saw, so nodding toward the door, ask, "You ready to face everyone?"

Her teeth worry her lip. "Not really. But I'll try."

I draw in air and let it out in an exasperated sigh. Not at

her, but at what's made her like this. "You'll be fine. They're your family. No one here is going to hurt you, you know that."

"I'm strong. I can do this. I can survive." She repeats the mantra I've made her learn.

"Too damn right."

"Just get today over with, then I can go home."

I press my lips together. Yeah, she can escape, but go back to half a life? I really don't want that for her. But she has made steps forward, I remind myself. Though it might not seem like it to her, she's not the complete mess she'd been three months before. That Amy wouldn't even step out of her apartment.

The clubhouse is full of delicious breakfast smells. Amy seems to follow the aroma of bacon, and we make our way across the room slowly exchanging Christmas greetings along the way. Amy gets approached by everyone, she's seems fine when the women give hugs, relaxed with her father. Then Zane, I think it is, puts his arm around her briefly and she goes tense. When she starts to pale I step up, pulling her into my side and away from an exuberant kid in his early twenties. I can feel her violently trembling, so guide her quickly through the kitchen and on outside to the backyard.

"Christ, Amy." I shake my head. "I didn't realise…"

She bows her head, placing her hands on her knees and breathing deeply. "Thank fuck you got me out. I was starting to go into a panic attack."

"No one," I remind her, sternly, "no one puts a hand on you without your permission. Everyone in there wants a part of you, Amy, it's for you to decide what you want them to have. Not for them, or anyone to just take."

"But they're my family," she protests. "They should be able to hug me without me freaking out."

"Tell them," I say, circling back to my favourite solution.

"Amy, just come clean. You can't go on like this. You've got a whole Christmas dinner to get through. You need support. Tell your dad."

"Tell her dad, what?" I swing around fast to see Heart and the older man called Drummer standing right behind me. Guess Amy's rapid departure from the clubhouse hadn't gone unnoticed.

Amy's slowly walking backward, her hand covering her mouth. Her eyes shooting to me, a wealth of pleading in them.

"Amy?" says Heart. "Sweetheart?"

Another woman pushes past Drummer and runs over to Amy, trying to take her in her arms. I stiffen and start to go over, when Drummer puts his hand on my arm, his fingers curling around and digging in. "Sam was that girl's mom for months. She'll be fine."

I shake off his touch, wanting to make sure for myself so I close the distance between us.

"Do you know what's going on?" Heart's come up behind me. "'Cause I want to know what's up with my little girl. Will someone fuckin' tell me?" His voice is getting loud, and Amy's shrinking into herself.

Ignoring her dad, I speak to her quietly, "Amy? Your dad wants to know what's wrong. I think it's best that they know. Then they can help." If they can understand. If not, we'll leave and I'll take her home. Back to her apartment where I've stayed for three months.

Her eyes flick to mine then behind me to where Heart and Drummer stand, arms folded and waiting for someone to give them an explanation. Suddenly she slumps in Sam's arms. "I can't," she insists.

Heart steps forward, he looks like he's making an effort to control himself, but his voice has become more even. "Whatever it is, Amy, we can sort it. Whatever's happened won't cause us to look at you differently. You're still my daughter and I love you whatever it is."

I see her back straighten and know she's making an effort. She pulls away from Sam. "Everyone will be busy in the kitchen," she tells us with a fake smile. "I'll go and help." She almost runs to get away.

When I start to follow her, Heart holds me back. "You and I," he tells me in a voice that threatens murder should I disagree, "need to talk."

"My office," says Drummer. Then he shakes his head. "Well, Wizard's."

I'm sandwiched between the two of them as I'm marched back into the clubhouse, Drummer pausing only to shout to the prez that he's going to borrow his space. He gets a cheerful wave back. Well, it's Christmas morning and everyone's in a good mood except for me, Amy, and the two men beside me.

Drummer walks in and sits behind the huge desk with a flag carrying their insignia behind it—the devil with a scythe hovering over three demons. It's an enlarged image of what they wear on their patch. If I'm honest, even to a big man like myself, it's intimidating. I don't need the reminder to remember, these men belong to an outlaw MC. Not the sort of people you'd cross.

Heart points me to a chair in front of the desk and takes a second for himself.

"Like old times," he says ruefully to Drummer.

"Like old times," Drummer repeats. Then his eyes sharpen and he gets down to business. "Right, come clean, Xander. We know something's wrong with Amy. I want to know what it is, and what we can do to help."

"And if that involves putting you in the ground, I won't hesitate to do it," growls Heart.

One look at his face shows he's making no idle threat, but he's making it toward the wrong person, what I've got to tell them will hopefully redirect his anger.

"You're fuckin' my daughter, and she's clearly not happy. What the fuck is going on, Xander?" Heart's face is tense.

I press my fingers to my brow, wondering whether it's my story to tell. But I've got to correct at least one assumption. "I'm not fucking her," I tell him, while wishing I was. If only for her sake, as it would prove her recovery.

Heart's eyes widen and he exchanges a look with the man behind the desk. "You're sleeping with her," he accuses. "The prospect tidying up said you only used one bed."

Seems like nothing's a secret here. "Sleeping with her, yes, but not having sex."

"Is that her problem? You won't give it up? You fuckin' gay or something? Not that we give a damn, only as far as it affects Amy."

I huff a mirthless laugh, then look at her father, and give it to him straight. "I sleep with her so I'm there to help her through her nightmares."

CHAPTER FOUR

Heart

On the surface there's not much to dislike about the man sitting in front of me. He's not one of us, he's a civilian through and through which makes me naturally suspicious. On the plus side, he's polite, well mannered, and overtly no threat and apparently a successful man in his field. There's a steel to him though, no doubt about that.

If he's the reason my daughter is unhappy, however pleasant he seems, I'll be carrying out my threat, and he won't be leaving the compound alive, or at least, unscathed.

The words he'd said filter through my brain. *He stays with her because she has nightmares?*

"What nightmares? What's caused them? Has something happened to Amy?" I rattle off the questions I want answered.

"How did you get involved with her?" Drummer asks. He focuses his steel-grey eyes on Xander, and I watch the man squirm. I know exactly how it feels to be subjected to that death stare. "Why are you the one she turned to for help? Okay, so you're a doctor and she's a nurse, but we know you don't even work at the same hospital. Did your paths cross because you're in the same profession?" We know that because of the research Wizard had done.

When Xander takes a moment to respond, I wonder whether he's keeping quiet out of loyalty to her.

"No, we didn't meet through our work," Xander gives an eventual and brief reply which explains nothing at all. His fingers rub his brow. "Look, Heart. You heard what was said outside. *I* think you should know, but Amy is worried it will change what you think of her."

"Nothing will affect my love for my daughter, Xander." I rest my elbows on my knees, clasp my hands, and look at him intently. "What I can't deal with is being left in the dark. Any problem she's got is mine."

Xander nods. It seems he needs a minute, we give it to him.

"She's got PTSD," he says after that moment.

"Sort of gathered that from the panic attack we saw and the nightmares you say she has," Drummer tells him. "What we don't know is why, and what the fuck caused it."

"Or why she didn't come to me," I put in.

Xander glances at Drummer, then at me. "You asked how we met. It's something a daughter wouldn't want her father to know."

"Why the fuck not?" asks Drum.

"How the hell did you cross paths?" I demand.

Xander purses his lips, then admits, "We met because we have a common pursuit. We both attend the same BDSM club."

Oh my fucking God no! I lurch forward getting into Xander's face. "What the fuck are you talking about? What the hell was my daughter doing at a club like that? Someone took fucking advantage of her? *You* hurt her?"

"Whoa, man." Xander holds up his hands as though

fending me off. I notice the already dark skin of his face deepening more. "I'm starting to see why Amy didn't want to tell you." He shakes his head as though regretting he'd opened his mouth. I almost wish he hadn't, I doubt I'll ever rid myself of the unpleasant images he's placed into my mind.

"Quiet, Heart. Amy's an adult, she can do what she wants." Drummer's snapped words attract my eyes. He's trying to send me a message. But it's not his little girl we're talking about. He doesn't know what it's like to have a daughter.

As I turn back to Xander, I feel my face burning. "Which club? What happened? Was it the first time she visited?"

Xander's eyes have narrowed. "Shit." He draws his hands down his face and looks unwilling to say more.

Abruptly I stand. "I'm going to speak to her. Find out what the fuck she was thinking of going to a place like that. Who fucking took her there in the first place? Was it you that suggested she go?" I'll strangle him with my bare hands if it was.

Suddenly Xander's on his feet as well. "You want to hurt your own daughter, Heart? Make her feel worse than she already does? You know fuck all about her life, and it would appear," he sends me a sneer, "fuck all about her and her needs."

"I know everything there is to know about my daughter. Starting with, she'd never go to a place like that. Not of her own volition." My hands start to rise, I'm aiming for his throat.

"Heart!" Drummer snaps in his old presidential tone. "Sit back down," he thunders. "Something's happened to Amy, and we need to hear what it was. You go off, rant and rage at her like you're doing now, how the fuck is that going to help?"

"But Prez… Drummer," I correct quickly, realising old habits die hard. "A pervert must have fuckin' hurt her, if it wasn't Xander himself." I glare at the man in front of me.

"Sit down now!" my ex-prez roars. "Both of you." He waits until we've got our asses back on the seats, then directs his stare at Xander. "Answer the question. How come Amy was in a fuckin' kink club?"

He's faced with two angry bikers staring at him, but he's got himself under control as he says calmly, "I'd left my phone in the clubhouse last night, so I walked back to get it. You know what I walked into? A live porn show. Women dressed, or should I say, undressed, with only one thing on their agenda."

Why the fuck is he telling us this when he should be talking about Amy? "Christ, man, you're talking about the whores. That's what they're there for." I doubt it was a good look for an outsider, but to hell with what he thinks. "What the fuck has that got to do with Amy?"

Xander's forward leaning posture shows that he's going on the offensive. "Amy was brought up in an environment where sex was on tap, pleasure casually given and taken."

"Kids were kept away from all that," I say scornfully, while remembering there was one occasion at least where Amy had not. I often wonder if that's why she left the compound. I push down my guilt, I'd done what I'd had to do, and Wizard had played his part admirably. Too well perhaps.

"And you're accusing us of… what?" Drummer says, eerily calmly. "That we set her up to meet an abusive fuck in a BDSM club?"

"Not at all," Xander refutes fast. "Heart, it might be hard for you to accept, but Amy is far from being a kid anymore, and we both know she's not stupid. From what you just said, you have whores on tap. No, don't get defensive, what I saw was women enjoying themselves." He pauses until I shut my mouth, then looks over the desk. "Drummer, I'm not accusing you of anything. What I'm saying is her background has given Amy a healthy outlook on sex." He shrugs, then continues, "A knowledge that there's pleasure to be had between a man and a woman—or even another woman, or multiple partners come to that. Exploring and having fun sexually was nothing she was, or is, or should be ashamed of." He levels that stare on me. "It might be Christmas morning, but if you even hint to her that what she's been up to is dirty or wrong, then I'm taking her away immediately."

I seethe at his threat. "I'm her father."

"You could hurt her… damage her, with just a few wrongly placed words." He rubs at his temples. "You don't understand her. Oh, I've no doubt you knew her as a child, but she's not been a kid for a very long time. What she does goes to the very heart of her."

"You're saying she's promiscuous?"

I don't like that word. But then Drummer got his name for banging everything in sight before he met Sam, and I wasn't shy myself before I got married for the first time. Xander's right, Amy's been subjected to promiscuity all of her life, why shouldn't it have rubbed off on her? But as I'm thinking maybe I can understand, even if I don't like the idea, Xander stops me with just two words.

"Definitely not." As both sets of eyes land on him, Xander continues, "BDSM clubs are not just about sex, or about sex at all a lot of the time. They are about letting someone be the way they truly are, giving them a safe place to explore not only their sexuality, but their psyche deep down inside, which maybe they normally need to keep hidden from the real world."

Put like that, it almost sounds respectable.

Until he says the next words, "Amy's submissive."

"Amy?" I scoff at him. "Fuck, she grew up bossing the little ones around, do this, do that. She'd stand up for them too. She's no doormat."

"Of course she's not," Xander counters. "But I bet her bossing was to keep them safe, and I would place good money that she helped her stepmom with the chores. Got pleasure from doing things for someone else."

"That about sums her up, Heart." Drummer's steel stare has dialled back from killing mode to maybe just permanently maiming instead.

Amy's man continues, "She's a nurse, and a good one. A typical role for someone who gets satisfaction from serving. Having direction and obeying rules."

Drummer's eyes meet mine, and he says in a dangerous tone, "And what role did you play, at this BDSM club? Where does Amy come in? Was something taken too far?"

It's a fair assumption to make, and I don't really need Xander's hesitant nod to confirm it. What I don't like is the image of him abusing her. I start to open my mouth, but Drummer gets in first.

"So you have fucked her?" He must have been lying when he said he had not.

Xander is adamant. "No. I've never played with her."

"Think you're toying with us. Spit it out, man." Drummer's growing impatient. "Did you or anyone else hurt her?"

Now both hands rub at his temples. "Yes."

"Details, man." I want to know who I'm going to kill, and from the look on his face, Drum does as well.

"Look, it's not my story to tell, but I'd rather this interrogation was directed at me, and not at her. Right now, she wouldn't survive it." He huffs. "I can't actually believe I encouraged her to come to you, seems she was right you'd have difficulty being able to understand."

"Well help us out, man," Drummer impatiently demands.

A quick grin crosses Xander's face. "I'm a Dominant, a Dom, and the excuse for the way you both are acting is that you share some of the same traits." My eyes narrow, and my brow creases. "You're protective to the extent of being overly so, you want to make it right for any of your family who are, or could be, hurt. I'd go so far as to suggest you prefer the controlling role in the bedroom and want to see your women take their pleasure first."

I find myself smirking.

"While a submissive has the desire to serve, a Dom prides himself on control, and that means above all, being in control of himself. A true Dom will never be hot-headed, will never lose his self-control. The safety and pleasure of his sub is paramount. Or should be." His lips narrow, but I don't interrupt, thinking he's getting to the gist of it now. "A huge part of BDSM is about communication. Before any scene, there's a negotiation, and how the scene will progress is agreed upfront."

"Doesn't sound very spontaneous."

"It's not," Xander agrees, "for the most part. And therein lies the safety element, the need for explicit consent. If the Dom is going to request oral sex, either give or receive, agreement is obtained before the fun starts. Same with whipping or flogging, bondage or anything else."

"You've whipped my daughter?" I stiffen.

"I told you, I've never played with her. But I can reassure you, Amy's no masochist, though there would be nothing wrong if she was."

Am I reassured? Fuck yes. I don't give a damn about

whether it's in a club or not, but I'll cut off the hand of any man hurting my daughter.

Xander seems to look at a spot above my head. "The club we go to is a good one, I've been a member for years. I've put in enough time and garnered sufficient respect that I've rights as a master Dom, and, take my turn at being a dungeon monitor. As I said, safety is a priority."

"Has Amy been going to the same club for years?"

His head moves in a negative direction, and his brow furrows. "Maybe for the last twelve months. After she joined, I began to notice her around the club, well, who could miss her, she's a beautiful woman. But as I said, I've never played with her."

"Not your type? Or you hers?"

Now the man shrugs. "Just didn't happen. I already had my established subs."

"She was new to BDSM?"

He chuckles. "Definitely not. She'd been a regular at another club, moved to ours because it has a good reputation." His mouth twists and I realise it probably hadn't lived up to its repute. "I said I was a dungeon monitor. Well, that involves going around, viewing the scenes, and making sure they are all performed safely, and that full consent has been obtained. The club is well equipped and some scenes can be very intense. Obviously the experience can be very sexual, but penetration is not allowed."

I shake my head, revising my opinion. No cocks in cunts? "So Amy didn't go to the club for sex?" I exchange a quick look with Drum.

"BDSM clubs are sexual, but sex isn't what, or all, they're about. They allow a person to be what they want to be, to relax and get out of their heads for a while. With subs, it's subspace where they totally let go, letting someone else take control and drive their pleasure. Doms, well, it's a heady experience to have someone place themselves in your care. I get off on that." He does a quick check to make sure we're keeping up. "In Amy's case, she has a demanding job. One where she has to make decisions, and direct other people, she's got sufficient responsibility where making the right call can be a matter of life or death." He looks up and meets our eyes. "She might be submissive at her core, but she's not when it comes to her daily life."

"But at the club, she can be?" I'm starting to understand. Starting. Not there as yet.

"It's a power exchange. When a submissive like Amy comes into the club, she can leave her worries at the door. For a few hours she can let someone else make all the choices for her. As I said, I didn't play directly with Amy, but I have a lot of experience with subs."

"So you know what type of... what did you call it, play? That Amy was into."

"I think we're entering the area of confidentiality, and I'm not going to cross it." Xander's voice deepens and what I suspect is the Dom, appears. "What she likes and wants is between her and her Dom, and none of anyone else's business. But," he holds up his hand when I go to speak, "I never saw... well, before... I didn't see her submitting to anything other than a light erotic flogging."

I realise I don't want to know. "So leaving aside the specifics, what sort of things would a submissive like Amy go there for?"

"If I was playing with a sub like her, I'd see that she liked to be restrained, maybe blindfolded, then I'd submit her to all sorts of sensations: feathers, a Wartenberg wheel, maybe even a little wax or a violet wand. Whatever I thought would arouse her and get her out of her head, so she can forget everyday life and her concerns for a while."

That doesn't sound much different to how I've played with Marc in the past and have to admit to there being handcuffs kept in my bedside table. Slick, God rest his soul, was more into that sort of thing, having had tips from Rope and Cuff in Vegas, and he hadn't been shy about sharing them. I glance at Drummer who's steadily looking at his clasped hands on the desk and suppress a grin. I reckon Sam probably knows a lot about restraints. I begin to become a little more comfortable with things Amy might have experienced. It isn't as bad as I first had thought.

"You've given us enough background." Drummer pointedly looks at the clock above the door. "Get on with the specifics. What went wrong in this idyllic club of yours?"

A dip and rise of Xander's head shows he's indeed going to get down to business.

"As a dungeon monitor I might not have played with all the subs, but I was aware of them of course. I knew the ones which have masochistic tendencies, and those which had none. I knew the Doms preferences as well, and their skill levels. If I thought a Dom was inexperienced or trying something for the first time, I'd make sure to stay close by to step in if necessary." He breaks off as though the memory is painful, and rubs at his temples again. "When I saw her with Flint, I was surprised. Flint is a sadist, and Amy wasn't into pain. I thought it an odd coupling. Flint had been away from the club for a while, I don't think Amy had met him before." Xander's voice has again deepened, and despite his iron control, a touch of anger comes into it.

"Both Dom and sub would have had negotiations, her consent would have been obtained for whatever he'd planned. As a club strict on safety, Flint had completed our training program before being allowed on the floor. That covers things like basic anatomy. It was unusual for him to target such a sub, but then, he'd been absent a while, and who knows what mood he was in that night. But I decided to keep a close eye on them. I even explained to the other dungeon monitor where my focus was going to be for the next couple of hours. Flint had taken her to a private room, but it had a viewing pane in the door, so that's where I was stationed."

"If you were keeping a close eye on them, what the fuck happened to my daughter?" He's admitting to some sort of failure. How much will determine his punishment to come.

Xander gives a quick shake of his head. "Flint had her restrained, on a bondage table. She was blindfolded. Nothing unusual there."

"Naked?" I ask, gritting my teeth for the answer.

But Xander's glare back shows he's not going to go there.

"What did this Flint do?" Drummer rasps out, sitting forward. Another man might have flinched, but not Xander.

"While I was watching, nothing unexpected. I noticed Flint had clocked me staying nearby and didn't seem pleased about it. But I just put that down to him thinking he was experienced enough to not need a caretaker. Well, to be honest, I didn't give a damn what he was thinking, I just wanted to see a happy and safe sub."

"While you were watching," Drummer snarls grabbing at his words, "you left her? Because this is where you're going, isn't it?"

Again Xander's head rises and falls, and again his already black cheeks seem to darken. "All hell broke loose. I had to leave my post, a woman was screaming. Turns out another Dom was doing knife play. The knife had slipped and the girl was cut." He shrugs. "It happens. Some clubs ban extreme play for that purpose, we don't. She wasn't hurt badly, but shocked. Just needed a few Band-Aids, no hospital visit required, but she'd freaked at the sight of her breast bleeding. I helped the other dungeon monitor calm her down, administered the first aid necessary. Then I went back to the scene I'd been watching."

As his eyes meet mine and harden, I realise I need to try and brace myself for what's coming next.

"When I went back…" his voice falters.

"Fuck." Drummer says, his gaze meeting mine. He stiffens slightly as though realising this is going to be hard hearing.

"What happened to Amy?" I rasp, caring fuck all about the other girl.

He fortifies himself with a deep breath. "When I returned, Amy had been gagged so she was unable to use her safe word or cry out to get help. Unable to prevent him doing whatever the fuck he wanted." He takes a deep breath, steadying himself. "It was only later I knew he'd beaten her with a crop, forced a butt plug inside her."

I forget to breathe.

"He was raping her, despite the rules of the club."

I stand and fly at him, but he's big and fast, and younger. He pushes me back against the wall and capturing my hands holds me prisoner.

"Sit the fuck down, Heart."

"You fuckin' bastard. You left her when you knew something was wrong. It's your fuckin' fault."

"Heart!" Drummer tries to call me off.

"Don't you think I know that? Don't you think I think about that every fucking day?" Xander's a strong motherfucker, he must work out. I struggle but can't get free, all I can do is throw words at him.

"So what are you doing about it? Keeping close so she

doesn't make a complaint? So you're fucking club doesn't get sued?"

"It doesn't work like that," he spits out, and I take some pleasure that he's at last getting riled. I'll take more pleasure when I'm able to do to him just what was done to her, stick a butt plug up his ass and then cut off his fucking dick.

"No." He eyes me, then Drummer. "Like your club, the BDSM community is close-knit. We sort things out our own way. He won't get membership at any decent club that we have contact with. But no, no one sues and we don't involve the authorities. Despite BDSM being around for years now, it's still kink and viewed with suspicion. Cops don't understand, and if he'd said she'd consented, it would have been his word against hers."

"Kicked out of the club? When he hurt my little girl?" I'm beyond angry.

"What did you do when you found her?" Drummer asks, his tone more reasonable than mine.

"She was my concern, I let the other dungeon monitor deal with him. Amy was distraught. I freed her, comforted her. Christ, all other play in the club came to a halt." He's staring at me as though willing me to believe him. "He'd used a condom at least, she refused to go to hospital. But I saw she couldn't be left alone. I took her home, stayed with her. She'd been violated and abused, had her trust taken away in the one place she should have been safe."

"You're still with her," I throw at him, and add sneeringly, "From fuckin' guilt?"

A dismissive shake of his head. "No, not from guilt. Because I care for her. Because I want her to learn to trust again. Because she needs someone to comfort her when she wakes from nightmares most nights. Because she needs someone there for her. Someone who understands and someone who—"

"Someone who…?"

Xander lets me go and turns to face Drummer. "That night, Flint had gone crazy when I dragged him off Amy. The other dungeon monitor took him from me, but as he was taken off, he was screaming that she'd asked for it, and he wasn't going to have her ruin his life. Then, that he'd see her around."

"And has he?" Drummer asks, tersely.

"He's stalking her. Giving her no chance to recover when she keeps seeing him in the places she frequents."

"He make contact with her?"

Xander's voice goes grim. "Flint hasn't done anything that he could be arrested for, but he's been scaring her. He appears at places she goes to and has her phone number."

"She got a new number…" She'd texted me it. It had been a couple of weeks back.

"He found it out."

Every word Xander says is tearing at the heart of me. Amy is mine to protect, why hadn't she come to me? Because she thought I wouldn't approve of the lifestyle she'd chosen. Because yeah, I don't like the thought of my little girl going to such clubs, having sexual encounters with random men. I have to admit Xander's right. If it was her in front of me trying to explain, I'd make everything worse.

Xander's continuing, "She's got so bad, she's terrified to go anywhere on her fucking own. She goes to work, but I make sure she gets there and back safely. If I can't do it because of my shifts, another dungeon monitor who I trust, steps in for me. When she needs to get groceries, she waits for me to get home."

"So this Flint's still a problem."

His face says yes, and his next words chill me. "My fear is that Flint's behaviour will escalate. He must know by now he's banned from other clubs, and he blames her. If he gets hold of her…"

"She's in danger? Why the hell hasn't she gone to the cops?"

"As I've said, there's been no threat, no basis for him to be arrested. Even the phone calls are innocent enquiries as to how she's doing. Flint could say he was a caring Dom wanting to check up on her."

"But he's not."

"He's not. For her to heal, he's got to get out of her life."

"And what have you fuckin' done about that? You say you care about her, why haven't you taken him out?"

Xander takes a deep breath. "I called him, told him to back off. He denied he was doing anything wrong. He said she was imagining things."

"And you left it at that?"

For a moment his eyes close, then he opens them and flexes his hands. "It's not enough, I know that. I'm a heart surgeon, these," he opens his palms, "these are my tools. I save lives, I don't take them. If he approached her while I was there, I'd see him off, and never mind the damage, but he's too clever for that. So I stay by her side, keep her safe. It's all I can do. I'm hoping in time he'll give up and stop. In the meantime I'll do whatever it takes to protect her."

Drummer's staring at Xander. His eyes narrow, and I wonder, if like me, he wonders why Xander hasn't stepped up. But he's a civilian. He might take on this Flint if there was a confrontation, but wouldn't start something, wouldn't approach a man from his rear. Unlike us, who don't play by the rules.

After a moment Drummer slams his fist on the table. "Sounds like a job for us, Brother."

It does. I'm just wondering why the fuck it's taken so long for Amy to ask for our help.

Then I remember, she didn't. It had taken her Dom to stand up for her.

Xander looks from me to Drummer, then, gives a sharp nod. If I could read his thoughts, I'd say he looked relieved.

CHAPTER FIVE

Amy

When I'd left Dad, Drummer and Xander, I hadn't gone to the kitchen as I'd said, fleeing up to the suite instead. I'd paced from side to side, and as the minutes passed and my protector hadn't reappeared, I realised Dad wouldn't have let him go without interrogating him.

Will Xander tell him my secrets?

I know how the Satan's Devils can be. While I doubt they'd use force to get Xander to talk, they won't make it easy for him to refuse. Xander himself thinks they should know. Of course, he can't see anything wrong with our chosen lifestyle, and being a good Dom, is hot on honesty and communication. Hence, his view I should come clean with my dad.

But what woman wants her father to know she's into kink?

He could just say I was raped.

But that's misleading. Facts are, I was there. Until it went wrong, I was an active participant. If I hadn't gone to a BDSM club, it would never have happened. *It shouldn't have happened there.*

What will Dad say?

It shouldn't matter. I'm an adult. I can do what I want. But what child wants to disappoint the people they're loved by?

Will Xander calm him down? Or will Dad try and find Flint? That's the other reason I didn't want to tell him, worried that he'd take matters into his own hands. *What if Dad gets arrested?*

I realise I'm going crazy just waiting here, and to keep up appearances should go down to the clubhouse. It's Christmas morning, and everyone else will be there. But do I still need to pretend I'm okay?

I stand stock still in the centre of the room as I consider the question. Dad will have got as much out of Xander as possible and maybe Drummer's heard too, he always made sure he knew everything that was going on. But will they be so ashamed they won't want anyone else to know? Or do I? Dad's bad enough, but the whole club?

I've grown up with these men, know what they're like, know their sense of humour only too well. It's that that decides me. I definitely don't want to be the butt of any jokes about being tied up or flogged, which I'd risk if they all found out.

Only one thing becomes clear. I need to show my face and keep up the pretence.

Can I go down there without Xander?

Looking down, I see my hands are unsteady. *There's no way Flint could get onto the compound.* I repeat that, then repeat it again, managing to open the door on my second attempt.

It's a hive of activity in the kitchen. There will be over thirty people sitting down to Christmas dinner later on, which means there's a mountain of potatoes to prepare. When I enter, Sam sighs with relief and puts a peeler straight into my hand. She sits me in a corner, out of the way, with a sack of the vegetables beside me.

She couldn't have done anything better. She's given me a mind-numbing task that means I have two choices, stay quiet and think, or join in with the conversation going on around me.

I choose the former, but in the background, the sounds of joking and chattering is a comforting one.

I can only assume the worst, that by now Xander will have spilled the beans, and my father will know exactly what his daughter is up to in her spare time. I can only hope that he won't be too disappointed. These men think women and men behave differently, one rule for them, one for us. While I know Dad was faithful to my mom, then to Marc when she came along, before that I don't doubt he made full use of the club whores. But heaven forbid, women should enjoy putting themselves into a sexual environment moving on from one man to the next.

These men I'd grown up around certainly aren't shy or try to hide that sex makes the club go around. I'd walked in often enough to full-on sexual activities unashamedly going on in the open. As I grew older, their exhibitionism didn't turn me off, but had turned me on.

When a college friend, my roommate, drunkenly pointed out an ad online for a BDSM club, and jokingly suggested we go, I was intrigued. I wasn't a virgin in any sense, but none of the men I'd been with had given me the satisfaction I was seeking.

I decided to do some research before diving in. I'd read up online about what happened in such clubs. I didn't think I'd enjoy being spanked, definitely not whipped, but sensual play? That sounded like fun. The idea of putting myself into the hands of a dominant man was definitely arousing, even just reading about it.

I'd looked up the club my friend had found and then

searched for what I could discover about others. I settled on one that emphasised safety and consent, and which had a play party coming up for newbies to attend.

We'd gone. I hadn't known what to expect, but quickly found I was in my element. The Dom I was paired with was fun, but knew what he was doing, and more to the point, how to arouse me to the point he'd made me come harder than I'd come in my life, and in doing so sent me soaring into subspace, where I was completely and totally relaxed, knowing nothing more until I was coming to in his arms as he provided what I understood was aftercare, gently bringing me back to myself.

My friend, not a natural sub like I found I was, didn't want to return. I, however, had.

I'm submissive, but I'm a confident person, comfortable in my own skin. For the past five years, I've spent at least one night a week being tied up and sensuously tortured. I love it. Even when play means I'm instructed to give service to my Dom, such as massages, I enjoy being told what to do, and bringing him pleasure. In that environment, I can give up all control, and my worries and day-to-day concerns disappear.

Do I want my dad to know that? Of course I don't. I doubt he thinks I'm still naïve and innocent, but knowing I'm sexually active with a variety of men, and that countless members of both sexes have seen me naked? Or, when I do wear clothes, it's fet wear, and worse than that worn by the sweet butts. No, I don't think he'd ever want those visions in his head.

A year ago, I heard about a different club, one more expensive, but hey, I've not much else to spend my money on. So, I joined and loved it, until Flint came along.

I've worked in a number of different wards while I'd been training, and now I give end-of-life care. It's hard, dreadful, when you're doing the little you can for a terminally ill child. That day, we'd lost a young man who'd been in a car accident and had suffered a severe brain injury. A lot of the time he'd been unconscious, but in his lucid moments, I'd talked to him, and found him cocky and amusing, despite his situation. When he'd gone, I'd felt a loss.

I'd needed somewhere I could go and forget, recharge my batteries for the next day, so I'd gone to the club.

That night had started normally enough. A Dom, new to me, had approached and asked if I wanted to play. He was in his thirties, a debonair attitude about him, and not bad looking. I'd said yes, then entered into the negotiation. Giving me no hint of what was to come, Master Flint, as he'd introduced himself, said he wanted to tie me up, and was I into sensual play? It sounded ideal. I've a weakness for the violet wand he was proposing to use, and excited to begin the night, like any good sub, I'd given myself totally over to my Dom.

He'd taken me to a private room, private except for the viewing pane in the door, so I knew our play would be monitored. After all, it's why I'd chosen that club, for their deference awarded to safety.

I allowed myself to be bound. While Flint was tying the velvet ropes, I'd glanced at the door and saw a dungeon monitor observing. *I'm safe.* Once I was blindfolded, my anticipation had started to build, and I felt secure in the knowledge that I could trust this Dom to get me out of my head and forget the young man's death.

The first sign something was different was when a ball gag was forced into my mouth.

I'd waggled my fingers in the safe gesture the club uses when gags are applied, but he hadn't seen. *Stop, I was telling him.* I frantically waved my hand again. Then again.

But he hadn't stopped…

"You want some help?"

I'm dragged out of my thoughts as Sophie sits down. "That's a bloody big pile of spuds to get through." She's also waving a peeler.

Still half lost in the past, I just nod.

"You hear about Olivia and Eli?"

I had. I force myself to speak. "It was always in the cards." I attempt to smile, pushing bad memories behind me. "I think they were meant for each other from the time they were born."

"Yes. It's strange to think of my little girl as an old lady."

She picks up another potato. With two of us we're getting through them faster now.

"Hey, you might be a grandma soon." Starting to relax I feel able to joke.

Her eyes widen. "Fuck that shit. No bloody way. I'm too young."

"Better tell Hawk to keep it wrapped up then."

"What's my son wrapping?" Sam overhears.

"His dick," says Sophie. "Don't want any grandkids anytime soon."

"Grandkids?" Sam stops with her hands on her hips. Then lets loose a chuckle. "Well, I suppose they'll come in time. Just as long," she points her wooden spoon at Sophie, "as they know when to stop, unlike some."

"What can I say? Wraith wanted a boy." She winks at me. "Talking of kids. Let me just go check on Eliza and Hilda, fuck knows they've been quiet too long." Putting down the peeler, she gets up and walks out.

"Teenage girls," Sam laughs. "I swear they're worse than boys." She takes Sophie's place and swaps the spoon for the implement Sophie had been using. For a moment I'm uneasy, knowing she'd witnessed the start of my panic attack earlier, but her warm smile shows she's purposefully keeping the conversation light. "Xander seems a fine man. So caring and attentive. Things serious between the two of you?"

How can I tell her it's all a pretence? How can I tell her there's nothing going on? How do I explain that Xander was the one who I saw as my rescuer that night, and that once he'd taken me home, I hadn't wanted him to leave, and he hadn't? He'd become my protector, the one I leaned on to keep me safe, pushing down he was only doing it out of guilt, that he hadn't stayed watching me. I didn't blame him at all, it hadn't been his fault.

Once Flint started stalking me, Xander had been there, keeping me out of harm's way. How can I tell her he's my safety net? How? When I don't understand what I feel for him myself. Do I like him because he's a Dom? Because he's keeping me out of harm's way? Or, do I feel more? Either way, I don't want him to go. So I settle for, "He's a good friend."

She eyes me carefully, as if she knows there's a hundred things I can't bring myself to say. But having witnessed my freak-out earlier, she doesn't press. All she says is, "Look, I know you've got your stepmom, but I'm here as well if you ever want to talk."

"You're my proxy-mom." I smile, remembering when Drummer and Sam had taken me in when Dad hadn't been able to cope. "Hey, remember that bike you bought me that Christmas?"

"Do I, heck?" she laughs. "Couldn't stop you riding it. You were a right little pest. Insisted on riding it around the club-room. Kept bumping into people's legs."

"It had training wheels on. It was bright red." I show I remember it well. At the time I hadn't understood why Dad had left me as well as my mom who'd had no choice as she'd been killed. Drummer and Sam had anchored me, opened up their home and hearts to a lonely three-year-old girl.

Now I better understand how loss and grief had almost destroyed my father. I haven't been a fully functional adult since the night Flint had raped me.

I don't want to think about him. "What time are they going on their run?" I ask, knowing it's what happens on Christmas day.

"*Our* run," Sam corrects with a wink. "Me, and my crew, Becca, Marcia and Charlotte are going along. And of course, the old ladies up behind their men, most of the kids are as well."

Charlotte is Shooter's old lady. Happened a few years back and yes, she's got the riding bug too.

"We're leaving at noon. The sweet butts will be down later to carry on the prep while we're gone. You want to come along? Jacob's got his own ride now, or you could go up behind Throttle."

I shake my head. "No, I'll stay here." I need to talk to Xander and find out what mood Dad's going to be in, and what exactly he now knows.

"You've reminded me. I left my jacket at the house. Think it's chilly enough I'm going to need it today. I'll see you later, okay?"

As she leaves, I hear a timid voice behind me. "Er, have you seen Mom or Dad?"

I swing around and give a big smile to the meek little Rose. She's far more like her mom than her father. Now she's standing, jacket already on, a helmet swinging from her hand. "No, I haven't seen Rock or Becca. You going on the ride?"

"Duh," she laughs, swinging her helmet.

"Who you riding with?"

"Mom," she replies glumly.

My brow creases. "What's wrong with that?"

"Dad's more fun."

Risk taker Rock probably is, but I can understand him preferring her with Becca.

"Aidan's riding his own bike. Dad won't let me get one."

I grin as she walks off. Any of the women have a fight on their hands when it comes to getting their own bikes. I was surprised when Becca wanted her own and even more so when Rock allowed her. I expect he'll give into Rose in the end, though. I know it won't just be that motorcycles are dangerous, it will be the thought of his sweet little girl riding alone.

"Amy!"

"Allie." I stand and give her a warm smile. "How are you and Truck doing? How's Hope? I haven't had a chance to talk to her properly yet."

Allie rolls her eyes. "She's currently trying to persuade Uncle Drum to take her on the ride on his bike."

"Will she succeed?"

Another look up then down. "Probably. It will be strange though. The first Christmas ride he won't be heading the pack."

Yeah, it was only a few months back that Wizard took his place as president, but I've noticed Drummer's more relaxed since he stepped down. Last night it looked like he was having fun.

"You going with Truck?"

"Of course. You coming?"

"No, I'm staying here with Xander."

It's then we hear the sound of engines revving outside. Allie gives me a wave and runs off.

I might not be in the mood for going along, or being close enough to a man to put my arms around him, but I go to the front of the clubhouse to see them off. It's always a sight watching them go on their Christmas run. Many of the bikes have been decorated with tinsel, and some of the bikers are wearing Santa hats.

"Amy."

"Dad?" At the sound of his voice, I turn, nervous.

"Come here, kid." I take the step needed to get to him and am enveloped in his strong arms. "Amy, it's going to be okay."

"Xander's told you." It's obvious.

"Everything," he murmurs and the tension I feel in his body warns me he might be saying the right platitudes, but what he's heard is not settling easy with him.

Shit.

He pushes me back slightly, holding me at arm's length. Then his hand brushes against my face, a gesture which sends me straight back to when I was a child. "Amy, you'll always be my little girl, but I know you've got your own life. What hurts most is that you're hurting, and I wasn't there to put it right. As for everything else? I know and I don't give a damn what you get up to in your spare time. You're a grown fuckin' woman. You can do naked pole dancing…" he breaks off, studies me carefully, then asks, "What?"

I've gone bright red. Yeah, I might have done exactly that.

"Shit! I did not need that visual in my mind." He shakes his head, but it's not with disapproval.

"You can't have that visual, last time you saw me naked I was about four years old."

"Jeez." He lowers his forehead to rest against mine. Then says more seriously, "You've got a problem, sweetheart. We're going to sort it. Then you won't be scared all the time. You'll be able to start moving on, okay?"

"I don't know. Flint's one problem, Dad, but the rest of it is mine."

He raises his chin at someone behind me. "Look, I'd like to stay here and thrash this out, but I've got to go on the ride. We'll talk when I get back, okay?" Then, with a gentle kiss to my forehead he goes to his bike and starts his engine.

I feel someone come up from my rear. Spinning fast, my heart rate slows down when I see it's Xander. "That's some sight." His head jerks toward the bikes.

Relieved that it's him, I turn back to watch. He's not wrong, it's impressive to see all the club, their old ladies and the women with their own bikes ride out together. The sound is deafening, music to my ears, shooting me straight back to my childhood.

Throttles are twisted, engines revved, even the electric bikes make an artificial roar, then Wizard circles his hand over his head and they start to move off. Hawk and Hound falling in behind their Prez, Dollar and Throttle close on their heels. Then in deference to their previous roles, it's Drummer and Wraith, Peg and Blade, Heart then… I lose track of them. But there at the back, their bikes adorned with rainbow flags are Lady with Maya up behind him, and lastly Joker as road captain bringing up the rear.

CHAPTER SIX

Xander

While I certainly didn't dream of ever stepping foot inside a one-percenter motorcycle club, I'm glad I've come here with Amy. Not just to chase away her nightmares, but seeing how she grew up has given me a deeper insight into her.

Even the meeting with Heart and Drummer had shown me how protective these men are toward their women, not unlike Doms in many ways. As for her freedom about sex, none of the people here seem to be shy. As last night had shown me, she's used to an environment where people aren't scared to show their sexuality, and where women are called property of the men.

Not that those women are pushovers. Like Amy, it would appear, it's just that sometimes they're content to give their control over, particularly sexually.

I've given her three months of my life. Three months where I've spent most of my free time with her, slept with her each night, while keeping my distance and showing my restraint. Like any self-respecting Dom, I take pride in how I can control myself, but like any man, there comes a time when a limit is approached. At that point you either need to walk away, or, take the reins.

Standing behind her as she's engrossed watching her friends and family ride out, I'm quickly calculating what I could do to earn her trust, not just continue as we are, but push her in different ways.

Gently, I rest my hands on her shoulders, feeling encouragement when she doesn't evade my touch. "How are you doing?" I can feel her tension beneath my fingers.

"You told him. My dad knows I'm into kink."

"He didn't criticise you, did he?"

"No, but… He wants to talk when he gets back."

"Amy. That's not about you or your proclivities, it's about Flint."

She's still watching the dust from the bikes swirling in the breeze. "I don't want them to hurt him."

"You need him off your back."

"I don't want to cause trouble for the club."

"I suspect a talk with Heart and Drummer will set him straight." Though I suspect they'll do more than exchange words with him.

There have been many times I've been tempted to do just that, but I'm a renowned surgeon, not a man who lives by his fists. Violence is an abhorrence to me, but I can turn a blind eye in circumstances like these, just can't bring myself to perform the deed. I'd tried talking to Flint, it hadn't worked. I doubt he'd ignore a similar message delivered by the Satan's Devils.

"You think they'll just talk?" she scoffs.

I change the subject, wanting her focus on me, not on what might happen to the man who abused her. I lower my head. "How long will they be gone?"

"A couple of hours."

That's enough. If she's willing to go for it. "How about we go back to the suite, and I'll take your mind off of that upcoming talk with your Dad?"

I've used my Dom voice so she can't mistake what I'm asking. She inhales sharply. *Too much? Too soon?*

Gently I move my hands from her shoulders and touch her arms, lightly wrapping my fingers around her biceps. I pull her back into my body, tiny movements, a calculated risk on my part. I tighten my hold. It's the most she's allowed me since Flint had trapped her.

"I'd never hurt you."

"I know." It comes out as a whine. "I know that, but I can't control my reactions."

"How about you give me control?"

"Why here? Why now?" she says, almost wonderingly.

"Because you're away from Phoenix. You're in a place where you know you are safe. Where men would kill anyone who dared hurt you. I know, because your dad just spelled it out."

A laugh is startled out of her. "Dad threatened you?"

"Yes. So where could you be safer?"

"What if, what if… I can't?"

"One, it's up to me to give you what you need. I'll take it no further. Up to you to set the pace. You know how this works. You can stop it at any time."

"I couldn't stop Flint." There are many things I could say in response to her statement, but I want her to be in the mindset where she'll understand.

"Come." I release her arms, turn her around, and with my hand resting gently in the small of her back, encourage her to move up the incline in the direction of our suite. The almost-there touch that she's become accustomed to over the past few weeks keeping her calm.

I open the door, then step back to allow her to precede me inside.

"What do you want me to do?" She sounds nervous.

I walk around her and go to stand with my back against the far wall. Leaning back, I cross one ankle over the other and fold my arms. "Stop will do as your safe word today. You say that, and our play will cease."

"We're going to play?"

"A short scene." Short will be more than enough.

"Strip for me."

Her eyes meet mine. I give her time to decide. To work through stuff. While I've never played with her myself, I've seen her naked in the club many times. She's also been part of the scene for years, so getting naked in front of someone shouldn't worry her. That it now does is sad, as it shows how vulnerable and exposed she feels.

Just when I'm thinking I'm going to have to call this off, she reaches down and pulls off her lightweight sweater she's wearing. With a quick half smile, she folds it neatly, and lays it on a chair. Next she kicks off her shoes, then removes her jeans. I suck in a deep breath, remembering just how gorgeous she is, as she efficiently takes off her bra and panties.

"Present yourself."

She stands, legs slightly apart, hands clasped behind her back. She's gone rigid. I push away from the wall. Her eyes, wide, watch me until I've moved behind her back.

My fingers lightly rest on her shoulders. "Pull them back." She does. "Good girl." I continue my inspection, touching her briefly in various places, allowing her to get used to the feeling of my hands on her.

"Remember you can use your safe word at any time." She

nods. "You don't need to stay silent. I want to know what you're feeling." I make another circuit, then pause when I'm behind her. "Amy. I want to make you come."

At my words, her breath hitches, and her skin flushes a delightful shade of red. Her body knows what it wants, she's just got to be into it with her head.

"I don't want to disappoint you."

"You won't." I'm certain of that. "You're beautiful," I tell her, moving back around to her front. Gently I run my hands over the sides of her breasts, trailing my fingers down her stomach. Her breath hitches, and even without being touched, her nipples start to bead. Leaning forward, I lick one of those peaks, then huff a breath on it, it hardens more.

"Keep your eyes open." I want her grounded, with me. Not thinking about anyone else, and definitely not Flint.

Her other nipple I take between my finger and thumb, rolling it until it too becomes hard.

Leaning in, I inhale deeply. "I think you're wet for me, pet."

"Yes, Sir. I think I am."

We hadn't discussed etiquette. But I'm easy on whatever she wants to call me.

"I'd like to make you come on my tongue."

"I think I'd like that, Sir."

"You can always tell me to stop." As I remind her, I sink to my knees and with my hands gently holding her hips, position my mouth so I lick her clit.

"I don't think I'll use my safe word right now," she replies in a not too steady tone. I ignore her mild brattiness.

I tap her foot. "Put your foot on my thigh." It allows me more room to work. She does.

"Fuck, pet, you taste so good."

"Tha-nnnk you, Sir."

"Can I make my pet purr, do you think?"

"Ooh, oh. Yes, I think you can."

Oh, I'm certain I can. The one thing about being an experienced Dom is that I know my way around a woman's body. Soon I'm having to grip her hard to keep her balanced on her shaking legs. Her clit is swollen and ready, and her muscles start to tense.

"Can I come?"

"Yes." My voice vibrates against her clit. Perhaps next time I'll make her wait, but now I want to see her let go for the first time in months.

A small cry, and her body folds as aftershocks sweep through it. Standing, I let her balance herself against me as my fingers take over from my tongue, bringing her down gently.

At last, her head relaxes against me.

"Thank you."

"My pleasure."

When she looks at me with half-hooded eyes and a small smile curving her lips, I feel on top of the world. She trusted me enough to let me give her this.

My hardened body accidentally rubs against her, she notices. "Do you want me to do something for you?"

I notice she's tensed. "No. I'll be fine." This isn't tit for tat. This is a Dom pleasuring his sub. This is his sub giving him her power. This is her Dom helping her find her way back.

I pass her, her bra and watch her expertly park her boobs in it, then hold her panties while she rests one hand on my shoulder and delicately lifts first one foot then the other. I pull her sweater over her head, then help her into her jeans, leaving her to pull the tight denim up. The act of dressing her almost more intimate than watching her undress.

There's a comfortable looking chair in the corner of the

room, taking her hand I lead her to it. I sit first, then with a gesture, invite her to sit on my lap. When she does, she leans her head against my chest, right over my heart. Very gently, I wrap my arms around her, a hold so loose, she can easily break free. She snuggles into me.

"I want to be your Dom, Amy."

"I thought you just were." She grins.

"I mean, exclusively." It's a conviction that's been growing on me for weeks and now seems to be the right time to tell her.

"You want me as a permanent sub?" She grimaces slightly. "I'm not ready to go back to that club. Or any club. Maybe I won't ever be."

"Not just at the club. We already live together, I just want us to build on that. Take the next step in our relationship."

"Have sex."

"No, not just sex, Amy. I want you as my submissive."

"I'm not a slave. I'm not always a meek, mild submissive," she warns.

I bark a laugh. "Hate to break it to you, Amy, but I'm not always an even-handed controlled Dom. Sometimes I leave damp towels on the floor of the bathroom."

She sits up and turns to stare into my eyes, and her hands frame each side of my face. "I won't lie, Xander. The girl who ends up with you will be the luckiest in the world. You're smart, good-looking, kind. You're supportive and caring."

I frown. The girl who ends up with me? "Why can't that girl be you, Amy?"

"Because I'm not a sub all the time, and I'm not looking for a full-time Dom. I want a man at my side who's my partner."

"Haven't I been at your side these last three months?"

"From guilt."

I brush her hair back from her face. "At first it was guilt, pet. But now it's because I want to be here. I chose you over my family this Christmas as I couldn't bear to be away from my sub."

She breathes in air sharply. "Really?"

"Really and truly. I want this."

She bites her lip. "You've only seen me at my worst, when I've been so weak and helpless."

I rush to correct her. "Amy, I've seen you so fucking strong. You've suffered something unimaginable, yet are starting to come out the other side. Just look how you gave me your trust just then. That takes strength." I give a little shake of my head. "Submissives aren't weak, they're strong. Willing to take that leap of faith and put themselves into the hands of their Dom."

"What if I never want to be restrained again, even with you?"

"Then we'll find other things to enjoy. And I won't need ropes or handcuffs to keep you in place. You'll do that because you enjoy doing the will of your Dom."

She snuggles back into me again, I relish the feeling of her against me. She toys with the buttons of my button-up shirt. "I suppose you've virtually moved in already, Xander. Wouldn't be too much of a change."

"Except you never know, I might give you my cock now and again." I say it light-heartedly, but don't want to hide my desires from her. It's been getting harder and harder to stop my hands from straying. I haven't wanted to push and have been respecting her boundaries not to touch her.

"You'll be my Dom, I'll be your sub." She sounds a little uncertain.

"Will that be enough for you?"

She's biting her lip. "Is this an arrangement or a relationship?"

I know what I'm capable of, and I won't mislead her. "An arrangement. As for anything else, we'll see where if takes us."

I'm the recipient of an intense stare. Knowing I've laid a lot on her, I cradle the back of her head with my hand. "Just think about it, Amy. I don't need your answer now."

A little nod.

I hope she says yes. I'd enjoy having a sub to come home to, one I know I could be a good Dom too. Amy needs a strong man in her life, and that, for however long it lasts, is what I could be for her.

CHAPTER SEVEN

Heart

I was torn, torn between acting as normal and going out on the Christmas day ride or staying and talking with Amy. I'd have preferred the latter, but that would have sent a loud signal to Marc screaming that something was definitely wrong in the life of the girl who's she's treated as her daughter for almost twenty-four years. I haven't missed a Christmas ride since I was patched in, and my clever wife would suspect I now possessed knowledge of what was the root cause of our eldest daughter's obvious unhappiness. She'd be desperate to know, believing she could help. But this is Amy's secret, one she can share or keep to herself. Fuck, I'm having a hard enough time processing what had gone on and am well able to understand why she tried to keep everything buried.

So to avoid suspicion, I keep to my normal festive routine, satisfying myself with a few quick words so Amy wasn't left scared I'd criticise the path she had chosen.

I am having difficulty processing everything, and hopefully getting some wind in my face will give me time to think how I should approach the fuller conversation with Amy. I'm not blind to my own weaknesses, my temper's quick to ignite, and I tend to jump straight in with both feet. My daughter deserves better than that. Somehow I've got to tamp down the anger of what's happened to her. She's fragile at the moment and could easily misinterpret any rage as fury at her. When I talk to her I've got to be calm and supportive. That will be hard.

My daughter's been raped, for fuck's sake. My hands grip the handlebars hard, and I'm glad Marc's riding her own bike. If she was behind me she'd be able to feel the tension in my body.

I'd left Amy with Xander. The talk Drummer and I had had with him had left me with a sense that he'd do nothing to hurt her, but instead is doing his level best to bring her back to an even keel. While he's not the type of man I'd normally brush shoulders with, I'm now convinced we have a common interest at heart. Amy's happiness.

Will they end up together? If what I've seen is the true man inside him, as a parent I probably couldn't wish for anyone better. A respected man with an incredible job. But it does irk me that he hasn't done more to sort Flint out for her. I, or any of my brothers, would have left her rapist beaten and bloody by now. But perhaps that's just our way, and not that of others.

Still, I think where it's within his abilities, he will protect her. Will he make her happy? That's for her to decide and not me. What concerns me about their potential union is the thought she'll never be returning to the compound except for the brief visits that have become the norm over the years. I'd always hoped she'd eventually get fed up with her life in Phoenix and come home. Nurses can work anywhere, can't they?

In the middle of the Christmas ride out, we stop off to let the old ladies stretch their legs, men to have a piss or just shoot the shit. Which is what it would appear I'm doing with Drummer while Sam and Marc are chatting, standing next to their bikes. But instead of chewing fat, we're having a serious discussion.

"This Flint needs to be taken out," I growl.

"I agree. Need Mouse or Wizard on board to track him down. See what we're dealing with first."

I can't deny that he's right, but I hate the thought of my brothers knowing her story. I glance around, shiver a little and pull my jacket around me. "What do you really think of this BDSM shit, Drum?"

"Each to their own. Xander made a good observation. His description of a dominant personality could describe many of us." His eyes fall on the various couples standing next to their bikes before coming back to meet mine. He waves his hand toward the people he'd been viewing. "Who d'you think wears the trousers in our relationships?"

I can't resist, "Er, Sam?" I deserve the clout around the ear.

"Well, okay, what about Joker and Lady then?"

"If we were putting them into Dom/sub roles?" At his nod of agreement, I continue, "I reckon Lady's the dominant one."

A burst of laughter gets my attention. Looking over I see Wizard slapping Throttle on his back. Hounds doubled up with laughter, and Hawk's watching with his sharp eyes. The younger generation are our equals now. More than that, grown up and leading the club. No denying they earned their officer patches and deserved the votes they got. A new chapter in the life of the Satan's Devils, and with Wizard heading it up, it's a good team who'll be leading us.

Drummer sees where I'm looking. "Suppose we ought to get Prez onside. Let him know what we're up to."

I shake my head. "Wiz would want to know why. It's fuckin' hard for me to understand the lifestyle Amy's chosen, don't really want to bring others into it, or at least limit the number who need to know."

Drummer stares at me for a moment. "Am I hearing you right? You want to do something under the radar? Without the backing of the club?"

"We're a big club now, Drummer. Old members have stepped down, but are still active, young'uns stepped up." Viper and Bullet's crew had to extend the meeting room a few years back. "While I trust all the brothers, this is personal shit. Rather keep it to just a few old hands."

He gives me a considering look, then turns away for a moment. When he turns back, he gives me a sharp nod. "Okay, so you're in the driving seat, Heart. Who d'you want?"

"Mouse, for information. Blade, 'cause he's good at this shit. Peg and… Wraith, of course."

"What you two old'uns plotting?" A hefty slap to my back gets me reeling. I swing around angrily at Blade. "Who you calling old?"

Still adjusting to his new position, no longer being an officer of the club, Drummer often veers between his old role and his new one, and now he slips back into being the prez. In a voice dripping with authority, he snaps, "Need you to come up to the house later, Blade."

The ex-enforcer pulls himself up straight. "Trouble?"

"Some law needs to be laid down."

"Wizard know?"

I shake my head. "Prefer to have a limited team on this." I eye him carefully in case he objects.

"Uh oh." Blade grins widely. "Mutiny in the ranks." But he doesn't sound unhappy about it. "Who else d'you want?"

Drummer rattles off the names we've just agreed on. "We'll get back, take a moment to freshen up then we'll all meet at my house. Sam and the kids will be down at the clubhouse so we'll have some space to ourselves."

I crack my knuckles together. Despite the worry I have for the reason we're doing it, getting the old team back together sounds like it's going to be fun.

A loud whistle gets our attention, and Wizard gets on and starts revving his bike. Drummer and Sam, riding their vintage bikes today, show him how it's done with real petrol engines and the genuine sounds of the exhausts rather than the electronic mimicry of the more modern bikes. As we get back into formation, I settle into my place. I fucking love this life, and wouldn't want anything different. When things go south like they have with Amy, I'm not alone, and have good men at my back.

When we return to the compound, it doesn't take me long before I notice something has changed, and this time, it's an improvement. There's a genuine smile, instead of forced one, on Amy's face, and seeing how Xander's got his arm around her, I think he was probably responsible for putting it in place.

"Amy looks brighter," Marc observes, nudging me in the side. "I like Xander for her."

"Yeah?"

"You don't?" She looks surprised.

"Jury's still out on that."

Marc stares at me, then grins. "I doubt, in your eyes, anyone would be good enough for our daughter."

She's probably right. "I'm going to have a word with her." I kiss Marc and then step away, heading toward the girl who looks so much like her birth mother. That she so resembles her had been hard at first, but now I'm happy Crystal lives on in her daughter. She left something of her behind when she was so cruelly taken from me, from us. And I'll never believe anything other than she sent Marc to save me.

"Dad." As she greets me, the smile slips away, instantly replaced by a cautious expression.

It reminds me I need to choose my words wisely. "Can we talk?"

"You go ahead." Xander places his lips to her forehead, suggesting I'm right. In the two hours we've been gone, something's changed.

"Grab your jacket." I jerk my head toward the picnic tables outside. It's cool, but not cold out, and it gives us the privacy I want.

She sits on one side, I sit on the other. Her arms go around herself.

I give her a long look, then ask her, "Why didn't you come to us?"

She counters with her own question. "How did you react when Xander told you what I do in my spare time?"

I stare down at the bench, suddenly realising the fact that it looks like it needs fresh varnish is more urgent than answering the question she's posed.

"I suspect," she says, her lips curving, "if he wasn't as big, fit, and strong as he is, he might not be standing now."

She'd be right. A quirk of my lips admits it.

I inhale deeply, then dive in. "He did say you were brought up in an environment where you saw people around you sexually active all the time. That that had an effect on you."

"He's right. It showed me sex was perfectly natural, normal and something to be enjoyed. It might have been different had I been raised in another club where women hadn't been treated so well." Her eyes crease. "I'm not saying that pushed me into exploring BDSM, but maybe it didn't make me fear it. It was part of growing up, discovering new things and experimenting. I went to the first club for a giggle with a girlfriend. Found I liked it and went back."

"I don't mind that you have sex—"

"Dad!" she rolls her eyes. "I'm twenty-seven and hate to tell you but it's been a long time since I was a virgin."

I shake my head and make a mock show of covering my ears. "I'm not even going to go there, Amy. What I was going to say, there's a lot of shit that goes on in those places. Just look how you got hurt." Christ, I can't even bear to think about it.

She reaches out and covers my hand with hers. "Dad, what happened to me was not normal. There are safety procedures, though this time they didn't work. It wasn't the club's fault, Flint was just one bad apple."

"Xander says you're still having problems with him." I stare into her eyes, making her look away.

In a small voice that shows me how scared Flint's making her she replies, "Yes."

"We'll make him leave you alone."

"I don't want you to hurt him." Her response comes fast and she sounds adamant.

"Sweetheart, we'll just talk to him. Let him know what he can expect if he doesn't leave you alone." We won't. She doesn't need to know, but we'll do one fuck of a lot more than that.

But even my innocent comment worries her. "Please, Dad, don't make things worse."

"Amy, I'm not going to do anything to hurt you or put you in danger."

She stares back at me with her intelligent eyes. "I know

you wouldn't knowingly, but I've got Xander now. He'll keep me safe."

He will as far as he can, but Flint needs to be taken care of. I drop that topic and raise the subject of the man she's with in its place.

"Is he good to you?" When she nods, I purse my lips. I always had hopes she'd end up with one of the members of the Satan's Devils MC. I'd even harboured the idea she and Wizard would get together, even though I'd played my part in forcing them apart when it wasn't their time. There's a ten year age difference which once seemed too high to climb, but nine years on, well, now I wouldn't mind. Is there still an affection between them? I'd seen his gaze go to her more than once as she grew from a child into a beautiful woman. Just yesterday, his hard prez's eyes had softened when they'd settled on her.

Christ, all those years back when she'd persuaded me to let her go to college in Phoenix, I'd half expected her to come back at any time. Anticipating at the least, she'd find a job in Tucson after she'd gotten her degree. But she hadn't, her visits were sparse even at first. It seemed she'd left us all behind. My last tangible link to Crystal taken away.

She shivers slightly, making me feel an ass for bringing her out here. "Get back inside and warm up."

"What you grinning for?" Her eyes narrow.

"What Beef would say if he were here." I wave up at the sun which is shining down. Though without the blazing heat of the summer months, while cold to us, isn't anywhere near what my brothers in Colorado go through each winter. For us to experience any of the white shit we have to make the trip up to the top of Mount Lemmon.

"He'd say we were a bunch of softies." Attuned to my

wavelength, she laughs, then stands. "I could do with some-thing to warm me up. You coming in, too?"

"Nah. I'll stay out here a moment." I've spied someone who looks like they're coming over for a chat.

"Drew!" Amy says delightedly as she sees him hovering by the back door.

"Amy," he starts, warningly.

She shrugs unrepentant. "Wizard," she corrects. "Or should I bow down, kiss your feet and call you Prez now?"

His hand curls around the back of her neck, pulling her to him and laying a fraternal kiss against her forehead. "You're still a pest," he comments, while I'm noticing she doesn't seem as nervous about him as she does the other men. If anyone else had touched her, she'd have flinched.

Hmm. I had noticed she'd seemed happier since we'd returned from the morning's ride, maybe she feels easier after whatever Xander's said or done to her. Or is it something about the new prez himself? Something to ponder.

"Prez," I greet him though it still seems odd giving him that title. "What can I do for you?"

He gives me a chin lift, then turns around to where Amy's retreating, watching her until she's opened the door and has disappeared from sight. Then, without rushing, he takes out the makings of a joint and starts rolling up. A habit he caught from his brother-in-law. I swear when they're working together, weaving spells on the dark web, you can barely see through the fog in the office.

It's only when he's lit the tip that he allows his eyes to meet mine. "You get to the bottom of why she's like a cat on a hot tin roof, and who that fucker with her is?"

I answer in the affirmative on both counts. "Don't like letting people into her business, so long story short, she ran into a sadistic motherfucker at a club she frequents. Xander has given her the support she's needed ever since."

"Club?"

I shake my head, but his eyes narrow, and then he casually says, "Will take me about zero point four seconds to find out the clubs she has a membership at once I sit down at my tablet."

Knowing he's right, I grit my teeth. Hating I'm giving Amy's secret away, but seeing no other option, I spit out, "A BDSM club."

His eyes widen, and his mouth curves. "Well, fuck. Innocent little Amy into kinky shit. Wouldn't have pegged her for that." Again he swings around and looks back toward the clubhouse, gives a shake of his head then turns back, his face now serious. "I'll keep it to myself, Heart. Don't worry about that. Her secret to tell if she wants it to come out."

I shouldn't have doubted him, but it will take some time before I give him the trust I'd not hesitate to afford Drummer.

"And Xander? He her Dom?"

He certainly knows the terminology. "He's *a* Dom, and I think he wants to be *her* Dom." Maybe he already is, something's altered since we rode out this morning.

"What did the fucker do? Hurt her?" When I nod, he asks lazily, "He still breathing?"

"For now," I tell him, then my own eyes narrow. "I've got this handled, Wiz."

"Like that is it?"

"She's my daughter."

"She's club." Wizard sighs heavily. "Never easy handing over to a new guard, Heart. But at some point, you've got to let Drum off the hook. May not have his experience, but my shoulders are as broad as his."

"I'm not questioning that, Wiz. Drummer's got a soft spot for Amy, she stayed with him while I was away."

"Before my time," he amicably agrees, before slamming his palms on the table between us. "Amy was five when I arrived at the compound, I was fifteen. She was the oldest of the kids after Jayden left to go to Colorado. It was Amy who stepped up to help with the babies and toddlers. You remember the things I did?"

"Took time to play with her."

He raises his chin. "Soon as I could drive and take a passenger, I took her out on trips. We went to the Arizona Sonora Desert Museum numerous times, fuck she loved that place. Took her to Old Tucson, down to Tombstone and watched the shootout at the OK Corral. Took her to the caves and other shit too. Got Mouse to let her ride one of the ponies at the riding stables he and Mariana took over."

He did. He reminds me that I'd felt guilty he was giving her the one-on-one time that with my other three kids and the club, I couldn't. "Marc and I did stuff with her—"

"Not saying you didn't. But wherever you went you had the twins and Alexis."

I feel my own temper rise. "You saying I neglected her?"

"No," he says, "but I saw she needed someone who would give her his full attention. I, too, was little more than a kid. Did me good to do kid stuff with her. Never had that before." His head moves side to side. "You know this, Heart. You know how close we were. Fuck knows why you don't think I'd want to know if there was something wrong in her life."

"Well, now you do. And you can rest easy, I got it handled."

He gives me a stare which comes close to rivalling one of Drummer's.

"Sure you do, Heart. Sure you do."

CHAPTER EIGHT

Amy

The sound of the door to the suite opening makes me jump. But then I relax. There's no way it could be Flint, it will only be Xander.

"BDSM? Really, Amy?"

I swing around with my hand to my mouth. "Dad told you!" I scream accusingly. "How could he?"

"Nah." Wizard steps closer and takes my hand away from my lips. "Well, he did, but only after I told him I could easily find out for myself."

"So am I in for a lecture?" My eyes spark in challenge.

He shrugs. "Your life, what you get up to is your business. For now I want to know what's between you and this Xander. Where is he, by the way?"

"He's gone to get his bag from the car." His toy bag as he wanted to play more later, but I'm not admitting that to Wizard. "And what's between me and him is up to us and nothing to do with you."

He walks to the door that leads out onto the balcony and stares out. I watch him. Drew—*Wizard is his name now, I remind myself*—had been my friend growing up. He'd also been the reason I'd chosen to move away to complete my studies and follow my chosen career. And why at first it was deliberate, then habit, that I hadn't often returned.

I'd first met Drew, *Wizard,* when I was five and he was fifteen. He'd come to the compound, not seeming to be too sure what to do. Of course, I hadn't understood what was going on then. But as often the way over the years, I'd picked up that something was wrong. He was here, his sister wasn't.

It had always been in my nature to help where I could, so of course, when I'd overheard that *Wizard* was worried about Mariana being missing, I'd tried to help, in the only ways I could. Back in those days, it was trying to occupy his mind by me parading my series of toys in front of him.

It seemed while there had been little I could do, he'd appreciated me taking his mind off of whatever problem he was battling with and we'd drawn close. When Mariana had returned, and things had settled back down on the compound, I'd often caught him gazing at me when I was helping my stepmom with the twins, and later my baby sister when she'd been born.

I still remember the day Dr… Wizard had come up to me.

In my memories, in my head, he's always been Drew. Damn it, unless he insists, I can't change how I think of him now, and anyway, he was the boy then, not a president of an MC. As he continues staring out and not speaking, I find myself back in time.

I must have been about seven.

"Hey, squirt. Fancy escaping this joint?" Then he'd added, "I'm going to visit the Desert Museum. Wanna tag along?"

I'd startled and jumped at his voice and then leapt to my feet. Drew's undivided attention for a few hours? Try and stop me. "Yes," I'd cried, then added remembering the lessons drummed into me, "Thank you."

I didn't even care where we were going. It could have been grocery shopping just to have some one-on-one time with the boy/man who intrigued me.

I could barely contain my excitement. I'd been there before on a trip with my school, but to go with Drew? "Can we see the lizards and snakes? And can I play in the playhouse?"

A chuckle had come from his throat. Deeper now, unbeknownst to me at the time, it was a perfectly natural progression of him aging as his voice had completely broken. All I knew is it had seemed to vibrate through my mind.

"You want to be a packrat, do you? We'll see what we can do."

"And get ice cream?"

"We'll see," he said again.

One thing I already loved him for was that most of the men tended to preface my name back then with the word 'little' in front of it. Drew never did, treating me more like an equal than a kid ten years younger.

I hadn't known it at the time, but growing up with Mariana, Drew and his illegal immigrant sister had flown under the radar, and were also dirt poor. He'd never been to the iconic desert museum just outside of Tucson, he'd never been to Tombstone, or spent time in the film studios of Old Tucson. Now independent with his own car, he was making up for lost time. Old habits had died hard, rather than make friends at school, he'd bargained with Mariana that if he got good grades, he could get a motorcycle, and, by giving Heart and Marc time to concentrate on the babies without me under their feet all the time, he was giving back to the Devils who had taken him in.

"One day, I'm going to be a prospect," he'd confided, on one of our trips out.

I'd felt a burst of excitement. That meant Drew would be staying around, even after he'd left school.

But things changed. I started to notice him in different ways as I grew into a teenager, noticing how handsome he was, his body so enticing and muscular, his chest a canvass of artwork as he began to add tattoos. My often made promises that I was going to marry him when I grew up, which had amused him and he'd laughed off while ruffling my hair, I began to keep to myself. My child's dreams turned into more mature ones and I started to believe they could become a reality. I'd sensed my personal time with Drew would come to an end, if he knew how much I wanted to feel his mouth against mine.

My seventeenth birthday had come and gone, and as I was seeing Drew as a man, I wanted to show him I was a woman. So I flirted with him, wore skimpy clothes, not put off when that didn't work. *He just needs time.* One day I was sure he'd notice me, and no longer see me as a little girl.

But he hadn't.

So I took it further, making it obvious what I felt. Gradually he started pulling away, our easy relationship changed for good. Gone were our times alone together, I never went out with him again. He was reserved, no more joking or fooling around, him tickling me or pulling my hair. But still I tried.

One night, Heart sent me down to the clubhouse to grab a couple of bottles of beer. I'd been behind the bar, directly opposite the pool table when I'd seen what he was doing to Silky. Well, it wasn't PG.

In fact, to me, it was downright disgusting. *Drew's fucking? He should have been waiting for me.*

I'd stormed out in a flood of tears, my dreams shattered into so many pieces they could never be put back together again.

Prior to that Drew had been pulling away, and I couldn't understand why, redoubling my efforts to maintain our connection. But from the moment I saw him with the whore our relationship was totally broken. I couldn't bear the sight of him, even a glimpse of him had hurt. It had felt too much like a betrayal.

It hadn't just been a child's crush, I'd been devastated. I'd lost my best friend. I knew I couldn't stay without my heart being broken, so I'd left for Phoenix as soon as I could. There, I found men who didn't say no. And I got over the man who one day I'd thought would be mine forever.

Suddenly the man himself turns. "Want to go for a ride?"

My eyes widen. "On your bike?"

He shrugs, as if it's of no importance. "Yeah."

I'm stunned. These men seem to have a rule, they don't take women on the back of their bike unless they're family or they're going to make them their old lady. But I shouldn't read anything into it. In his eyes, I'm like the little sister he never had.

"Xander will be back soon," I remind him. "A bit rude for me to go and leave him alone."

A sound, suspiciously like a growl, comes from his throat. "We won't be gone long. Thought some wind therapy might be just what you need."

Xander wants me, I know that. As a submissive, I balance out the Dom in him perfectly. He's been so supportive and good, doing everything for me since the incident with Flint. Suddenly I ask myself a question, *Do I love him?*

A voice inside says it's enough to enjoy the thought of serving him. It will settle that uneasiness inside me.

Can Xander really give me what I want from life? Sure, he can give me orgasms, but he hadn't even said it was permanent. What had he called it? An arrangement. It sounds cold when I'm faced with Drew's warmth.

Damn, I shouldn't have come back. Should have stayed

away. There's no way Drew's changed his mind. Nothing's different in that there's still a vast age gap between us, more than that, he's now got far too much responsibility to want an old lady. If I hadn't come home, I'd have been more than happy with Xander, now speaking to Drew is resurrecting dreams I should never have had.

"Come on. You know you want to."

Glancing up, I see Drew's mouth quirking, his hand pushing back his hair. In that instant he looks more like the teenager who first took me out, than the president of an outlaw MC.

Biting my lip I wonder whether I should be doing this. But the day is fine, albeit with a nip in the air, and while going pillion on a motorcycle is far from new to me—I've been on the back of Heart and Marc's bikes since my feet were able to reach the foot pegs—the thought of riding behind Drew holds a certain attraction. *To feel my arms around him, just this once?* It's a chance I can't give up.

"Sorry I took so…" Xander's words trail off.

So intent on wondering whether I should or shouldn't, I didn't even hear the door opening behind me. Now I'm blushing like a child with her hand caught in the cookie jar, and I'm not even sure why.

"…long," he finishes his sentence. He walks forward, politely holding out his hand. "Wizard. We haven't really met as yet."

"No." Wiz draws himself up, and even I can see the persona of the prez as his palm meets with Xander's. "We were at opposite ends of the table last night." Completely unapologetic, and showing no guilt at all, he continues, "Amy and I have always been close. I wanted to check how she was doing."

"She's doing fine," Xander answers for me.

I just turn to him, raising an eyebrow. Not what I'd call it. Better than three months ago, and sure, he's helping me get to a better place, but I'm still far from that destination.

"I also offered to take her for a ride. Isn't much shit that a bit of wind in your hair can't blow away. Amy hasn't been on a bike for some time, and I know how much she'd like to get out."

I can tell Xander is torn. If he protests, he's denying me a pleasure that, as Drew has said, I've loved from when I was a child. I wonder if he's got suspicions about me and Drew? If he has, he can shut them down fast. Drew's made it clear he doesn't want me, pointedly so when I was in my late teens.

"Wizard, do you mind if I have a word with Amy first?"

Now it's Drew put on the spot. He's unable to say that he does. His face remains unreadable, but there's a flare in his eyes. A sign I've seen before which demonstrates there's something he doesn't like.

But all he answers is, "Sure." Then confidently adds, "I'll be waiting down by the bike."

The two men shake hands once again before he leaves, holding on a second or two longer than would be polite. I'm wondering whether it's a test of some sort. Xander's a Dom by nature, and Drew didn't make prez without being a strong and confident man.

The door closes behind him. Xander walks over to me, and I immediately lower my eyes.

"Look at me, Amy." His finger rests gently on my chin as he encourages my face to rise. "Are you comfortable going off with this man?"

"I've known Drew, *Wizard*, since I was five. I grew up with him. He was good to me then, watching out for me. He'd never hurt me now." That's the honest truth. Out of all the men here, possibly with the exception of Xander, Drummer and my dad, he's the one I feel most comfortable with. He'd protected me as a child, saw I needed some me time without the babies around, and gave it to me. He might be the prez now, but in our conversation there were flickers of the connection we once had before he went and destroyed it. One thing I won't admit to Xander or anyone, is that Drew's the reason I left the compound.

Xander stares at me for a moment. "Okay," he breathes at last. "I don't like the thought of you being on the back of a motorcycle. You know only too well what medical staff think of them."

I do. When I worked in ER, I saw a few *motorcycle organ donors* come in from a bad crash, end up with life changing injuries, or even die. I also have to live with the fact my mother was killed and my father almost joined her after their bike was run off the road. It hadn't put Dad off riding, nor prevented him taking me as a passenger as a little girl. His love of bikes greater than his fear of the danger they represented. Some risks you don't take, but it's a thrill, like riding a roller coaster, a bug which gets its hold on you and won't let go. While I know all the sensible reasons for not getting on a two-wheeler, I also know there's nothing better than the freedom and excitement of riding on the back of a bike, being one with the elements, and seeing the scenery up close. It was so much more personal than driving in a car.

"It's Christmas day, Xander. There won't be much traffic around, and Drew is a safe rider, he's ridden for years." Coming up on twenty if my memory's right. I nibble at my lip then tell him, "But if you really don't want me to go..."

"I'd be selfish denying you a pleasure that I can't give you myself. You go, Amy." He pulls my head back by taking a firm grasp of my hair. "Later tonight we'll continue the conversation we started earlier."

I shiver, by which he means he wants an answer to his question. Wants me to agree to becoming this dominant man's submissive.

That's what I want too. Isn't it?

I grab a jacket and walk out of the suite, at first head down, then I feel a bubble of excitement growing inside of me. I'll be riding with Drew, a first. Suddenly I itch to experience my arms around him, a dream I'd had before everything came crashing down. Of course, all that's behind me now, but for just one moment maybe I can allow myself to pretend it all turned out as I originally desired.

CHAPTER NINE

Amy

As promised, Drew is waiting for me by his motorcycle. He's polishing his bike, or at least, as I can see from the distance, wiping off a speck of dust that had dared land on it. As if he can sense me coming, he turns and stands, leaning back against his bike, his arms folded across his chest, and a smirk on his face.

God but he's handsome. If anything, he's grown into his skin over the years. At thirty-seven he now looks like he's entering his prime.

It seems he's not going to waste time. He walks his bike out of the parking space, then, holding it upright, jerks his head toward me.

When he passes me a helmet, I place it on my head and buckle the strap, knowing there's no point in admonishing him for not wearing one himself. Then, with one hand on his shoulder, I sling my leg over the pillion seat, muscle memory taking over, even though it's been years since I've been for a ride. Suddenly nervous, I place my hands on the sissy bars, getting ready to hold on tight.

He tsks, then reaches back, his hands closing around each of mine, and then my arms are pulled tightly around his waist. Confident in his knowledge I'm an experienced passenger, he says nothing as he starts the engine and heads down the track. The gates open automatically, I presume there's some sort of remote control on his bike, and then we're out. I breathe deeply as we turn onto the I-10.

Coming home had been hard carrying so much baggage with me. Knowing at least some of the men here now knew more about me than I ever wanted them to know, and that Xander had shared the details of the worst night of my life, had opened the wounds once again. It had been as difficult as I'd expected it to be, so to have a reprieve if only for a short while is welcome.

As I expected, traffic is light, and there are no holdups as we make our way along familiar roads. I notice new estates, which have sprung up since I was a child, and a large store which I thought would be there forever, closed down. The changes strike me as sad, and a sign the years are passing. A world I'd willingly left behind was moving on without me.

After half an hour, Drew turns down a familiar track, and I realise he's taking me to the stables that Mouse has owned for twenty years now. He'd taken it over when the old man who used to run it retired. Mariana, Mouse and their children live here now. I remember it had been Drew's home too, from the time his sister and the computer guru married until he'd become a prospect and moved to the compound.

It's quiet and peaceful. Drew pulls up in the now paved parking lot and taps on my leg.

Mouse, his wife and their children will all be at the compound. The horses aren't left unsupervised though, there's a couple of hired hands I can see mucking out. I remember Mouse taking on people to help as he couldn't dedicate his time to the place full-time, he was too useful on the compound. But he and Mariana had built a new house, replacing the ramshackle building that the previous owner had lived in.

"Come." Drew holds out his hand. With his other he gives a wave to the hands who give us just a cursory look and a nod. First, he leads me into a barn and leans over a food bin, coming out with some carrots in his hands.

I grin widely. As a young girl I'd loved feeding the horses and doing so now takes me back in time. In my head, Drew's not an MC prez, he's just the friend that I'd grown up with. He was the one who'd taught me to ride.

"It's years since I've been on a horse, Drew," I observe, breathing in that smell that's unique to a stable yard.

"When are you going to start using my road name?" he asks with a boyish grin.

"You'll always be Drew to me," I remark, challenging him with my eyes. "Is it really that important to you?"

He's quiet for a moment, thinking, before he seriously replies, "If it was anyone else, I'd give them a beatdown. Disrespect shown, punishment dealt. But you? Nah. As long as you're not calling me an asshole, you can call me what you like."

"And if I call you an asshole?" I can't resist finding out.

"Then I'd spank you." His eyes sparkle, and I notice he looks and sounds relaxed, but moves quickly on. "Come, let's give the horses their Christmas treat."

Still holding fast to my hand, he takes me past each stall. Some horses I remember, some, he tells me, had reached the end of their lives, including Patch, the plodding pony on whom I'd learned to ride. I remember the whole family had been heartbroken when Niyol, Mouse's stallion, had died.

"Sunny?" I ask him. She'd been a palomino pony, my next

step up. She was gentle with the children, but younger and livelier than Patch.

"Here." He leads me to a stall.

My eyes open wide when I see she's still here. "How old is she now?"

"Thirty-four," he tells me proudly. "Retired now, but Mouse will give her a home as long as she lives."

As I feed her an extra carrot, one of the hands calls out, "She's due for turnout."

"We'll take her," Drew shouts back. Expertly he puts a halter on her, and old as she is, she still does a little prance, anticipating her freedom.

"Want to take her?"

I do. Leading her to the field, waiting while Drew opens the gate, taking her inside, undoing the halter and freeing her seems to loosen something within me. Watching her trot away in search of a good place to graze, my worries subside. I feel tranquil for the first time since I was broken, and possibly for a long time before that.

Standing next to each other in a comfortable silence, I rest my arms on the railings and just watch the pony munching.

"I hate that you live so far away," Drew says at last.

"Why?"

"Because you're not here. And that's where I want you to be, right here at my side."

I'm really not sure what he means with his pronouncement until he turns me to face him and I see heat in his eyes.

"I wouldn't be saying anything if it weren't for the fact that I'm scared I'm going to lose you to that fucker who came with you."

How can you lose something you've never had? Or does he just mean as a friend? Yeah, that must be it.

As my eyes show my confusion, Drew continues, "When

you left, I was having inappropriate feelings toward you. You were seventeen, I'm ten years older. Seemed like far too much of a gap. I felt a pervert for my thoughts toward you."

He'd had thoughts about me?

I don't trust myself to say anything.

"I knew you had a crush on me." He looks over at the pony, then to the next field where some horses are kicking up their heels. "I didn't feel I could admit to feeling the same way. Well, I couldn't. Heart would have killed me."

My eyes widen. "You certainly didn't show it," I say, tightly.

"Oh, your Dad saw the way the wind was blowing and told me to put an end to it. He said you needed a chance to be you and to follow your dreams of becoming a nurse. I understood, it wasn't unlike Mariana making sure I finished my education before doing anything else. Christ, Amy, you weren't even of the age of consent."

"You didn't look like you cared much about me when you fucked that whore."

"I knew you were there," he admits. "But never dreamed of the result. You barely spoke to me from then on until you went to Phoenix."

He's being frank, I'm equally so. "You broke my heart, Drew."

His lips quirk. "You know? I like that I'm Drew to you." He muses for a moment, then says, "I like that balance. To everyone else I'm Wizard, have been since I patched in. Christ, that was fifteen years back. Until you came back, I'd almost forgotten who I was. You calling me Drew reminds me I'm a man and not just the prez with responsibilities."

"You've done well," I tell him, giving credit where it's due. To rise through the ranks in an MC, to be voted into the top spot by all members is no small achievement.

"The MC saved Mariana, and myself," he tells me bluntly. "We both could have died were it not for their help. Such a big debt owed, I wanted to give something back. So I prospected and became a member." His face tightens. "When you went away, I was lost, adrift, made to re-evaluate my life. I fucked up, Amy, I admit it. I'd lost my friend and realised I'd lost the girl worth waiting for. All I could do was throw myself into the MC. I aimed at becoming an officer when the old regime eventually retired. I lived and breathed the club, and I still do. Got to admit that."

"How did they save your life, Drew?" I ask, curious. I'd been so young at the time, I hadn't known what was happening.

He stares at me, and shakes his head, simply saying enigmatically, "Not sure the statute of limitations ever runs out when it's murder. Let's just say Mariana and I never had to worry about our psychopathic father again."

He's told me everything and nothing. But it's was more than I could expect.

I've always known how important the Satan's Devils were to him. Now having some inkling of how far they'd gone to save him and his sister explains why he owes them so much. Is he saying the club still takes precedent? That now as the prez, he's no time for anything or anyone else? Having admitted his feelings, is he pushing me away once again? "What do you want from me, Drew?"

Again he seems lost in the view, and at the point when I wonder whether he's going to continue speaking, he does. "I want an old lady. Someone to ride with me through life. Someone to share the worries and the triumphs with me. Well, except for when it's club business of course. Someone to settle me, someone to come home to. Something more than just the club to live for." He smiles a small smile. "Maybe even have a family of my own."

Well, it sounds like items to be crossed off a shopping list. Then I wonder, "Have you found her, Drew? Is this what this is all about? Because you're a free agent, you're not tied to anyone, and don't need to explain to me."

He's doing it again. Once more he's pushing me away, though at least this time he's using words and not giving me a demonstration of what he can do with his cock. I suppose I should be grateful he's given me an explanation, when he owes me nothing at all.

I'm curious. If there's a woman he cares for, why have I not seen her around the club? She wasn't there yesterday, I'm sure of that. I don't come back often, but I'd have noticed a stranger. It can't be any of the other kids I grew up with, if age is a problem, as they're all younger than me.

"Yeah, I've found her."

"Has she been voted in?" I'm proud I'm able to keep my voice steady as I wonder whether I'm the last to know. A pang goes through me, a hurt I didn't expect. It's so deep, I can hardly bear it.

"Nah. No one knows my intentions."

"Who is she?" I murmur, half to myself. Wondering whether she's good enough for him. The first old lady needs to have a backbone, just like Sam, Drummer's woman. She needs to lead the other old ladies and keep the sweet butts in line. She needs to be the prez's rock, his anchor.

Now he turns, and his hand pushes gently on my shoulder, so I am forced to face him. "Never stopped having feelings for you, Amy." He swallows, then admits, "It's you that I want."

Me?

Utterly stunned, I'm speechless, and my heart misses a

beat. "Me?" I ask out loud, my voice almost a squeak. Surely it's too late, and our time has passed.

He just stares at me, intently, making me list all the reasons why it's a bad idea and incredibly bad timing.

"I'm not the woman I was, Drew." I pull away from him, and it's my turn to stare out over the scenery. "I've discovered who I am, and what I want."

"And Xander can give you that?" He sounds annoyed.

"Xander's a Dom, and I'm a submissive." I know he knows that.

"So you like kink. I can tie you to my bed anytime you want to be restrained." When I swing around, it's to find him smirking as he goes on, "I can spank that ass as red as you want."

"I'm not into spanking," I say fast, while trying to ignore how his voice has deepened, and how what he's suggesting is turning me on.

"Oh, I think you would be, when it's my hand on your ass."

As my nipples harden at just those words, I think there's a good chance of that. Then I mentally slap myself. "It wouldn't work, Drew."

Instead of protesting further, he seems to change the subject, taking me by surprise when he asks, "Why, Amy? Why did you want to get into kink?"

He's been so honest with me, I'll give him what I can to explain. "I grew up in the clubhouse, Drew. Sex was never something shameful. Men used the whores just to get relief, and, well, the whores enjoyed what they were giving them. Mutual satisfaction, no strings attached. Not that I'd ever want to be a whore," I say quickly. "The way you were fucking Silky that night, well, I wanted some of that. Sex, with no strings attached."

A hand brings out another pony, and we step aside to let him enter the pasture. Sunny gives a whinny in greeting, the other snickers in return. Then the man leaves us to get on with his work.

"I wasn't frightened of admitting my sexuality, saw nothing shameful in going with a man, but not stepping into a relationship." I feel my eyes glaze as I look back, knowing I've got to tell him the truth, wondering whether he'll reconsider his position once he knows. "I lost my virginity soon after I got to Phoenix. I wasn't a party animal as such, my studies were too important, but for relaxation, I'd hook up with someone. Oh," I get in first before he has a chance to offer the observation he's sure to make, "I was always careful. Never got drunk and went with someone on a whim. I always knew the men personally or by reputation via my friends. But yeah, I had plenty of variety if you know what I mean."

I sneak a glance at him, seeing a muscle tick in his jaw. As I thought, my confession is making him ready to rescind his invitation. "It was never enough. I soon learned vanilla sex didn't give me what I was looking for. When I went to a club, it was different. That's when I learned I was submissive, I liked a man taking charge. I liked being able to trust him to focus on my pleasure."

Drew's so quiet, I don't expect him to respond. In fact, I anticipate his next words being that he's going to take me back to the compound, understanding now why I'm with Xander.

He responds after a couple of minutes, but in a way I didn't see coming. He comes up behind me, and *my God,* presses a rock hard cock against my ass. "Feel what you do to me, Amy. And everything you ask for? Well, I can give you that. I don't give myself a fancy title, but I take charge in bed. Once you've had my cock, you won't want any other."

His confidently spoken words, his closeness, and the

evidence of his arousal at my back, send sensations through me. I can't trust myself to speak.

"But I can give you more than that. I can give you my heart, Amy. Fuck, you've owned it since we first met. Has anyone else given you that? Has Xander?"

All I can think is no one but Drew has ever made such a promise.

I can't speak. I don't think I even dare breathe, fearing I'll I wake up to find that this is all a dream.

CHAPTER TEN

Heart

"Whatcha got, Mouse?" Drummer asks when he walks in carrying his tablet.

Drummer had given us an hour after we'd returned from the ride—enough time for me to have a talk with Amy—and then we assembled at his house. His sons, Hawk and Zane are partying down at the clubhouse, his old lady Sam is supervising the preparation of Christmas dinner. Me, Wraith, Blade and Peg are currently sprawled on sofas and chairs, while Drummer strides across the room and back, his hand toying with his mostly salt beard now, a gesture he often employs as he thinks. Though I didn't particularly like sharing Amy's secret, I'd brought the men I'm closest to up to speed.

"Found shit out about this Flint." Mouse purses his lips, and Peg, taking the hint, shifts up along the sofa, making room for the tech guy to sit. At Drummer's raised eyebrow, he continues, "He's married with a wife and a kid."

My eyes narrow. "She know he plays at kink clubs?"

"Who knows? But she spent some time in a women's shelter a year ago back."

"She left him?" Peg asks, his brow creased.

"After a couple of visits to the emergency room, yes," Mouse confirms. "But it would appear she's living with him again now."

"Why the fuck did she go back?" Blade asks, shaking his head. "Fuck, some women are gluttons for punishment."

"Maybe she didn't have a choice," I put in. "Man like that is used to getting what he wants." Just like he took from Amy. "If he wanted her back and was able to find her, he might have enticed her back somehow."

"He probably laid on the charm, convinced her he could change," Drummer says decisively. "He had to be compelling and/or persuasive else Amy would never have trusted him. Fuck knows I respect that girl and she wouldn't step blindly into something that didn't look right. He'd have had to have been convincing to get to her. What hope would his wife have?"

Blade suddenly takes out his knife and plants it in Drummer's coffee table, then, his arthritic ravished hands pull it back out and he looks around sheepishly. But Drum's table's got scars from over the years, sure Sam had complained when she'd seen the first one, but she's given up since then. Blade expresses his anger in one way.

When he realises Drummer isn't going to admonish him, his eyes roam the room, landing briefly on each one of us, settling finally on mine. I feel like an insect pierced by a pin with the intensity of his stare. "He's got to die. Are we all agreed?"

"Vote?" asks Wraith, quite reasonably.

"Fuck yeah," I say with feeling.

"No choice," inputs Mouse.

After a moment, Peg gives his verdict, "Yes."

"Sergeant-at-arms?" Drummer fixes his steely glare on him, having noticed his delayed response. "Got concerns?"

Peg chuckles. "Ain't SAA anymore, *Prez*."

"I ain't enforcer," Blade puts in. "But I'm still ready to tear off this fucker's balls. He hurt one of ours, one of ours who we all but saw birthed."

"One who I cared for like one of my own," agrees Drum. "VP?" he raises his eyebrow toward Wraith, who's gesturing he's got something to say.

"I agree with everything said. Amy's club, but more so to us than the youngsters. I don't want the kids fighting our battles, taking over and spoiling our fun." Wraith gives an evil smirk. "As Heart suggested, I'm happy we keep this discussion and outcome between ourselves." His gesture encompasses the six of us.

I'm often touched by how my brothers rally around. Fuck, they'd had to when I went off the rails for six months, and before that when I was in a coma and then away recovering. Meant I hadn't had any interaction with Amy for all but nine months, but even in my darkest moments I knew they were all watching out for her, like they're still doing.

"Shouldn't we at least tell Prez what's going on?" Mouse looks concerned. He unties the long ponytail he still always wears his hair in and ties it with the same leather thong, the only change visible are the white strands which now pepper his long straight locks. "We go take out a man up in Phoenix, what if there's blowback on the club? Shouldn't we be doing it with his blessing?"

"My concern hit right there on the head," Peg nods. "Looking out for the club has been my habit for more than thirty years."

"How would you feel, Drum? If you were still prez and several members went rogue?"

"I'd have fuckin' killed them." Drummer's lips curve.

"If Wizard knew, he might stop us," I add my two-cents' worth. "I can't let this fuckin' lie, Brothers, I just can't. Fuck, the damage that's been done to her, I'm not sure she can find a way back from it."

"Amy will get there," says Blade firmly. "What she needs is a good man beside her to build her back up."

I put my head in my hands, drawing my fingers down my face. *Will that be Xander and is he up to the job?*

"Heart?"

Slowly I shake my head, remembering. "She could have had a fuckin' good man beside her, but I warned him off early on."

"She was seventeen at the time, Brother. Not even legal."

"She saw him plowing one of the sweet butts," Mouse reminds me. "Wasn't long after she left for Phoenix. Wasn't your fault. Down to Wizard if you want to put the blame on anyone."

I grimace. "Yeah, well I might have set that up. Backfired spectacularly."

"No," Drummer contradicts, pausing in front of me. "She was too young, there was too big an age difference. Going away to college was the best thing that happened to her. Allowed her to spread her wings, become a woman we can all be proud of."

"Until it all went wrong," I remind him.

"Who says she wouldn't have gone to a kink club in Tucson?" Wraith suggests. "There's always a risk there'll be someone in that type of place with the wrong motive."

I stand, move swiftly to the armchair he's sitting in and leaning my hands on the arms either side of him rasp, "You saying it's her fault because of the places she likes to frequent?"

"Whoa." Wraith raises his hands in surrender. "Walking down the street can be fuckin' dangerous. And the only fuckin' fault lies with that motherfucker, Flint. None with her."

Slightly appeased, I straighten.

Drummer claps his hands to get us to listen to him, well, all he can do without a gavel and table. "So, we're agreed we take him out, and that we doing it on the QT."

"Tomorrow," Wraith suggests, with a quick grin, "we're just old-timers wanting to go for a Boxing Day ride while all our brothers are sleeping off today's overindulgences."

His old lady, Sophie, was originally surprised the day after Christmas wasn't an official holiday in the United States. Must admit those Brits have got it right, after eating too much and heavily drinking, let alone the partying, not many people are up for much after Christmas Day. Over the years her approach has rubbed off on us, and we all put down our tools and don't pick them back up until we get back to work the day after.

"I like that plan," says Drummer, his lips curving up in a grin. The one you don't want to be on the wrong end of. "Ten a.m.?"

"Wait, we need to find Flint's whereabouts…"

Mouse looks to the ceiling and back down. "Tracking his phone, Brother."

Of course he is. But I've another concern. "What if he's with his wife and family?"

"We draw him out."

Easy to suggest, but how would we get to him. "Saying what?"

"Blade, your knife skills still good getting air out of tyres?"

Blade snarls, "Of course they fuckin' are."

His knife throwing skills have only been honed over the years. Not the first time he's slashed tyres at a distance.

We let Mouse keep the floor, all leaning forward to hear what he's planning.

He doesn't disappoint. "Took a good look at where he lives." Leaning forward, he repositions some drink mats and glasses. "Here's where he keeps his car, around the side of the house where there's a blind spot. High hedges between his and the houses either side, and a privacy fence out front. We slash his tyres, and one of us goes to the house and like any good passerby tells him they saw kids doing it and running off."

"He comes out to check the damage and we nab him." Peg's looking animated now. He tugs at his beard. "Need the crash truck." He raises his eyebrows at Drummer.

"Blade, you okay to drive it?"

The ex-enforcer closes his eyes briefly, then reopens them. Truth is with his hands the way they are, a two-hour ride there and then the same distance back will be a stretch for him. "I'll drive," he confirms, and fuck knows I won't be the only one feeling for him. Time's coming up in Blade's future when he won't be able to ride. But he'll keep going as long as possible. If he can't handle a bike, club regulations say he can't stay a club member. But he's got a good woman beside him, like we all have, and Sabrina and Mason, his kids, will be there for him.

"Mouse," Drummer steps back into the role of prez and starts issuing instructions, "you look for a suitable location where we can take him locally to have a discussion with him." He flexes his hands suggesting how that chat will go. "He's got to know that he messed with the wrong woman. Heart, not a word of this to Amy."

"She suspects, Prez," I interrupt him. "But I promised we'd just have a conversation."

"Needs more than that, he needs out of her hair. Only way she'll feel safe in Phoenix," Wraith tells me.

I nod to show that I'm well aware. I just wish she'd come home. Hate having her away from me, albeit only a two-hour ride.

"Peg," Drummer glares at us all for interrupting, "make sure everyone's tooled up, will you? Anything we need isn't there, take it from the armoury… What the fuck's that grin for, Heart?"

"You sound just like the prez," I explain, unrepentant. It makes everyone laugh and even Drum's lips quirk. Old habits clearly die hard.

He waits for the mirth to die down, then continues, "I'll let Joker know we're going for a pleasure jaunt, get him to spread the word if Wizard asks questions."

"What about the old ladies? They might want to tag along."

Wraith's got a good point, but Blade's got an answer for him, "Fuck them hard until they can't walk and won't want to ride tomorrow."

I smirk. Won't be any hardship fuckin' Marc. From the leers and comments, everyone's taken it as a challenge, and the puffed up chests suggest no one feels they'll have any problems.

"On the off chance anyone fails," Drummer grins, "just say boys want to be boys for a while."

"When's Amy going back to Phoenix?"

"Tomorrow," I answer Peg, glumly. I'm going to miss her. Especially now when I'll be doubly scared for her knowing what can happen to a woman alone in a different city.

"You think she's tight with this Xander? What's your read on him, Heart?"

"He's a good man, Drum, but he's not what I'd want for her. Though it's hard to tell right now, I think she'll be happy enough. Seems a man like him is just what she wants."

Drummer considers for a moment, then nods. "Okay, we all know what we're doing. Meet ten sharp in the morning. Now, you fuckers, get the hell out of my house."

We laugh as we're meant to, stand, and leave him with waves of our hands and chin lifts. Outside in the weak winter sunlight, I stop Mouse.

"You okay with this, Mouse?"

His eyes narrow. "What do you mean?"

"Us keeping Wiz out of it." Mouse is tight with his old lady's younger brother. He'd become his legal guardian back when Mariana had her immigration issues and has treated him more like a son than a brother-in-law, being as proud as punch when he was voted in at the head of the table.

"Wiz means one fuck of a lot to me, Brother. He might be my brother in the true sense of the word, but so are you all. You, Heart, I've known even longer. I don't know that he would stop us, but he would, at least, try to take over. I know you need this, and so do we all." He waves to indicate the rest who've just left Drummer's house and are walking back down through the compound. "What Wiz doesn't know about what the Secret Six are getting up to, can't hurt him."

I bark a laugh at his appropriate reference, and nod at the point he's made. He means Wiz can rightfully distance himself if we put a step wrong and get ourselves arrested. I slap Mouse's back, understanding his boy might be the prez, but he's still the kid Mouse always looked out for.

CHAPTER ELEVEN

Amy

Xander had suggested we live together, that he'd be my Dom, but he mentioned nothing about love. Now, here, where the only sounds are of birdsong and ponies munching, in the place I'd loved as a kid, Drew's offering it all.

Bad timing. Only earlier Xander had laid a future before me in terms of something I'd thought was exactly what I wanted. Now it dawns on me, I would be settling for second best. A Dom/sub relationship which would be comfortable, but lacking. Xander would be fair, kind, caring and faithful. We'd communicate with words, there would be no misunderstanding, our expectations agreed and contracted between us.

Drew's offering everything, a dream I've long thought was out of my reach. A relationship which would probably have flaws in it, where things were spontaneous and doubtless mistakes would be made. It would be exciting, unpredictable, a ride of a lifetime, and a lifetime to kiss and make-up when we got out of step.

I stare at him wide-eyed as he waits patiently for my answer. It's hard, but I try to think rationally.

I might not have been back to Tucson much over the nine years we've been apart, but there's nothing about Drew I don't know, or not the important stuff. I know he's loyal and trustworthy. I know when he gives his word he means it. Even as a kid he'd never stand me up when he'd promised to take me on an outing. I loved him since I was a kid, if I'm truthful, I never stopped, just gave up any hope of ever being able to show him how much.

He's tempting me with a vision of a future so perfect, I'm almost scared to reach out and grab it.

"But I live and work in Phoenix," are the words which come out of my mouth.

"You're a good nurse," he says fast, dismissing my objection. "Any hospital in Tucson would be grateful to have someone like you."

He's right. It probably wouldn't be that hard to find a local job.

"Of course, I'd prefer you barefoot and pregnant."

Oh, I'll be fucked if that didn't get me right in my lady parts. Even though the feminist side of me tells me, I should feel insulted.

But then he winks. He. Winks. God, that undoes me, and I have to turn away, not knowing what I want. No, that's wrong. I know what I want, I'm just not sure if I should take it.

He turns me back to face him and smirks. "Think we ought to check if we've got chemistry? I'm giving you just this one warning. Unless you say no, I'm going to kiss you now."

His words, so dominating while not being a Dominant, give me exactly what I need. Not for one second do I think about Flint, or that I should be scared.

I don't utter any refusal. I make no objection when he lowers his lips to mine, slowly, but determinedly. Then his mouth is pressing against my mouth, moving gently side to side. My hands move of their own accord, pressing against his chest. My touch excites him, and he increases the pressure, his tongue intruding into my mouth. For the first time ever, I taste him, and it's pure heaven.

His arms come around me, holding me to him, crushing my hands between our bodies, giving me no chance to get away. I don't feel trapped, but cared for. The aroma of leather and oil filling my nostrils is the perfume of home, the scent of him being the cherry on the top.

He's held me before. To comfort me when Grunt, the wolfhound cross that seemed to have been in my life forever eventually died when I was thirteen. He'd held my hair back when I was vomiting, having snuck alcohol out of the club-house just to try it, making excuses for me so my dad and Marc never found out. He'd stopped holding me, stopped touching me when I began to mature. This is the first time we've come together as man and woman.

I lose myself in his kiss, even trying to follow his mouth when he eventually pulls away, then cradles my head to his chest. "Tell me yes, Amy. For fuck's sake, say yes. I'll never knowingly hurt you, never step out on you. Make it my life's purpose to make you happy, well, after the club of course." There's mirth in his voice as he adds the last. "Make me a better person, Amy. Be at my side as my old lady and my wife, and on top of everything, accept my love."

So many declarations my head is spinning. "Does Dad know?" Was this something they've cooked up? I know Dad wants me home. But Drew wouldn't make declarations of love if it was that.

"Know that I'm going to step in and sweep you out from under that… Xander's feet? No, that's between us, so you can say no or yes. Won't be any comeback on you. But do they know what I feel about you? Yeah, doubt there's anyone in the club who hasn't got some sort of inkling. You might not have noticed Amy, but whenever you come back, I've only got eyes for you."

"Why now?"

"Why now?" he repeats. "Because up to now the time hasn't been right. I've known for years that Drummer was grooming me to eventually take over as the prez, setting me up so a yes vote was on track. Had to keep my eye focused on that. Knew you were doing okay in Phoenix, thought I'd leave you to make your mark. If I was going to be a man worthy of you, worthy of the club, while you were establishing your career, I needed to step up and concentrate. There wasn't the space in my life to keep a woman happy by my side."

"And now you're the prez?"

"Now, I'm the prez," he admits. "And I need a first lady."

"Maybe anyone would do."

He chuckles, but seriously responds, "Nah. No one could be more perfect than you. You understand the club, know all the men, are loved and respected by everyone. But no one loves you more than me. I couldn't see myself with anyone else, no one has ever measured up to you, Amy."

We need to get back. We've been out longer than I expected, and Christmas dinner will be served soon. I'm feeling guilty that I should have been there helping, alongside all the old ladies. Alongside my brother and sisters, and my MC cousins with whom I grew up. But I push my thoughts of attrition away, I wouldn't, couldn't have missed this. Now, when our age gap no longer matters between us, there is only one answer I can possibly give, despite all the difficulties which come along with that.

"Yes."

Drew waits for a moment as though stunned. "Yes?"

"I've loved you forever, Drew. So yes, but," I add with my

sensible head on, "let's see how this goes. We're moving from friends to having a relationship, maybe I'll find out you snore in bed…"

"I don't snore if that's your only objection." He smirks.

"Well, you might fart or leave pubes in the basin…"

"The basin? What the fuck…?"

"How do I know what bad habits you have?"

He taps the end of my nose with his finger. "I already know I'll love your little quirks, Amy. Even if you're the one who farts in the bed."

"I don't," I start indignantly, and then see him trying not to laugh. "Seriously, Drew, I'll have to go back to Phoenix, turn in my resignation, look for a new job in Tucson. I'm not going to be a stay-at-home wife, or not until…" I don't finish that statement as just the thought of having a baby with Drew fills me with a sense of rightness. "Let's take it one step at a time for the next month. I'll come down, or you can come visit. Let's get to know each other again, as adults, not with one part of this partnership a kid."

He's grinning, an evil look, as though he's plotting. I narrow my eyes as he leans in.

"You say you don't mind casual sex? Well, come to my bed tonight. I'll make sure you never want to leave it. Might even get you knocked up so you have to come back."

I poke my finger into his chest. While the thought of being in his bed is exciting, which is strange as I haven't wanted even to be touched for three months, I've got some conditions. "If you want to fuck me, you're going to have to glove up."

Another of his smirks and then he raises an eyebrow, the bastard. Oh, I'm sure he'll take precautions while I insist, but I wonder, if I go through with this, how long it will be before I end up pregnant? He knows how much I love children, and how I always said I'd wanted six. I may have revised that down a bit as I've grown up, but I'd loved looking after the twins and Alexis.

Suddenly he grows serious. "I'll give you a month, Amy. But I'm warning you, when we're together you'll be in my bed as of tonight."

My face falls, I hadn't realised he meant what he said, I'd thought it was just a joke. "I've not been with anyone since…"

"Not Xander?"

"No, though…" I go red, but why I don't know. I'm not exactly shy talking about sex. I frequent kink clubs after all which are all about communication and being upfront and truthful. "This morning, he pushed me, and gave me an orgasm orally."

"Pushed you?" Drew's face has gone tense.

"No, not as in forced me. I've not been ready for anything, so he started slowly."

"Today," Drew repeats. "On my compound." It's not a question but a statement.

Is he going to take my dreams and smash them? Part of me regrets being honest, but I couldn't go into anything based on lies or things kept hidden.

I purse my lips. "And when was the last time you fucked on the compound, Drew?"

His lips curve. "It was just sex." Then his mouth turns down. "Have I got this wrong, Amy? Do you love him?" He rakes his hands through his hair. "I thought nothing about swooping in and taking you from him, as I didn't see any intimacy between the two of you."

He was right. The relationship with Xander is nothing like the one Drew is offering.

"Amy, I've got a past, you've got one, but it's here on in that's important. In fact, I'm delighted to know he hasn't given you his cock."

"I didn't want it. I'm… scared."

Again, he raises an eyebrow.

Fuck. I just kissed him. Was held tight in his arms. Felt his erection behind me and all it did was turn me on. I stare up at him with wonder in my eyes and place my hands against his cheek.

"I'm not scared of you, Drew." I feel I have to admit, unable to believe from the moment I wrapped my hands around him on the bike, what happened with Flint and my reaction hadn't crossed my mind once. "But I am worried I'll get flashbacks… Especially if we make love." I think he'll be the first man I've ever made love to, and I know that's what he'll be giving me back. It won't just be fucking, not with our hearts involved.

"I can be dominant, I can be gentle. I can be anything you want or need." He presses his lips together. "I can do slow, and if you want to stop, I'll stop. No need for," he puts it in air quotes showing he does indeed know about kink, "safe words."

I lean my head against his chest again, realising I'm resting my cheek on his cut, but he's not protesting. He raises his hand and gently rests it against the back of my head.

"I have to admit I hate what happened to you, sweetheart. But we'll work through it together." He thinks for a moment. "Are you sure you're okay with going back to Phoenix?"

I don't answer immediately, turning to view the vista that stretches up into the Coronado forest. If I allow myself to be honest, Tucson was and always will be my home. But I've enjoyed my time in Phoenix, apart from the last couple of months, as the independence helped me grow. The progression in my career, as well as the ability to strike out on my own raising myself in the eyes of my dad, Marc, and most people on the compound was necessary. Perhaps the respect I'd need as the prez's old lady, is already there.

Even if I have another meltdown, there are enough brothers here who suffer from PTSD having served, they'd be hypocritical to criticise how badly Flint affected me.

Drew deserves an honest answer.

"You asked me if I loved Xander, the answer is I don't. I'm grateful to him, I feel a lot of affection for him. I would have tried to make a relationship work and have no doubt we would have got along. But love? You're the only man I've ever felt that emotion for. You thought I was just a kid when you were responsible for me leaving, and it's true, I was. My love may have been that of a young girl's, but I gave you my heart then, and it could never belong to anyone else."

He goes to speak, I stop him.

"I would have said yes. I'm fine with returning to Phoenix, and that's the answer I'd give anyone else. But to you, I'll admit, the thought of going back scares me. What if Flint comes after me again? I keep seeing him, Drew, at the grocery store; I saw him one day hovering outside the hospital where I work. Sometimes I freak out and then find he's not there at all, that it was my imagination summoning him up." I'm not stupid, I know my dad has something planned, whether he's shared that with Drew it's not my place to ask. Family loyalty trumps friendship until I say an unqualified yes. "Even if he's made to back off, I'll still be nervous about going to my car, going to the store." I bite my lip and admit, "I've never been a victim before, I didn't realise how much it would affect me."

"You don't need to worry—"

"Easy to say, but I do." He's not the one who's got a rapist stalking them.

"You don't need to worry," he repeats, "because I'm sending a prospect back with you."

"You can't do that." I look at him wide-eyed.

He leans in and gives that boyish smirk once again. "I can, because I'm the prez."

With that pronouncement which I can't argue with, he takes my arm and leads me back to his motorcycle. On the drive back, I have conflicting thoughts going through my head. Elation at the future that's just been offered to me, and sorrow at parting with the man who's been my rock for the last three months.

I hate to let anyone down, and now I'm going to bring disappointment to the man who I respect, although, compared to the resurrection of my feelings for Drew, I know I don't love, or maybe I do, but only superficially, as one would a dear friend.

"I'm coming with you," Drew says, after he's parked the bike and dismounted.

I don't pretend not to understand. "No, Drew. I'll speak to Xander." Whether or not when the month's out I'll have a future with Drew, I know from this afternoon my feelings for Xander aren't enough. If there's one thing Drew's shown me it's I want a partner, someone who can take charge, but not take over. And that's what Xander's been doing, making choices for me.

Up to today, I was in the headspace where I needed that, but even after the short time with Drew, I can feel my confidence starting to come back. I was always looking for a play partner, not a full time Dom. Xander can't turn off what he is, just as I have to accept I can't be what he wants.

Drew's hand curls around my neck. "Okay," he says simply, and I'm grateful he doesn't insist or try to take over. "But remember, Amy, I want you in my bed tonight. Don't want you alone with another man, however much you trust him to keep his hands off."

"What if I'm not ready?" It's not just the upcoming confrontation with Xander that's already eroding some of my briefly found self-assurance. It's returning to the compound and all the thoughts and fears I initially brought here with me. I wish we could have stayed at the stables, it had been like being cocooned in our own little bubble of safety.

The memories of why Xander's been close and protecting me slam hard into me. Flint stole my control, he was caught raping me. And worse, he'd abused me, in ways I'm too ashamed to voice.

I turn my watery eyes up to Drew. "What if I'm not ready?" I repeat, my voice sounding small.

"I don't give a fuck, Amy. If you want to just cuddle, or not even touch me, then that's what we'll do. You're in the driving seat for now. I've waited all these years, I can wait a bit longer. But never doubt your place is with me. You need support and protection? I'll be the one giving it to you." He leans forward and places a platonic kiss to my forehead. His eyes though, they flare with desire and promise, showing that mindful of people watching, he's diplomatically keeping things casual. "I'll see you later, okay?"

I give him a tremulous smile, then at his confidence-giving chin lift, walk slowly up to the suite we've been allocated, dragging my heels rather than rushing into this difficult conversation. I still haven't found the right words to say as I open the door and step inside.

Xander puts down the book he's been reading, his welcoming smile slowly slipping off his face. He's on his feet in seconds, standing in front of me, his forefinger and thumb going under my chin and raising my head to face him.

"What's happened?" he says urgently. "Did you have another episode?"

"No," I shake my head adamantly. "Nothing like that, but we've got to talk, Xander."

You don't get to be a heart surgeon by being stupid. Xander lets out a heavy sigh, and states, "He cares for you."

"I've only just found that out." I don't want him to think I've used him.

"And you care for him," he continues.

My voice sounds weak, breathy. "I always have. But I put it to the back of my mind. I thought I lost my chance with him, a long time ago. I haven't been lying to you, Xander. I thought I was a free woman."

"But you're not," he replies in an unreadable tone. "At least not in here." He places his hand lightly over my heart. "Do you love him, Amy?"

"Yes," I admit.

"And he loves you back?" He carries on after I give a small nod. "What has he offered you?"

"Him. He's offered me himself, completely. To be his old lady, his wife. To have his children."

"I see." I'm certain a fleeting flash of pain crosses his face, but he hides it fast. "Is that what you want?"

"Yes," I say quietly, unable to say anything else.

Xander mumbles something which sounds suspiciously like *fuck*, though he's a man who's so in control of himself he rarely resorts to swearing.

He moves away and stands with his back to me, his head slightly bowed. Then he pulls back his shoulders and starts talking. "I offered to be your Dom, Amy, and you agreed to be my sub. We would have lived together, and I could see us making a go of it. There's already affection between us that could have grown stronger. But I can't promise you anything, I can't promise you a future in case it all comes to nothing. Don't get me wrong," he swings around, "I'll miss you, I've kind of gotten used to you being there, of holding you and easing your nightmares. I like someone depending on me, having someone to protect from the world. But maybe I'd have stifled you, and maybe my demands would have eventually proved too much."

That he's not fighting for me now, either shows he's a good man or that he doesn't have deep feelings for me. I hate making someone hurt, but the picture he's painting isn't anywhere near as attractive as what Drew had laid out.

"I'm sorry, Xander."

He comes closer again. "I'm not, pet." He sounds sincere, and one side of his mouth turns up. "If bringing you here has made you discover your destiny, then my job as your Dom is done. I could never take you away from a man who loves you, when all I can offer is a relationship that's transactional." He chuckles softly. "I knew you'd be a brat, knew you'd balk against my strict imposition of rules, but I was looking forward to punishing you. But if that's not the relationship you truly want, then it's best we find out before making a commitment."

"I'll miss you," I spit out fast. It's the truth, he's been there for me through my darkest days.

"I'll miss you too, pet. But don't doubt I'm happy for you." He starts opening drawers and taking out his neatly folded clothes, carefully placing them in the case he brought with him.

"What are you doing?"

"Going."

"Now? But it's Christmas, there's a dinner—"

"And I'd be a third wheel." He looks up and meets my eyes. "If you want me to stay, just one word will make me."

But I can't think of saying it. He knows. Within minutes, he's packed. Like Drew had done earlier, but for entirely different reasons, he places a kiss to my forehead. "Say goodbye here, don't walk down with me."

I was going to at least walk him to his car, but I think he knows by the way my eyes glisten, I'll be crying after he's gone. He might not have turned out to be my one and only, but he's been such a good friend it's hard to see him walk away.

"Will I see you again?" I ask, as he opens the door.

He hesitates for just one moment. "If our paths cross, if you come back to the club, then yes. But I won't seek you out, Amy. Not because I don't want to see you, but a clean break is best. You've got a different path to tread now, and I wish you every happiness."

When the door closes behind him, I fist my hands to prevent myself running after him and after a moment, throw myself on the bed, tears flowing freely, wracking sobs going through me, remembering him lying spooned behind me, comforting and supporting me through those dark long nights. I go over everything in my head that he's said or done. Xander's a good man, I probably didn't deserve him.

But while I allow myself time to grieve, not for one moment do I think I've made a mistake. My future is with Drew now, just for this moment I'll dwell on the past, then move forward and put it behind me.

CHAPTER TWELVE

Amy

A knock sounds on the door. Throwing myself off the bed, I rush to open it, thinking it might be Xander coming back to say we'll always be friends. But it's not him, it's the man I want to see much more.

"I saw him leave, about half an hour ago. Gave you some time, but not giving you anymore. Any tears you cry, you cry them with me." He uses his thumb to wipe one such tear from my eye.

"I think I hurt him," I say, biting my lip. "He was so good, Drew. He didn't blame me, he gave me his blessing and good wishes."

Drew tilts his head slightly. "His job's done now, Amy. It's now mine to protect you and keep you safe."

"He doesn't even want to stay friends with me."

Drew's sigh sounds like it's one of relief. But there's also understanding in his eyes as he comes closer. "He was there for you in your worst time, saved you from the worst experience of your life. He saw you at your lowest point, and, of everyone, has direct knowledge of what Flint did, and the impact on someone like yourself. Of course you're going to miss him. But he was right to make a clean break." He pauses and rubs the side of his nose. "His being with you served as a reminder. Perhaps, now he's gone, you can move on."

I look down at my hands, wondering whether he's right. I could never forget that night with Xander there to remind me. It's true, sometimes I look at him and remember the fury in his eyes when he'd seen how Flint had taken advantage of me.

"Babe, it's time we made an appearance at the clubhouse."

I glance up fast, it's the first time he's called me something other than Amy or sweetheart which he'd used when we were younger. Now he's holding out his hand.

"Uh uh." I shake my head. "You go down first, and I'll follow in a few minutes."

His brow creases, and his hand goes to his temple. "What's up Amy? Why do you need more time to yourself? I think you need your family around you."

He's misunderstood. "Drew, if we walk in together, what will people think? We agreed we'd give it a month before making a commitment. Everyone will get the wrong idea. I don't want to make it difficult for you."

"You think I give a fuck?" he rasps. "You and I are together, and I've no fuckin' doubt we'll stay that way. If it doesn't work out, well, I won't be the first man jilted."

"You jilt people at the altar," I say with a small laugh.

"Oh, I'll get you to the altar sooner or later." Drew sounds solemn. "You'll be my ol' lady *and* my wife." His tone lightens as he adds, "Going to tie you to me in every fuckin' way that I can."

I cover my mouth with my hand, then manage to get out, "Is that a proposal?"

"Nah," he sounds serious again. "That will come at the end of the month. Then you can start planning our wedding."

I stand open mouthed. He wants everything. I remember the first time I said I'd marry him, I'd been about six. He'd laughed. When I'd repeated it a few years later, he'd looked awkward. Now that everything I wanted since I was young is being handed to me on a platter, I'm beginning to think he's right. At the end of the month I'll be able to commit to him completely. I can't now. I need time to get my head around the whirlwind changes. Time to think when I'm not under pressure to make a decision.

"Come on then." Again, he holds out his hand.

This time I take it, but resist his little tug to get me moving. "What are people going to think, Drew? One minute I was with Xander, and now…"

"I don't give a fuck, and you shouldn't either. You and me, babe, that's all that matters."

I stare at him for a moment, then realise he's right. We shouldn't need to sneak around hiding our relationship. I'm the girl who walked into kink clubs alone, I can walk into a clubhouse full of my family with my man by my side. *My man?* Jeez, he's already got me thinking that way.

It's not as if we have to rub people's noses in it. All we need to show publicly is that our friendship has been rekindled. Take things slow. Then, at the end of the month, it won't come as a shock to anyone. Me sitting beside Drew during Christmas dinner shouldn't raise any eyebrows at all. I did it enough when I was a kid. Me sleeping in his room? Again, I can slip down to his discreetly when everyone thinks I've gone back to my own suite.

This time his pressure gets me putting one foot in front of the other.

The walk down to the clubhouse only takes a few minutes.

Drew stops me outside and chuckles. "Sounds like Peg's got control of the music again."

I smile back as I hear strains of Wizard's *I Wish It Could Be Christmas Every Day* bellowing out. Then I start giggling.

When Drew looks at me as if I've gone mad, I point out the coincidence. "You do realise this is your song, don't you? It sounds like they're expecting you to make an entrance."

"Apt," he agrees, smirking. "Now, come on."

He opens the door to the clubhouse, and then guides me through with his hand at the small of my back, a tactile comfort which no one else can see. *That's right, be inconspicuous, let them get used to the fact we're friends once again.*

But it seems Drew has different ideas. As soon as we're inside, he pulls me against him, my back against his front and holds me tight to him, in a sign no one can interpret incorrectly.

Dad gets to his feet and comes across, looking behind us. His eyes narrow. "Where's Xander?"

"Gone," Drew answers for me.

"What the fuck is this Wizard?" I notice Dad doesn't respect him with his title.

Drew holds me tighter and replies, "This is me doing what's right. What's always been in the cards. Me and Amy, together."

Dad's eyes now find mine. He's searching my face, trying to read my expression. Then he says sternly, "You alright with this, Amy? Is this what you want? Because if it's not, don't fuckin' care if he's the Prez, he's going six foot under."

My eyes widen as I see his hand rest on the butt of his gun. *He wouldn't shoot him, would he?* Drew hasn't tensed, as if he's unconcerned with a threat issued by one of his members, but while it might not be to the death, I don't want a fight between Drew and my dad. I swallow fast and realise much as

I wanted not to immediately go public, to avoid bloodshed at Christmas, I have to admit the truth.

"I've wanted it forever, Dad."

"Wizard's the reason you fuckin' left in the first place." He rakes his hands through his hair.

I gasp. *Had I been that transparent?* "But it was right, Dad. I was too young, and Drew put the club first. You should understand that."

I notice the room's gone quiet, and even the music has been turned down. I view everyone looking on, the main expressions are bemusement and surprise—it's not an everyday occurrence that the prez takes an old lady. Even more not so, that said old lady's dad threatens his president.

Dad's moved his gaze to the man behind me. "You're serious, Wizard? Have you thought about this?"

"I'm serious as a fuckin' heart attack."

"And a heart attack is exactly what you'll be getting if you hurt Amy." Drummer steps up. "You may have taken my place, but I'll still order a beatdown, and I'll have brothers at my back who'll jump to comply."

"If I hurt her, I'll deserve it," Drew replies earnestly and sounding unconcerned. Then he nuzzles my neck and places a kiss there.

"We're giving it a month," I say quickly to Dad, trying to reassure him. "I've got to go back to Phoenix and close that chapter of my life."

"You're not claiming her?"

"I'd claim her now, but she's not ready."

As Drew's deep voice booms close to my ear, I can feel the vibrations. What woman wouldn't want to be claimed by a man she's loved all her life? Perhaps I should admit that I am ready.

No. I need time.

"Well, fuck." Drummer's shaking his head. "I didn't see this coming. Thought you were with that Xander."

"I stole her away," Drew admits, putting the blame on himself. "Perhaps it took seeing her about to put me out of her life forever to bring me to my senses. I've always known it was her, and I did what I could to make sure I didn't lose her."

Dad's face is unreadable. Then he says, "Step away from my daughter."

I gasp as Drew does so, watching Dad, trying to analyse his body language. I know violence is part of these men's lives and fully expect him to hit his prez. Out of the corner of my eye I see the VP, Hawk, stand up. When he nods at someone, I see it's at Hound.

Drummer steps up to Dad's side, and behind him, is Peg.

Oh shit. I *knew* we should have been more subtle. There's going to be a fight in the clubhouse, no one will let Dad get away with harming their prez. *Will Drum stop it, or take on his son?* What a clusterfuck this is turning out to be.

But as soon as Drew is clear of my body, Dad shows he's got different intentions to those I had feared. He holds out his hand. When Drew takes it, he pulls him to him and slaps his back. "I couldn't wish for a better man for my daughter," he admits. Shocked, I see his eyes glisten. I suspect he's realising I'll be back and living on the compound. Then I see him take a step back and glare viciously. "You hurt her? Then you better prepare to meet Satan." Almost immediately his expression softens again, this time when he takes Drew's hand it's to shake it. "Welcome to the family."

It's a signal for everyone to make their reactions known. Hawk and Hound step down, and join in with the hollers and shouts, stomping of feet, and banging of fists on tables. The noise is deafening as everyone shows their approval. Dad holds out his arms, and I step into them, hearing his voice in my ear, "Welcome home."

When he lets me go, I see Mouse. His hand is firmly resting on Drew's shoulder. "This sit right with you?"

"Oh, so fuckin' right," is Drew's simple answer.

"Amy!" I swing around to find Mariana approaching. She's got tears in her eyes. "I couldn't be happier. You were meant to be together." And then I'm engrossed in another hug, the first of many tonight. Well, from the women at least.

Whether it's Drew being over-protective or whether he's jealous, he stands by my side warning the men off with low growls emanating from his throat.

"You're being a bit obvious," I tell him, while deep down I'm relieved not to make my own excuses.

He pulls me into his body and speaks softly into my ear. "I don't mind my brothers hugging you, Amy, but you stiffen when they get close. It'll come, babe. You'll get there. But for now, I'm keeping them away, okay? And if they think I'm just being ultra-possessive, I couldn't give a flying fuck."

I stare up at him in wonder. "I didn't think it was possible to love you more, Drew."

Suddenly Peg whistles loudly and calls out, "Sam's just told me, dinner is ready."

I hold Drew back. "Thank you," I tell him softly. "I hate being like this."

He holds my gaze for a moment, then places the gentlest of kisses against my forehead. "You'll get there, babe. You'll be okay. Now shall we get some plates while there's still some food left?"

With Drew's arm firmly around me, I step forward and join in what can only be described as a stampede as people rush to fill their plates with the delicious food the old ladies have cooked up. Well, I think it was delicious. I cleared my plate, but I couldn't tell you what I'd eaten.

All the time I'm seated, Drew's got his hand on my thigh. I can feel the warmth of his palm, and I keep sneaking looks at the handsome man sitting beside me, finding it hard to imagine if he has his way, we'll be like this for the rest of our lives. It's a heady thought, and one that's hard to get my mind around.

"Hey. Ever wonder why Santa doesn't have his own kids?" Joker's loud voice cuts through the air.

"'S'pect you're going to fuckin' enlighten us," calls out Rock.

Joker certainly does. "'Cause he only comes once a year."

On cue, everyone groans.

Joker doesn't care, but continues, "How does Santa stay free of the clap?"

I notice Sophie covering Hilda's ears, and the young teenager shrugging her off. I also see Mouse glaring at his daughters Maria and Tanya, while the expression on the face of Yiska, his son and eldest child, leaves no one in any doubt the fourteen-year-old knows exactly what Joker's talking about.

"'Cause he wraps his package before shoving it down the chimney." Joker snorts as he gives the punchline.

There are a few chuckles at that one. I grin, and looking over, see Lady shaking his head at the antics of his man. He slaps a hand over his partner's mouth, but Joker pushes it away.

"A whore was lying in bed waiting for Santa to come. Then he got dressed and went back up the chimney."

There are a few grunts but mostly groans at that one.

Then Joker's eyes find mine. "Hey, Amy? Is your name Jingle Bells?"

My brow creases as I hold myself ready for the answer.

"'Cause you look ready to go all the way." Joker's head drops to the table and his shoulders shake at his own brand of humour.

"Lady, how the fuck do you put up with him?" Blade shouts out.

Lady winks at their daughter, Maya, and then pulls Joker in for a long, deep kiss eliciting cries of *put him down* before he answers, "Because I love him."

Awws go around. Drew takes it as his cue and his arm comes around me, then his lips find my mouth.

"Christ." Dad's eyes have opened wide. "You're going to be fuckin' my daughter."

Marc slaps his arm, while Drew answers calmly, "You can bet on that."

My face must resemble a beetroot.

Suddenly another voice sounds, "Who says oh, oh, oh?" Then he spoils it by immediately giving us the answer, "Santa walking backwards."

This time there's genuine laughter, and Wraith slaps Tommy on the back. Tommy starts beaming. His eyes catch mine and he grins even wider. I haven't seen Tommy since I arrived home.

As they're sitting opposite, I hear Wraith as he asks, "Tommy, why didn't the skeleton go to the Christmas party?"

He gives Tommy time, then when Tommy's shoulders rise and fall, then looks at him wide-eyed with his head shaking, continues, "Because he had nobody to go with."

It takes him a moment then Tommy slaps the table and gives a belly laugh. Still chuckling, he turns to the joke teller. "Good one, VP."

Seems the child/man can't understand the changes as he gives Wraith his old rank. But no one here gives a damn.

Everyone is here tonight, old ladies and children, and there's even a table for the whores who are fully dressed for the occasion. I don't think anyone's missing. Watching my family, my stomach full of good food, I lean back in my chair and feel myself relax. Then a thought hits me. If Xander was here, I'd be on edge, wondering what he made of the people around me. I don't think he'd have fit in. Oh, he'd have been polite, but as the drinks flow and people become rowdier, I think he'd have been uncomfortable.

Suddenly, the door to the clubhouse opens, and a few hands go to their guns. Then there's a shocked silence, followed by roars of greeting.

"What the fuck?" Drew gets to his feet, nods at Drummer, and the prez and ex-prez go to greet the visitors.

"Sorry, we're late." Paladin nods at the baby he's carrying. "This one wouldn't stop fussing."

"I didn't fuss, Daddy," a toddler calls out.

"I was good too, Dad," the oldest boy says.

"Hank, you only behaved yourself because Santa was coming." Pal rolls his eyes at his wife.

Hank. Paladin had called his first child the name of the man he once prospected with, and who was killed protecting Sophie. I glance over at Wraith's wife to see her wiping a tear from her eye.

A girl about four stares up at Paladin, her arms folded across her chest. Another girl, clearly her twin, copies her sister's example.

Pal just shakes his head. "I told you two before. You couldn't bring your new bikes. There wasn't room in the car. Now stop sulking."

As Pal competently deals with his brood, I count them.

Five kids, and standing behind Pal is a very pregnant Jayden, and, well, look at that—I'm delighted to see Ella and her daughter Faith.

"Jay!" I call out, then I, too, am running across, greeting my old babysitter.

"Is there any fuckin' food left?" a loud voice behind Pal asks.

Another roar as Beef, the VP of the Colorado chapter, enters with his wife Steph, and her latest guide dog. I swear Rock has tears in his eyes, as he slowly stands, then quickens his pace. Within moments, Beef and Rock are hugging.

"Sunny side up, Brother."

"Dirty side down."

Even Drummer seems choked up as the old team is back together.

Once the newcomers are settled with plates—there were plenty of leftovers—Drummer stands and raises his glass. "Merry fuckin' Christmas, Devils." People drink, then there's another toast. "Let's raise our glasses to people who can't be with us tonight." He looks up at the ceiling, then back down. "Here's to Tongue, Viper, Slick, Hank, Adam, Kidder and ShortAss. They may be gone, but there'll ride with us forever." As Drummer mentions the men who've been lost over the years, silence descends. I cast my mind back. ShortAss only rode with the club a few years. He prospected when I was a teenager, got into an argument with an eighteen wheeler and lost just before I left for Phoenix. Kidder joined later, he'd been shot, but I never heard the details of who, why, or how.

As everyone spares a moment to remember, glasses are raised and drinks are sampled respectfully.

Drew takes my hand, his eyes settling on all his members, then he looks back to me. Brushing my hair back from my face with one hand, he leans in. "Merry Christmas, baby."

CHAPTER THIRTEEN

Amy

I go to return his Christmas greeting, but the words dry in my throat as I see the fire in his eyes. There's such promise in them that I shiver. This is real. I'm going to be in this man's bed tonight, and, if he has his way, forever.

"Babe, don't look at me like that," he warns. "Else I'm going to forget I'm the prez and that I ought to stay here, and instead drag you back to my room right fuckin' now."

I love my family. Despite the misgivings that came with me to the compound, because of the man beside me, I've enjoyed the evening immensely, the celebrations and fun exceeding my expectations. But now I'm more than ready to leave and have Drew to myself. "Yes."

His eyes sharpen. "Yes?"

I raise my head slightly, then let it drop.

Fulfilling his threat, he grabs my hand and leads me through the partygoers, moving so fast I struggle to keep up with him. Hawk slaps him on the back and winks, Hound chuckles as we rush past, and Throttle stops him for a second and says something in his ear which I can't hear, but makes Drew snort.

Our progress is slowed as one by one the men want to talk to him. On my part, Sophie gives a hand wave, and Sam a thumbs up. Even Ella, who earlier I'd managed to have a brief chat with, grins and mouths *good luck.*

Eventually we're outside in the fresh air.

I hold him back. "What did Throttle say?"

Drew taps the side of his nose. "That's between me and Throttle."

I narrow my eyes at him suspiciously.

"Babe."

"So, you're 'babing' me now," I accuse. But my lips are curved upwards.

Drew draws a deep breath and remarks, "Alone at last," as he puts his arm around me and we start to walk up to his suite. "Just you and me. Fuck, I've waited years for this."

We don't have far to go, as prez, he stays close to the clubhouse. His bloc is one of the nearest.

Just you and me. Damn him to hell. Flint had said something similar that night when he suggested a private room. As Drew's words filter through my brain, a flashback slams into me and his expectations of the night ahead suddenly don't seem as enticing as they had previously. *Alone with another man. This time there won't be a dungeon monitor watching.*

My steps falter, I can't breathe.

Drew stops, his stare homing in on my face which I feel has been bleached of all colour.

"I, I… I d-d-d-on't think I c-c-can do this, Drew." I'm trembling so much, I'm sure he can feel my body shaking as I gaze off to the side.

He turns me back so I have to look at him, his eyes now softened. His hand brushes my hair back from my face, such a gentle touch it starts to calm me. "Heart didn't give me any details, left me to fill in the gaps. All I know is that you suffered abuse in that BDSM club you went to." He pauses, then gives it to me straight. "I'm going to guess you were raped in a place you should have been safe."

I can't look at him, instead, once again, I turn away, finding the darkness more interesting.

Pulling my head against his chest, he murmurs softly, "Will you tell me what happened? I want to help you."

I hesitate. An owl hoots in the distance, a common sound here, but not one I hear in the middle of Phoenix, usually it's sirens instead. It reminds me where I am. As I breathe in the scent of Drew's leather cut, I realise he deserves to know how damaged I am and what he's proposing to take on.

"I trusted him, Drew. He was a new Dom to me, but not to the club, though he hadn't been there for some time. To be allowed to play, he'd have to have completed their training programme. Other Doms had greeted him like an old friend. There was nothing to make me suspicious." I pause and sob. I've tried, God, I've tried to work out if there'd been some sign that I'd missed, some inkling I should have had that Flint wanted more than I'd been prepared to give. "I trusted him because he was a Dom, and Doms look after their subs. I knew it could only be a light play session, anything else was on my hard limits list. Penetration was banned in the Feathers club, other than hands and mouths. Part of the reason I went there." Again I break off, wondering whether my words are too much for him to hear, but his hand is rhythmically stroking my head, and the movement doesn't falter. My hands clasp the edges of his cut as though it's an anchor. "We negotiated a scene, the type I like. I'd be tied up and blindfolded, and then there'd be sensual play."

"You like that?" There's no censure in his question.

"I did." I take a shuddering breath and spit the worst out quickly, "I was restrained, blindfolded. I was expecting to feel a gentle touch, was waiting with anticipation. I couldn't see… I couldn't see what he'd taken out of his bag. It was a gag." I huff mournfully. "I even opened my mouth when he told me too. It was to fucking gag me." A moment of anger, swiftly chased away by the guilt at how easy I'd made it for him. Drew's arm tightens around me, and under my cheek, I feel his heart race.

"Go on," he says, gruffly. "No secrets between us, Amy. I don't want to not know and something I do trigger a reaction."

"You still want me?" My voice trembles.

"Fuck yes. Nothing, nothing you can say will change how I feel about you."

The owl hoots again, ensuring I stay in the present, even though the vision in my head is of the past.

I swallow and summon up the strength to resume. "He gagged me. I'd told him I didn't like pain, but it didn't stop him using a crop on me. It stung, he hit my breasts… He was strong, stronger than me. He untied my legs, turned me over and secured me again, even though I tried to fight him. He flogged my buttocks, then…" Drew's hand keeps moving, never stopping. "He used a butt plug, forced it into me. All the time I was trying to make sounds, using the hand signals to tell him to stop. Then, he, he…"

"Shush, shush."

I'm sobbing, I hadn't realised. But I want to get this all out. "He was raping me when Xander pulled him off."

"Why did no one fuckin' stop him before it went that far?"

"Xander was a dungeon monitor that night. He'd been checking on Flint and me, but he was called away when someone else got hurt. He felt so bad, Drew. He took me home and then stayed. I think at first it was out of guilt, a Dom's disappointment a sub got hurt on his watch. I get nightmares, Drew, so he slept with me to comfort me, but that's all he did in my bed."

Behind us the door to the clubhouse opens and someone steps out, laughing in the way people do when they've had enough drink to get merry, but aren't drunk. I recognise the 'goodnight' called out as coming from Joker.

"'Night," Drew replies, and waits until the trio of Joker, his man and their daughter, walk past.

"You've got a lot of fuckin' baggage in your head, babe." Drew's body has gone tense. *Is he angry? Upset? Disappointed?*

"I'm sorry, I shouldn't have laid that on you." I was wrong to tell him. What man wants to hear the details of how their woman had been abused?

He takes a shuddering breath as though to bring himself back under control. When he speaks, his voice is even and calm. "Amy, babe." He lifts his hand away from my hair and uses it to raise my face to his. "We're going to be lovers, but more than that, friends and partners. Any burden you carry is mine to share. Thank you for being brave enough to tell me."

"I'm not brave."

His head shakes. "Oh, you fuckin' are, Amy. You've survived, and you'll get better every day. I'm here, and I'm here to stay. Nothing you can do, nothing you can say, will push me away. I'm not going to be pressuring you. One day you'll be my woman in every sense of the word, but when will be driven entirely by you. For now, I'm happy you'll be in my bed, and I get to lie beside you. I promise on my fuckin' life you can trust me."

Drew's never given me a moment to think I should have any concerns about that. "I do trust you."

When I shiver again, it's not from fear, but the chill of the night air.

"Come on, let's get you inside." Keeping his arm around me, he leads me the final few steps to his suite.

"No pressure," he reminds me, pulling me close, hesitating to open the door. "Whatever you need, babe. What I'd really like to do, what I've been thinking of all evening, is feeling those lips again. Is that alright with you?"

God, yes. Especially when I'd been scared knowing what happened would indeed push him away. The fact that it hasn't is a relief. What I hadn't realised is the knowledge there are now no secrets between us, that he knows the worst and has stayed, is freeing. I'd felt used and dirty, but Drew now made me feel clean. Part of the power Flint has held over me for the past three months drifts away. Flint's in the past, and this man I've desired forever is my future.

He's waiting.

"Yes." My permission is gasped and breathy.

Then he lowers his mouth to mine, slowly, deliberately.

The taste I'm still learning is tinged with whisky and beer, but I know, like me, he's perfectly sober, both of us staying so, intentionally. His touch, so gentle, his tongue dancing with mine. I shiver again, but it's not from the cold, nor caused by my nerves which are receding, memories of that awful night lessening their grip on me as I hold on to dear life for the man who's always been kind, and apart from the once, has never done anything to hurt me. Instead of no, I begin to ask, can I? Could I allow my fantasy to come true? Could I let Drew make love to me?

Eventually he pulls back from me and leans his forehead against mine. "Slow as you need or nothing at all, okay?"

I nod. He opens the main door and I get my first look at the place Drew calls home. Both interior doors are open, bedroom furniture is in one, and the other has been turned into a sitting room, just how I remember Peg's back in the day. It's the room containing a large king-sized bed which Drew guides me into, his hands resting on my shoulders.

Something catches my eye. "Hey, where did that come from?" My eyes narrow as I spy my suitcase by the side of the bed.

"Got a prospect to bring your shit down. You don't need to go back to that suite. Your place is with me, Amy, whenever you're on my compound."

I'm slightly annoyed he's telling not asking, but why should I object, when deep down it's what I want. I don't want to sleep alone, and I'd prefer not to be where I'd remember Xander sharing my bed, and how I disappointed him.

"I go back to Phoenix tomorrow," I remind him, the idea not attractive in the least. "I've a shift tomorrow night. I was lucky to get these three days off." I only managed it by getting my request in early.

He sighs deeply. "I know, Amy. Believe me, I fuckin' know. I spoke to Nathan, he'll be driving back with you and staying in your apartment. You won't have to go anywhere alone."

"Are you sure you can spare a prospect?" It's lucky I've a two-bedroom place.

"Not letting you go, otherwise. I want, need you to feel safe, babe. Now why don't you use the bathroom first?"

I nod, nervous again. *First.* I know he means before him, but it also signifies it's before I get into his bed.

I enter the en suite, do the necessary, clean my teeth, then eye my bag I'd brought in with me. I've a t-shirt and shorts that I sleep in. Making a quick decision, I slip them on. There's no way I'm going to walk back into the bedroom naked. I shake my head at my reflection in the mirror. I'm the girl who doesn't mind walking around completely unclothed in a BDSM club, but I'm scared stiff of letting Drew see me. How fucked up is that?

"Babe?" Drew calls out, a reminder he's waiting for me.

"Coming."

I nod at the woman staring back at me, then, taking a deep breath, open the bedroom door…

Drew hasn't got the same nerves as me. He's already undressed, lying naked on top of the covers. I stare, grin, and then let out a loud laugh as I see what he's using to maintain his modesty.

"It's Christmas." He shrugs when he sees where I'm looking.

Then my mirth fades. I'd often seen Drew dressed only in a swimsuit when we'd played around in the pool, cooling off in the scorching heat of summer. But I haven't seen his bare chest for years. He's changed, grown into the body of a real man. Christ, I knew he had muscles, I've felt them as he's held me, but he's bulked up and has a well-defined six pack leading down to that mouth-watering V. He's got tattoos almost covering the whole of his chest, on his back, while I can't see, I'm certain he'll have a replica of the Satan's Devils colours.

He's the most magnificent specimen of a man that I've ever seen.

Then I'm laughing again. Full belly laughs which have me bent double.

"What?"

I point out a finger that's quivering, not with fear, but as a result of my amusement. "It's moving!"

"Well, looking at you eating me with your eyes, seeing you in those tiny shorts. That's what you do to me." He looks down too, and chuckles.

The Santa hat covering his cock is slowly rising. My God, he's making hormones go wild as I get an idea of what he's packing. If only I can summon up the guts to go through with this, I'm going to be one lucky woman tonight.

It's then I realise I've made my decision. Drew, making me laugh, making me promises he'll never hurt me. Suddenly the remaining power Flint has over me starts to fade. A burst of rage goes through me, chasing the remainder away. Why let him ruin this? What I've wanted since I became a woman? *No, I tell myself with determination. I won't allow thoughts of him to intrude.* It's only Drew and me here. Drew, the man of my dreams.

"Why are you staying over there? Come lie beside me." He pats the sheets.

But I don't. I do something else. Taking a fortifying breath, I go to the end of the bed and climb on. Then, on my knees, I crawl until I'm sitting on his thighs, one leg one side, one the other. I look down at the red hat with the white bobble on the top, it's still twitching.

I smile, then grin as I look up at my man. "I think this is on the wrong head." Brazenly I remove his covering and place the Santa hat on my own head, my action exposing a very erect, thick, long cock.

Gingerly, I reach out and touch it, enclosing as much in my hand as I can, noting my fingers can't close around it, relishing the feeling of steel covered velvet.

He gasps and throws back his head.

I stroke him, up and down, my hand grasping him firmly.

"Babe," he says hoarsely. "While I love your hand on me, I'm going to blow if you keep up what you're doing. Come up here."

But before I obey him, I lower my mouth, licking the drop of pre-cum that's escaping, then kissing the tip of his dick.

"Babe," he grates. "Here, now."

Now I move, inching my way up the bed. For the first

time, it's me initiating the kiss. He lets me lead for a short while, but man that he is, he can't resist placing a hand to the back of my head and taking over. His taste is in my mouth, his scent fills the air. His fingers grip my hair as our lips move together.

Then he lifts my head away, his eyes searching mine. "Are you ready?"

"I think I am," I admit, my voice soft and low.

"You can stop this at any time, Amy. We can take it at your pace."

His reassurance, his care for me and the love shining from his eyes starts me thinking that we're taking things too slow. "I need you, Drew."

In an unsteady voice, he all but begs, "Show me those tits, babe. Show me what I've been dreaming of."

Crossing my arms, I grab the hem of my tee, and with only a second's hesitation when I worry he'll be disappointed in me, I pull off my top.

"Brown," he says, reverently. As he reaches up a hand, he gently brushes his knuckles over my nipples. "I always wondered."

God, his light touch is doing things to me. My stomach clenches.

"Mouth, babe."

Interpreting what he means, I lean forward, balancing my hands on the headboard while his lips and tongue work what he doesn't know yet is one of my most erogenous zones. His teeth nip gently, then he moves my body to the left and applies the same attention to my other nipple.

I close my eyes and give a low murmur of appreciation.

"Are you wet for me?"

"So wet," I manage to get out.

"Babe, I've got to taste you."

I find I have no objection at all.

"Take off your shorts."

Logistically, I can do nothing else but unwrap my hands from the headboard, lift my left knee rather ungainly, and roll on my back. Then, putting my thumbs in the elastic, push my sleep shorts down my legs, toeing them off completely.

"Bare," he says softly. "I like." He's on his side, gazing at me. "Fuck, Amy, you're even more beautiful than I imagined you'd be." His fingers gently caress my skin, while his eyes feast on me. "What's this?"

"Appendix scar."

"Jeez. While you were in Phoenix?"

I nod. "Three years back."

"I didn't know. Were Heart and Marc with you?"

"It happened so fast. It was an emergency. I was in too much pain, then in surgery. When I came around… Well, there didn't seem any point. Luckily I didn't have any complications, and I had the best care. One of the perks of being a nurse and being taken ill in your own hospital."

"You'll never have to cope on your own again."

I honestly don't know why I did. Dad and Marc would have been there like a shot. But it warms me that he cares so much.

Then I forget to breathe as I realise he's moved, now he's on his knees between my legs.

"So fuckin' pretty."

His fingers trace my labia, gently parting my lower lips, then he lowers his head and I suck in a lungful of air. It makes him pause. "You doing okay?"

"No," I tell him, making him tense, so follow it up fast, "I think I'll die if you don't get your mouth on me."

He places a kiss to the inside of my thigh, sucking so he'll leave his mark there. A mark I'll wear proudly.

"My mouth, here?" he asks, his voice shaking as he laughs.

"No," I say, desperately.

"Where do you want my mouth, Amy?"

"On my clit," I gasp, my experience in clubs means I'm not shy about using the word.

He takes his time, marking my other thigh first, then, when I'm about to pass out from frustration, he at last moves to the spot where I want him.

"So fuckin' wet for me. Fuck, Amy, I could die a happy man now."

"I'll die if you don't suck me," I manage to rasp, my hands clutching at the blanket, my hips rising.

Then he stops torturing me, but soon he's tormenting me in delicious ways. His fingers are inside me, one, then two, curling around and finding that spot unerringly. He sucks and licks at my clit, driving me mad, I'm reaching for, reaching for…

He stops.

"You doing okay?" His question rumbles against me.

"Drew!" I admonish.

He chuckles before starting his sensual assault again, this time taking pity on me and not ceasing until I go over the top, my back bowing off the bed. *Christ, that was amazing.* My head flops down as he slowly brings me back to earth. Only to start all over again.

After my body's stopped quivering, he raises his head. "Are you ready?" he asks once again.

"Would you stop?" Though I try to force them away, memories of Flint entering me assault me. But then, I wasn't turned on, I remind myself.

"Amy, I'll stop any time you want me to. If you're not ready…"

"I'm ready. Drew, I'm so ready." I want him. Need him.

He'd obviously had a condom prepared, and I watch as he slides it on carefully. Then he lines himself up, an intense expression on his face. He leans over me. "I'll stop," he repeats. "If it gets too much."

"You think you're too big for me?" I widen my eyes in mock challenge.

"I didn't mean it that way," he laughs. "But yeah, that too."

"Do your worst, big boy." Again my hips flex.

He starts pushing in. He is big, no denying that. I breathe through the initial burn. There's no one else in the room with us, and for the first time since it happened, there's no one in my head. *This is Drew.* How did I get so damn lucky? I've spent my life waiting for this moment all my life.

He doesn't disappoint in any way, and when he's fully in and says, "Amy, you were made for me," I know exactly what he means.

"Gonna move now."

"Please." I'll resort to begging if I have to.

Christ, has this man got moves. At first he thrusts gently, when I open my eyes briefly it's to see him watching my face, checking that I'm right there with him. Then he starts speeding up. My hands tangle in the covers once again as my body starts to clench.

"Fuck, Amy. Fuck. You feel so fuckin' good."

But I can't answer him, not when he swivels his hips, making sure he's hitting that special spot inside me. Then he does it again, and again.

"Drew, I'm going to…"

"Come for me," he commands. "Come on my cock."

I do, the orgasm hitting me so hard and fast that I scream.

"Fuck, Amy. Fuck, babe. I'm coming." He thrusts hard and fast. Again, I open my eyes to see his closed, his jaw clenched tight, his face reddened from exertion. Then he stops, groans, throws back his head, and with a final short jerk reaches his own peak. I don't think I've ever seen anything so beautiful in my whole life. Drew, in the midst of his pleasure. Drew making love to *me*.

He takes a shuddering breath, then another. Then opens his eyes and looks down. "Never, ever felt this good, Amy. Never. I was right. You were made for me." Then he ruins, or enhances the moment when he adds, "Looks like all I need to do to get you in my bed is to wear a Santa hat on my cock."

I punch him lightly, but am soon chuckling, then I stop. "You're the best Christmas present I've ever had," I tell him, my eyes conveying my earnestness. Reaching up, I place my hand against his cheek, the skin warm and still flushed from his release. "You're my very own Santa."

CHAPTER FOURTEEN

Heart

"You were tossing and turning all night," Marc tells me. "You're planning something, I know it. Do I want to know what this ride today is really about?"

Marc's sharp, she's still got the nose of a cop for sniffing out trouble. I try to throw her off the scent. "Just a chance for the guys to get some fresh air," I reassure her. But one look into her eyes shows she doesn't believe me. After all the years together, she can read me like a fucking book.

Her lips press together as if she's trying to hold words inside. After a moment she says, "Just take care." That that's all proves how good an old lady she is.

"I will," I promise, intently. I move my body over hers, letting her feel the cock that, even after all these years, is always rock hard for her.

"Have you got time?"

"I'll make time," I promise.

We move in practised unison. My cock finding her pussy, the vasectomy I'd had after our third child, meaning I take her bare without worry. In tune with each other, it's not long before she cries out, and I roar as my cum rushes from my balls to my cock, and into her.

"Messy." But she's got a smile on her face.

"Always," I tell her, planting a kiss to the tip of her nose. Leaning back on my haunches, I watch my cum running out of her, her pussy glistening with the evidence of us coming together. It's a sight I never get tired of. After placing my finger briefly in her cunt, I bring it to my lips and taste our combined juices.

"Pervert."

I grin. "Always," I repeat. Then after a glance at the clock beside the bed, "Fuck, I've got to get a move on." Drummer might no longer be the prez, but I still don't dare keep him waiting.

As I move around the room pulling my clothes together, she lies there, unashamed in her nakedness, watching me.

"You could take my rat bike."

Barking a laugh, I try to imagine it. "Peg would go mad. He hates that fuckin' thing." I'm actually tempted for a moment to wind him up.

"Only because you'd leave him in your dust."

Too fucking right I would. I'm still scared when I see her riding it, though I know she's a good fucking rider, and I trust her to take care. But that thing can accelerate fast, and I don't even like to think of its top speed. As for cornering, she can almost lay it over. I will admit though, it's a blast to ride.

"I'll be back late afternoon, maybe tonight." I lean over to kiss her, tempted to take my chance for a second morning fuck and to hell with the outcome if I make Drummer wait. With difficulty, I restrain myself and straighten up.

"I'd like to catch up with Amy before she leaves. Check she's alright. She seemed happier last night."

"She did, didn't she? Marc, can you believe it? Our little Amy, marrying the prez and living on the compound."

When she reaches out her hand, I grasp it. "It's perfect, Heart. They've always been close. I know he'll never hurt her. But Amy, the first lady. How about that? Hey, I'll always remember the time she called me Mom for the first time."

Unfortunately I do as well. I frown, "I was an ass."

"Water under the bridge now, Heart." She giggles. "Me carrying your twins brought you to your senses."

I tickle her ribs. "And you didn't fuckin' believe me. I was right, you were wrong." If it comes out in a sing-song voice, I don't care. Have to keep stock of my few victories.

She bats my hands away. "It was the first and only time, Heart."

"You think you're always right?" But I've nothing to support any argument. She's probably correct.

Stopping my torture, I lean down and kiss her sweetly, then raise my head back up. "Now all we've got to do is make sure Isabel and Alexis never leave the compound."

Her eyes roll. "What is it with men and their daughters?"

My eyes fall again on the clock which has been mercilessly counting the minutes. "Shit, darlin', I gotta go."

Lines appear on her brow. "Promise me, you'll come home."

She's not stupid, and I'd rather not say anything than lie to her. I settle for a simple, "I promise. When you see Amy, give her my love, will you?" Knowing it was quite possible I wouldn't see her this morning, I'd said goodbye to her yesterday evening.

"I will, Heart. But she won't be gone long this time."

I hope not, trusting that when the month has passed, she'll be home forever.

Closing our bedroom door I descend the stairs. When I

get to the bottom, Isabel waves a cup of coffee in my direction.

"Dad, aren't you getting too old for you and mom to—"

I put my hand over her mouth. "Never." The kids are all of age now, and I don't feel the slightest remorse that she heard me and her mom. I'd rather she heard us making love than growing up with parents always fighting.

I'm still chuckling at her audacity as I walk down the incline.

I find the others already waiting outside the auto-shop.

"Finished getting your dick wet?" Peg calls out.

"Like you didn't," I throw back, and his smug grin shows I'm right. I glance at Wraith.

The ex-VP shrugs. "Sophie insisted."

Blade shouts out, "Tash is insatiable, what's a man to do?"

Mouse barks a laugh.

"You too?" I ask. His smirk confirms it.

"Alright, alright," says Drummer. "Enough about your morning fucks."

"Sam not put out?" Peg challenges him. "That why you're in a mood?"

"I'm not in a fuckin' mood," he snaps back. "And as if it's any of your business, she always does. Likes to see my engine revving."

Hmm. TMI. I know he has a V-twin tattooed on his chest, but I really don't want to think of how that might move when he's getting down to business.

"Right, gather around." When Drummer uses that serious tone, we fall silent, and stand in a group around him, why we're here taking precedence over any joking. "Mouse has confirmed Flint's got the day off work, so we'll assume he's at home. We all know what we're doing?"

We take a few moments going over the plan again. When

Drummer's satisfied we're as prepared as we can be, he signals we should go to our bikes. My mood changes, and I'm focused on just one thing. I'm going to find the man who hurt my baby girl and get my revenge on him. By tonight, there'll be one less bastard breathing.

"Mornin'," a loud voice shouts out.

We all swing around. Fuck, if it wasn't so serious I'd laugh at the look Drummer's sporting. For the first time ever that I can remember, he's gone a bright shade of red, and his eyes are shifting to the side. Embarrassment and guilt written all over his face.

Prez is wheeling his bike down the track. Hawk, his VP, is alongside him, behind is his sergeant-at-arms, Hound, and finally Throttle, his enforcer.

"Mornin'." Drummer recovers fast. He leans back against his bike and folds his arms. "You going for a ride out as well?" he asks deceptively casually.

"Thought we'd tag along, it's such a nice day."

Nice day? I glance up at the sky where dark clouds are forming, glad I've got my wet weather gear in my saddlebags. I realise our problem and wonder how the fuck Drummer's going to get out of it.

"Nah," he tells Wizard with a shake of his head. "Us old-timers are going to take it slow and steady. You'll just get bored."

Prez looks around at his companions. "We don't mind a gentle ride. Be good for us to lay off the throttle for once."

Fuck.

Even Drummer seems stumped about how he's going to handle this. What can we do? Go for a short ride, say we're turning back and hope they go off on their own? I really don't want to cancel. I raise my chin toward Drum, directing a pleading look at him. But he responds with a shrug and a shake of his head.

Wizard kicks down the stand of his bike to support it, then walks the few steps to join us. Hawk, Throttle, and Hound also leave their rides and gather behind him. A show of support for the prez.

"I know what you're doing." Wizard addresses Drummer first, then his eyes fall on us one by one.

Fuck.

"You can't stop us, Wiz." Drum lays those steel eyes on him.

"Can't I?" he says, deceptively lazily. "What if your *prez*," he emphasises the word, "forbids it?"

Fuck me. I raise my eyebrows in horror. If he did that, there's no way we can go through with it. *Amy,* I vow, *I'll get rid of Flint on my own if I have to.* But that would mean going against my prez which could lose me my patch and get me thrown out of the club. Fuck. I've given thirty years of my life to this MC, could I really walk away from it? What would I do without the Satan's Devils behind me?

Wizard's allowing us a moment to think. Suddenly he barks a laugh and claps his hand down on Drummer's shoulder.

"Fuckin' old men," he says without malice, then turns his head to address his companions. "Thinking they can get away with shit without needing babysitters." His face hardens and his voice becomes deep as he looks toward me, then addresses Drummer, "This concerns the woman who's going to be my old lady. You're going after the fucker who *raped* her, for fuck's sake. You think for one fuckin' second we're staying behind?" *He knows.* Amy must have told him. I suppose it's a plus they've a relationship where she's able to confide.

Wizard waits a moment for that to sink in, while I let out the breath I hadn't realised I'd been holding. Finally he finishes with, "So," he grins evilly at Drummer, "what's the plan?"

We discuss what we'd decided for a few minutes, and Wizard makes some adjustments as is his right.

When we all know what we're doing, Peg asks, frown lines on his face, "How the hell did you know what we were doing? What gave us away?"

Wizard glances at Mouse. "I checked what you'd been searching. Flint's address, his work schedule…"

"Fuck, Wiz." Mouse is shaking his head.

Two hours later, we're riding around the back of an abandoned office building in Phoenix, stopping at the rear parking lot which is hidden from the road. Mouse had somehow managed to find a suitable place to use at short notice. As we get off our bikes, I notice Peg's hands massaging the middle of his back and he's rolling his head to get the kinks out of his neck. Drummer's shaking out his hands. Blade, having driven the plain white crash truck, grins as he steps down.

A light drizzle is falling, not enough to make us stop and suit up in our wet gear, so while my leather jacket kept my body dry, my jeans are damp which is playing hell with the leg I'd shattered twice in the past. I flex it, rubbing my thigh and calf when I bend down.

To give him his due, Wizard and the officers with him give us a moment making no witty comments about old men.

Wasting no time, Blade's already switching the plates on the truck.

Our new plan is that just four of us will go to Flint's house in the truck with Blade, while the rest stay with the bikes. This many bikers would stand out, even if we're not flying colours. Wizard had also suggested another amendment, one which made Blade and Throttle exchange grins.

We'd agreed I would be one of the ones in the truck—well I wasn't going to miss out on visiting the bastard's lair. Same goes for Wizard. With us will be the current and ex sergeant-at-arms. It was a good move. No one in their right minds would face off against a big fucker like Peg, and that also goes for Hound.

The next step in the plan requires me swearing on my children's life not to punch Flint in the face immediately upon seeing him. My word had been necessary; we'd agreed that I'll be the one to approach Flint's front door as I apparently look the least threatening. That's okay, I've been underestimated many times.

Having switched plates, Blade checks with Mouse and programs the GPS. Then, with back slaps and instructions to get the fucking job done, we pile into the truck.

Five minutes later and we're at our destination. I'm tense as we first take a casual drive up the street to give us a chance to assess the house and the surrounding area. Mouse though, I'm pleased to see, had got it right, and the privacy Flint clearly desires is going to be his downfall. I share a twisted grin with Prez. Blade pulls the truck over and parks.

"I couldn't see any cameras, and the hedge will give us some cover," Wizard offers.

"When you get there, keep your head down, Heart," Peg suggests, "in case he has security on the front door."

Appreciating the unnecessary warning, I give him a sharp nod. "I'll keep my eye out."

"His car was parked to the side of the house. I couldn't see any windows along that wall," Hound comments. "He wouldn't see the damage from inside."

"Then we don't need to actually slash the tyres," Prez says. "We'll just tell him that's what's been done. Blade, make sure you're ready to come on Heart's signal."

"Here." Hound hands me the overalls he'd grabbed from our auto-shop. Awkwardly, as there's not a lot of space, I slip into them. Now I'll just look like a mechanic on his way home from work.

"You got your head in the right place for this, Heart?" Prez checks, his eyes hardening as they find mine. "Remember, success hinges on you keeping your cool. Trusting you, Brother."

Raising my chin, I give my silent promise.

"Okay. Let's get this show on the road." Prez opens the door and gets out, we follow him. "Ready boys?"

I rise up on the balls of my feet then let my heels down. "Never been readier."

"Ready, Prez," comes followed by two more affirmative replies.

As Prez bangs twice on the truck, Blade drives off to find somewhere to make a U-turn and will return so he's facing the right way down the street. Next Wizard, Peg, and Hound start walking sharply in the direction of Flint's house. While I give them a minute to get into position, in case anyone's watching, I bend down and pretend to tie an imaginary bootlace.

Time. I stand and take a deep breath. My job is getting Flint out of the house unharmed and without arousing his suspicion. But knowing the fucker has had his hands on my kid means it's a mammoth task to remember not to punch him in the jaw at first sight. But I've promised my prez, and if I want him dead, and want to live life as a free man, this is the way I'll have to play it.

Nonchalantly, I walk down the street. I walk past the house, stop then turn back. Then moving to one side, I make myself look like I'm trying to stay out of sight of the garage. Then I approach and ring the front door.

It takes two presses of the button before I hear movement inside.

Fuck. A woman answers, her face tightening at the sight of a stranger. Her presence may be a complication which could fuck up the plan. Then I notice the yellow/greenish signs of a healing black eye and wonder if maybe, it won't.

She eyes me up and down and makes her own assumptions from the clothes I'm wearing. "I'm sorry, you must have the wrong house. We didn't call anyone out."

"Is the man of the house home?" I lean forward and almost whisper, "You've got a problem." I jerk my head toward the side of the house where the car is parked out of sight. Behind my back I cross my fingers, if he's not, hopefully my brothers will find something to use as an excuse if it's her that goes looking.

I'm dressed as a mechanic, maybe she thinks I spotted a puddle of oil under his vehicle, but whatever, she doesn't seem suspicious.

Instead she half turns. "Malc? Someone for you."

When he comes, she sidles away, giving a pointed glare to his back. She's leaving him to my mercy, not that he's going to get much of that.

"Who are you and what do you want?" he demands in an authoritative voice. The sound of someone used to getting his own way.

I motion with my finger against my lips. "There are three men, they look like they're trying to get into your car."

"What the hell?"

I nod. "I was just passing and saw them." I look him up and down. "I didn't want to approach them by myself, but the two of us can probably chase them off."

"Damn right we can." He puffs up his chest, then pushes me aside and strides off to where his car is parked.

I follow, surreptitiously sliding my phone into my hand and shooting off a text to Blade.

Damn but Devils are good. In the few seconds head start I've given them, by the time I round the corner it's to see Flint lying on the ground, tape over his mouth. Though it's not necessary right now, but will keep him quiet when he regains consciousness.

"Who hit him?"

"Peg." Hound pauses, looking at the front yard which as Mouse had said, has high hedges and a security fence all around. "Fucker went out like a light."

He would have. Peg might be nearing sixty, but he still works out and has got a lot of power in his right arm, as I've found out when I've been pitched against him in our ring.

Then it's all action as Blade backs the crash truck onto the drive in such a way as it looks like he's chosen this driveway to turn around. It goes smooth and fast. Hound fast has the unconscious man in a fireman's lift and deposits him in the back of the truck while we pile inside. Then we're off, the whole thing taking only seconds. Our only problem is if the wife is looking out. I'd glanced back, but hadn't seen any sign of her.

We reverse our tracks to the parking lot where we left the others and our bikes. Quick as a flash, Blade changes the license plates back to the normal ones, then he's just driving a plain white truck, no different from a million others on the road.

"Any trouble?"

"Nah, Drum. Went like a dream," Prez tells him with a wide grin. "In and fuckin' out fast."

"The wife was home," I warn them. "It's possible she saw us putting him in the truck if she was looking out."

"We're not wearing cuts. She could report the make and

model of the truck, but even if she clocked the plate, it won't matter."

I listen hard but can hear no sirens, which is good. She could give a description of me. But hell, I don't care. We've got the fucker who hurt Amy, mission fuckin' successful. Even if she's asked to look at a photo line-up, they're unlikely to find me.

"I don't want to hang around," Prez starts, then turns. "Blade, he's trussed like a Thanksgiving turkey, gagged to boot. If he comes round, he shouldn't give you any trouble. If he does, pull over, and we'll knock him out again."

Blade nods and grins at Prez's instructions. "I can manage that myself." He waves his hands. "Fists are fine, it's straightening my fingers out that gives me problems."

"Mount up, Brothers. Let's go home."

We ride out, Blade following behind in the crash truck. I grin to myself. Blade looks more cheerful than he has for some time, that arthritis in his hands is a bitch. I hope, when we get Flint back to the compound, Throttle steps back and lets his predecessor have some fun. He deserves it.

CHAPTER FIFTEEN

Heart

Instead of following through with our original plan to do what we had to do in a discreet location in Phoenix, it had been Prez's idea to take him back to the compound where we can take our time. It's safe to say everyone was on board with the changes Wiz had suggested. One benefit of him insisting on coming along with us.

We ride carefully in formation back to Tucson, Prez and his boys leading the pack, Drummer and Wraith behind, then Peg and Mouse, and finally, myself. When I hear a siren behind us and a squad car comes into sight, I'm tempted to twist my throttle, but Wizard signals that we're to go into single file and slow down. Blade pulls over to the side, and the cops go whizzing past, with only a cursory glance in our direction. Then we resume our journey, me with a loud thumping in my chest.

I sigh with relief when we reach the compound and offer up thanks that before his death, Viper had the foresight to put pavement down all the way to the storeroom. Just for occasions such as this, though as far as the women knew, it was to bring shit in and out without carrying heavy boxes up from the gate. So Blade carries on driving while we back into our parking slots outside the clubhouse.

I glance in the window, see some of the women looking up expectantly at the door, but as no one enters, they go back to what they're doing. I grin at the sight of the huge Christmas tree in the corner. What we're going to do now is incongruous with the spirit of the season. Or is it? Flint's going to welcome the gift of death in a few hours' time.

"Coming?"

Try and keep me a-fuckin'-way. Alongside the others, full of anticipation, I walk up the track that leads to the isolated and soundproofed storeroom.

"Fucker's come round," Blade informs us as we arrive, but the thumping and banging from the truck render his words unnecessary.

Hound nods at Throttle, and they go to the back doors, open them, and then together they pull the bound man out by his feet, uncaring as his head smashes to the ground. Watching, I feel no sympathy as he's dragged into the storeroom, my head full of how he'd hurt my little girl. There, expertly as if they're masters at this, they soon have him strung up, and Throttle's slicing off his clothes.

I raise my eyebrow at Blade and grin. Seems the new guard is just as competent as we used to be, and still are, given half the chance. Blade's returning grin back is reminiscent of that you'd see on a Halloween decoration. *He's getting ready to go to work.*

Finally, Wizard strips the tape gag off, taking facial hair with it. Again, I don't wince on his behalf. I don't give a fuck how much he's hurting. It will be nothing to how he'll be feeling soon enough, and less than he deserves.

"Who are you?" Flint starts shouting. "Let me go. What

the hell do you want? Money? Huh, haven't got much of that. I've done nothing to you, let me go."

I tap Wizard on the shoulder, it's clear he's tense as he tries to hold himself back. But in deference to my being her father, he raises his chin toward me.

Stepping up in front of the man, I stand still for a moment. When I've got his full attention, I spit out, "You fucked with the wrong woman." At his look of confusion, suddenly aware that Amy was probably not his first, I clarify, "Amy Norman."

Flint stills, then protests, "I don't know anyone by that name. You've got the wrong man. Now let me go and I won't say anything."

It's him alright. But it's possible he's not lying. In such an establishment she could have used a fake name, so I refresh his memory. "Three months back at the Feathers BDSM Club. The woman you abused and raped. The woman you've been stalking ever since."

He sneers. "Abused and raped? It's a fucking BDSM club for God's sake. Women go there to be abused and have sex."

Wizard's lost his patience and steps up beside me. "Penetration's not allowed at that club."

Flint pouts. "Well damnit, it should be. It's a sex club."

"It's a kink club," I correct.

He shrugs as if there's no difference; however, I know there is.

Prez growls loudly, "There's a thing called consent—"

"It was consensual," he protests. "She wanted it that way. If she says anything different, she's a liar."

"Then why were you stripped of your membership? And why did the dungeon monitor who pulled you off, confirm her story?"

He blusters. "It was all a mistake. I broke the rules of the club, but I did nothing she didn't ask for. Look, when a bitch is gagging for it, you give it to them."

"I don't believe you." Prez's voice has gone eerily calm. Wiz has learned a lot over the years from his old prez, it's a bit like watching Drummer at work. "None of us," he indicates the men standing around, "believe you." He points to me. "This is Amy's father. Do you think he's going to show you any mercy?"

There's a flicker of fear in Flint's eyes, but still he tries again. "I didn't hurt your daughter. Well, not beyond what she wanted."

"She wanted to be raped?" I approach him having seen Prez's chin lift. "If she wanted sex, why was she at a club that banned it?" When he opens his mouth, I give him the answer myself, "Because she wanted a safe place to play, where she could be herself, where she could relax and have fun, knowing there were limits."

He must see something in the expression on my face, as he shouts out, "She wanted it. I swear. She wanted it!"

Knowing there was no fucking way she asked for anything of the sort, my fist smashes into his jaw. So hard, I have to give it a shake to remove the sting from it, knowing Marc will question why my knuckles are broken and bleeding. *Must have hit a fucking tooth.* And I'm right on the money, as he spits one out.

Wizard gently moves me out of the way and takes his place in front of Flint. He waits patiently while Flint spits more blood out of his mouth, and for his eyes to focus on him. "Now you've… met… Amy's father, let me tell you who I am. I'm Wizard, President of the Satan's Devils MC. Amy was born into this club, and unlike you, we'll do anything for one of our own." He pauses to let that sink in for a moment, the coldness in his tone emphasising the implication. Flint seems to shrink back into himself. His eyes open wide as it appears to dawn on him, if we've told him who we are, he's not getting out of this.

"I'll give you money. I'll give her money. I've not got much, I'll mortgage my house..." Christ, I wouldn't be surprised if he offered us his children.

"Rude," Wizard states. "You didn't let me finish. Amy's club property, ours to protect. More than that, she's my old lady. You think money can fix what you've done? You believe the nightmares she still has can be wiped away with a handful of dollars? You fuckin' know a submissive gives control to a Dom because she trusts him. She trusted you Flint, and you took that trust, tore it up and shredded it."

"You let your old lady go alone to a kink club?"

Prez stops him talking with a fist to the opposite side that I'd hit, his Satan's Devils' ring contacting with his eye. Right on target.

"You've taken out my fucking eye!" Flint screams, shaking his head, trying to rid himself of the stinging pain.

"Not yet I haven't, but it's an idea," Wizard says drily. "Blade, would you like to do the honours?"

Blade gives an evil and chilling chuckle and, as well as he can, flexes his gnarled hands. "Sure would. An eye for a rape. Sounds fair." Then he snaps out, "Hold him."

"No. For the sake of God, no." Flint's screaming. "No, you can't. No!"

Throttle and Hound step up. It takes them a moment to subdue him, but soon Hound's holding his head in a headlock and Throttle's holding a knife to his throat.

"Move and this is all over," he warns. "You might survive losing an eye, but I'll cut your fuckin' throat if you keep fighting.

Flint squeals like a stuck pig. He's gone completely white and Blade hasn't even touched him yet.

"Not my eye. Please, I beg you. Not my eye. Anything but my eye."

Then he's screaming again, forgetting the threat of the knife at his throat, he jerks back against Hound who just grips him more tightly. The ex-enforcer approaches, gripping a stiletto blade firmly. With one hand he parts the eyelids of the swollen eye, then waits.

"No. No. You…"

Blade strikes. Christ, I don't think I've heard anyone scream so loudly as Blade proudly brandishes Flint's eyeball in front of him still pierced by the stiletto. With his other hand, he takes another knife from his belt and calmly slices through the ligaments still attaching it to the socket.

"My eye. You've blinded me," Flint sobs. "Christ, my eye." All the time Blade's holding the eye in front of him as though it's a trophy.

"You're all crazy," Flint sobs, blood dripping from his empty socket, and tears streaming from his one remaining eye.

Prez is tapping his chin, looking thoughtful, his face gradually darkening, betraying the direction of his thoughts. "I had a chat with my ol' lady last night. You know what she fuckin' told me?" He pauses and looks around at each of us. "You know what I had to hear from my woman? Do you want to know how this man gets his kicks?" He blanches as though even the thought pains him, and his gaze meets mine, sending an apology. "This man tied her up, gagged her. She couldn't scream for help, he ignored her non-verbal signals. He fucking hit her, abused her, and he dared to put his cock inside her. You think one eye pays for what this scum did? I fuckin' don't. In fact, I don't think Flint deserves to see another pretty girl ever again in his life."

As he spells out what she went through, Throttle, Hound, and Hawk clearly hearing the details for the first time, swear loudly. It's almost too much for Hawk, who turns away, hurling his fist against the wall. Throttle's vibrating with anger, and Hound's gone still.

Prez's calm, cold, retelling had been hard hearing to even my brothers who already know most of the details. Drummer's stroking his beard, pain showing on his face.

Eyes come to me, her father. Then go to Prez, her old man. I catch his gaze and say simply, "Blind him, Prez."

"My turn," says Throttle, tightly. "Blade, walk me through how you did it."

If I thought Flint was shouting loudly before, his bellows are almost deafening as Blade takes his time, and makes a show of instructing Throttle just how to insert the blade and twist. I'm sure Throttle could work it out for himself, but Flint's begging, promising us everything he owns, just to leave him some vision.

I'm glad the room's soundproofed. Christ, the scream as Throttle takes out his one remaining eye is ear piercing.

"Fucking shame he can't see this." Throttle shakes his head in disappointment as both he and Blade display their prizes.

"We could let him go free," Wraith suggests. "He wouldn't last long if we dumped him on the freeway." We all start laughing. I'm picturing him stumbling in front of a truck.

"No, no, no…" Flint's got blood running down his face from his empty eye sockets.

"You want to die yet?" Wizard asks him seriously. "You ready to beg for us to end you?"

"You know what Slick would suggest?" Mouse refers to our brother who's passed over.

Drummer, Wraith, Peg, Blade, and I grin at each other, while Wizard cocks his head, not certain of the answer.

"Cut off his fuckin' dick." Blade's jumping on the spot, looking cheerful.

"Christ yeah," says Throttle. "Always wanted to try that."

Peg's shaking his head at his son, though the grin shows he's proud of him.

"He wouldn't be able to fuck anyone again," Hawk observes. "Good fuckin' idea, Mouse."

Flint's screamed pleas for mercy are now almost drowning us out. It's getting hard to hear each other.

It's annoying Prez. "Throttle, cut out his fucking tongue, will you? Fed up with hearing this piece of shit."

Hawk and Hound step up. It takes them a moment as Flint is surprisingly not cooperative. But they get him in position for the enforcer, and soon his tongue is out too. Now he's making odd sounds and is definitely quieter and spitting blood out of his mouth.

"He could bleed out from that," Blade observes casually and certainly with no pity.

"I want to make him hurt." I raise my eyebrow at Wizard, thinking cutting off his dick probably would. But it seems it's not enough. "I want to send him to Satan with every part of him screaming."

Prez's eyes land on me. "He raped your daughter." He points to himself. "He raped my ol' lady." Now he looks at each of the others in turn. "He raped our property. He left her broken, and she'll never completely recover from that. I think we all deserve a piece of him."

None of us mistake what he means. It's Drummer who steps up first, cutting through the tendons in one leg, Wraith goes for the other. Hawk slices off one ear, and Peg attacks his left arm, then Hound his right. Mouse, with a wide grin at Blade, goes behind the gurgling man, and slowly, and deliberately, uses a suspiciously old looking knife to slice off his scalp.

An arm's been left for me, I take my own knife from my belt and slice through it. Flint flops like a grounded fish, only the ropes holding him up, his body twitching like a marionette.

Wizard has retrieved the bat we keep for such purposes, now he lets his rage loose, breaking both his legs, well, to be accurate, smashing them to pieces. I grimace, remembering how much that hurt, but maybe it's too late… no, I saw movement, he's still conscious.

"Can I go for his dick now? Can I, can I?" Throttle sounds eager, just like his predecessor.

"Wait," I say, taking the bat from Wizard, wanting something to satisfy my burning anger. The satisfying crunch tells me I've broken his ribs.

"Now?" Throttle tries again.

"Yeah," Prez says.

There's an attempt at a scream from the broken body. It's more of a gurgling strangled sound.

"Christ. His bowels have let loose," Throttle complains, gingerly picking up the limp cock with his now latex covered hands.

Drummer comes up beside me, laying his hand on my shoulder. This is the end, we all know it. A man can't exist without his dick, or not unless he has pretty quick treatment.

He's dying already from the punishment we've inflicted. Maybe he won't even feel it, but the thought of removing a rapist's dick is highly satisfying.

"Slice his balls, Brother," Blade offers helpfully.

The enforcer wastes no time in doing just that. Then he

raises his knife one last time. "This is for Amy. Goddamn your soul for ever touching our sister."

His cock, which he used to rape my daughter, is now lying on the floor. I view it for a moment, then turn away, disgusted. Not at what we've done, but at what the man did.

But he's no longer a man, he's a bloody broken mess. All I feel is relief and a sense that he'd gotten off lightly. His suffering lasted an hour or so at most. Amy has got to live with what he did, forever.

"Get the prospects up here," Wizard instructs.

"He's not gone yet," warns Peg.

"Don't give a damn if he's breathing or not when he goes to his grave. He'll be dead soon after."

"Nathan will have gone with Amy," Hawk reminds him. "But I don't mind helping with clean up."

I glance at Wizard seeing him grimacing. Yeah, by now, Amy will be back in Phoenix, but at least she's got a prospect to protect her even though, while she may not know it, the threat is gone.

"I don't mind giving them a hand to dispose of the trash."

"Yeah, I'll help too," offers Hound. He nods at Hawk.

No one needs any instruction on what to do, we're practised at this. And yet again, Road's track will be extended a little bit, the name still sticking even though he's with another club and, like the rest of us being older, doesn't ride in trials any longer.

Drummer slaps his hand on my shoulder again. "The girls are laying out a buffet. Anyone want food?"

"Sounds good," I reply, turning my back on the thing in the chair.

"Not me," Blade shudders, and Mouse goes over to him. "Come on, man." With his arm around his shoulders, he leads the ex-enforcer out into the fresh air.

"He's never gotten over that, has he?" observes Wraith.

Nope, surprisingly he hasn't. He always pukes after he's done his job. I reckon, myself, it's something to do with the adrenaline hit, rather than him being squeamish.

The rest of us? Well it turns out we've worked up quite the appetite.

CHAPTER SIXTEEN

Amy

There was never really any doubt what my decision would be after the month Drew had given me had run out. Somehow, my subconscious had known what I'd do, as the very first day I went back to work after Christmas, I'd handed in my resignation.

But I did use the time to do some serious thinking. One side of my brain was telling me, rushing headlong into a relationship with Drew was a mistake. On the other hand, it wasn't as if we'd only just met and I didn't know everything about him that's important—his loyalty, the depth of his commitment once he makes one, his truthfulness and reliability. That in conversation he gives weight and consideration to anything I say, something that goes back to when I was a child, and he'd taken notice of my opinion, even if it was an uninformed thought from a young mind.

If I listed everything I wanted in a life partner, Drew would tick every box, all but one. I worry if I'll be settling for something less than I want if I commit to him.

My perfect man would be dominant—not in day-to-day

living, but definitely in bed. I can't deny vanilla sex is amazing with Drew, but at the back of my mind worry I may become bored if it descends into a routine. I don't need to be tied up or blindfolded every time we make love, but occasionally I like to feel I can totally relax, and feel myself drift away into subspace, where I lose myself completely in the moment.

Can I live without that? It's the question I ponder when I see Drew at least once every week. He's fitted in with my shifts, often making the journey up to Phoenix and staying over for the night. On one occasion I'd driven down to Tucson, and it had felt so natural being back on the compound.

We've made love, but Drew's always been so careful, mindful of what happened with Flint and trying to do nothing that would bring back bad memories. On my part, while I trust him completely, my brain screams at the thought of experiencing the things I previously enjoyed. But one day, I hope to get to a better place where I'll want him to restrain me, where I'll want him to be inventive, but if he were to make such a suggestion now, you wouldn't see me for dust. But in time, I know, I'll want him to dominate me. Will he be able to be the man I want?

Vanilla sex with Drew? Or kink with someone like Xander?

I've come to the conclusion that there's no comparison. Maybe a month ago I'd say something different, but I love everything about Drew, and should he turn out not to be the most exciting lover, then what he can give me in everything else will more than compensate. He's a complete package, not just what he can offer in bed.

As well as deep thoughts about our relationship, I find myself damning Flint every day for how he's ruined my life. I hope one day his will be in tatters too.

I was shocked when Xander called me, not having expected to hear from him again, even though I yearned to call and apologise, and see how he's doing. The reason for him making contact was that the police had been making enquiries at the BDSM club. Apparently, Flint's wife had reported him missing a few days after Christmas, but they can't find out where he's gone. Most think he might have left her for a girl-friend, apparently his wife saw nothing suspicious, just that one minute he was there and the next he left. I wonder whether she's glad to be shot of him, and whether she'd ever had a taste of what he'd done to me. It wouldn't surprise me. Even if she hadn't, she might not know it, but she's better off without him in her life.

That he's missing doesn't make me feel easier. It would be better if someone was keeping tabs on his every move. I constantly worry I'll see him when I come out of the hospital, or that he'll be waiting for me back at the apartment, or even one of the stores I visit.

At least I'm never alone, Nathan's been my shadow, always there when I leave work, and accompanying me back home. I'm sure it must be the most boring job in the world being my babysitter, but he assures me he'll obey his prez's instructions to the letter. It's a sign of how much he wants his patch. Nevertheless, his being here has allowed me to have some semblance of peace of mind. He's also good company. As I've come to know him better, we've shared a few laughs.

Nathan told me he'd served in the army, and anyone can see he's tough and trained. If Flint did turn up, he wouldn't have a chance up against the taller more muscular prospect. His presence is what enables me to sleep at night—until I wake up screaming. Even there, Nathan's been a great help, waking me gently and making me a cup of hot chocolate. All part of his job, he tells me, when I apologise for disturbing his rest.

I'm hoping when I leave Phoenix and I no longer have to keep an eye out for Flint, maybe the memories will be easier to bear and the nightmares will ease up.

Drew tried to tell me I don't need to be concerned about the man who ruined my life, but he wouldn't explain how he could tell me that with such sincerity. It's probably just that he'd disappeared—maybe he got wind that the Devils were after him? He's out there somewhere, so my worries are only eased slightly. *I wish he were dead, then I wouldn't have to worry.* But I keep that to myself, remembering that while he's my Drew, the club named him Wizard because he can find out information that even eludes Mouse. If he knew what I wanted, he'd probably discover his whereabouts and kill him, and I don't want blood on the hands of the club. Heaven forbid Drew be arrested for murder. No, I shudder. Drew can't be responsible for taking Flint's life, so I'm not going to tell him I'd prefer the ultimate solution.

Once again, I think back to Xander's call. After he'd told me about Flint, I asked him a question.

"Are you doing alright, Xander?" Hearing his voice makes me feel guilty. "I owe you so much, yet I left you after I promised I'd be with you."

There's a sigh. "Let's get this straight, Amy. You weren't the love of my life, but I could see us together because we fit, and I have a lot of affection for you. I'm the type of Dom you want, and you're my ideal submissive. Of course, not how you are now, but before… when I saw you playing in the club. As a dungeon monitor I watched your scenes, seeing the reactions I like. Yes, I think we would have made a go of it, but love?"

He goes quiet for a moment, as if he's gathering his thoughts, then he continues, "I was born dominant, learned to have tight control over myself.

I don't allow myself to feel emotions, I'd never strike out in anger, and everything I do I give consideration to first, assessing the pros and cons, the best way to go about it, and what could go right, or wrong. I don't think I'm capable of feeling the unconditional love I know Drew has for you. That's why I left and didn't fight for you. I'd have been kind, respectful, given you everything you wanted, but I couldn't have given you the depth of emotion Drew clearly has to offer. If you want more than a Dom in your life, for you, he's the right choice."

"Will you find someone else?"

There's a pause. "Amy, you know how tightly I'm tied to the club. Yes, I'll play with the submissives, and maybe eventually find one I want in my life."

"I hope you do, Xander."

His voice deepens, becomes the tone used by Doms when they instruct. "Delete my number, Amy."

"You don't want to hear from me again?" He'd been my friend. Or perhaps, that concept is equally as alien to him as love.

"You've got Drew, Amy. Wipe the slate clean and explore what you have with him. Don't give him a moment of doubt."

I hadn't thought about it that way, that Drew might be jealous if I kept Xander's number on my phone.

"Thank you," I say, quickly to get it in before he ends the call. "I couldn't have gotten through those months without you by my side." He did so much for me, giving up a lot of his life. Giving up his precious club because going there would test me. Holding me at night but never pushing me to give something I wasn't ready to bestow.

"You were a sub in need, Amy. As a Dom, I needed to provide comfort and support. If I hear any more about Flint, I will let you know."

"What do you think happened to him?"

"With luck, he's left town." Xander might not allow himself to get angry, but I'm certain I hear a touch of that in his voice.

"Goodbye," he says.

When I try to say it back, he's already gone.

I'd deleted his number and had then cried.

"Well that's the last of your shit boxed up."

Startled out my reverie, I look up and smile. "Thanks, Nathan. You've been such a help." Having gotten to know the man over the past four weeks, it's not unexpected when he shrugs off the fact he's dismantled furniture, taken it to storage, and helped get everything in order, patiently waiting for me to decide what to take and what to store or what to give away. When it comes down to it, I won't be taking a lot.

"Have you finished in here?"

I'm in my living room. The walls are bare except for the boxes stacked against the wall. In my hand is the picture of Drew and I when I was a kid, and he'd taken me yet again to one of my favourite places, the Desert Museum. It's one I cherish. I slide it into the 'to take' box.

"That's it, I think." Looking around as I make one last check. I'm not particularly attached to this place, it was a two-bedroom apartment that I could afford to rent, but not one I'd have chosen if I had a choice. But I've lived here three years and have mostly good memories except for the last four months.

Nathan's moved to the window. "Good timing." He looks around and grins. "Prez is here with the truck."

As always, my stomach fills with butterflies fluttering around. It's not nerves, but anticipation. We've been apart for a week. But from now on, we'll be together, forever. It's a heady thought.

If I hadn't had the last month to consider what a fool I'd be to turn Drew down, I might have asked myself whether I was doing the right thing. But the time has only strengthened my original yearning to say yes.

A pounding on the door signals his arrival. I run across the room, throwing the door open with no caution.

"Babe," he admonishes. "Did you even check?"

I roll my eyes. "Nathan saw you arriving, so it was a safe enough bet."

He peers around me, seeing the place empty and bare. "Fuck, I'm glad you're coming home. I'll be able to sleep easier in my bed. Been worried as fuck about you."

I just shake my head. He'd assigned Nathan to me, he'd done all he could to keep me safe. Nothing was going to happen to me with that big man around. But that's Drew, and I doubt I'll ever change him, and don't believe I want to.

Then, at last, he kisses me deeply, with all the emotion he possesses. I lose myself in him, his lips moving across mine making me feel loved and cherished, even without hearing the words. *I've missed him.*

Nathan gives us a moment, then coughs. I pull away and swing around to see him smirking.

"Just wanted to know whether you want me to start loading up."

Drew plants a kiss to the tip of my nose before he answers the prospect, "Yeah. Just give me a moment and I'll help."

"I will too," I tell them, being quite capable of carrying boxes myself.

It's over quickly with the three of us pitching in. Soon the apartment is bare and empty, and in some ways it feels anti-climactic, with no sign that I ever lived here.

Drew interprets my expression as one of regret. Walking over, he smooths my hair back over my shoulders and his stare into my eyes is intense. "I'll spend my life making you happy, Amy. I won't allow you any regrets."

"I don't have any," I tell him, "and I don't expect to. I know what I'm doing is right. It's just that I've been in Phoenix for nine years, and now it's all gone in a flash."

He pulls me into him and holds me close. "I love you."

"I love you too," I give back completely and utterly. But then, I always have.

Then, with one last glance back at my old life, I step into my future.

Nathan's driving my car behind us, and I'm in the truck with Drew. It seems he can't bear to be apart from me, even if it will only take two hours.

"Anything new happen on the compound?"

He barks a laugh. "Fuck, yeah. Hawk's gone and knocked up Olivia."

"Oh, that's great." I'm really happy for Eli and his old lady.

He chuckles. "Tell that to Wraith and Drummer. They're horrified at the thought of being grandparents. Wraith even marched into the clubroom armed with a shotgun. Well, you can imagine what Drum thought when he saw him threatening his son. Thought there was going to be a throwdown right there and then until they came to their senses and realised they were on the same side. Hound took the shotgun away from Wraith, just in case. Fuck, everyone was doubled up laughing. Two F.O.Gs circling each other with their fists up."

I can actually imagine that, and the picture in my head makes me giggle. "F.O.Gs?"

"In the services a green recruit is called a Fuckin' New Guy, or F.N.G. So," he waggles his hand, "Fuckin' Old Guys seems to fit. They're like a bunch of unruly kids at times."

Even at Christmas I'd seen he was right. Drummer, Wraith, Peg, and Blade have had their responsibilities taken away, on their own account, as no one forced them out. But lightening their load means there's more time for their mischief.

"They give me fuckin' hell." He's shaking his head, as if there's something in particular he's recalling.

"Are you going to tell me what just went through your head?"

"Club business."

He turns and sees me raising an eyebrow, and grins.

"Anyway, Wraith got his way. Olivia and Eli are planning a wedding in just a few weeks."

"I'll have to ask Olivia for tips."

His head spins in my direction, and his hand reaches over to clutch mine. "Yeah?" He clears his throat and repeats firmly, "Yeah?"

"It was your idea," I remind him. "You said I had to be ready to plan a wedding when I moved back."

"Too fuckin' right."

He's beaming from ear to ear.

CHAPTER SEVENTEEN

Wizard

*U*ntil Amy was sat next to me, her belongings piled up behind her, and we were heading to Tucson, I'd found it was hard to believe this day would arrive when I'd be taking her home for good.

She'd been right to insist on giving us this month, not just so she could wrap up her old life in an orderly fashion, but it had also allowed me to fortify my impulsive decision in my head. But each day we were apart, I only wanted her more. I hadn't been wrong in anything I'd said. She's the only woman I have ever wanted.

I'm in an MC, I lived at the compound since I was fifteen. I wasn't quite seventeen when I lost my virginity to a sweet butt. The influences in my life showed there was nothing wrong in sleeping around, as long as both partners had the same expectation. The sweet butts, well they knew the score, but I made sure to be careful with the occasional women I had in town, moving on when they started talking about kids or a future. As far as I know, I may have caused regret but no hurt.

None of them had tempted me to stay around longer, and I hadn't seen myself committing to them.

Amy? Well, I suppose it's a story of a friendship changing to be something more. Had I fucked up when I'd so blatantly pushed her away from me? Many times I've regretted it over the years, but not enough to rectify it. I was married to my club, had no room for anything else until I'd reached the position I have. I'd have been unable to give her all of me if I'd gone to her sooner.

Not that the club means anything less to me now, but rather than thinking an old lady would distract me, now that I'm the prez, I know I need her to balance me. It's fucking hard being president of the Satan's Devils MC, and I know I'd give it my soul if nothing stopped me. Amy will remind me I'm a man at the times when I forget, and not just prez. The fact that we're more than compatible in bed is only the icing on the cake. I grin to myself as I think of the handcuffs I've bought for her especially, and will use when she's in the right headspace. My dick twitches as I imagine the woman beside me tied to my bed.

I adjust myself slightly and try to concentrate on driving, but thoughts keep invading my head as she seems happy to watch the passing scenery.

She's perfect, I adored her as a kid in her pigtails, admired her when she was in her teens. I was fucking terrified of her when she developed a crush on me, which was why I'd played my part in making her leave. I've missed her, all these years. Missed her easy company and simply knowing she was around.

I hate how it happened, that such dire events brought us together. But have to admit it was seeing her with Xander and realising I risked losing her to another man that made me pull my head out of my ass. It was her I wanted and needed by my side.

Now I'm bringing her home for good. Christ, I'm the luckiest motherfucker alive.

"Any news on Flint? Have you been looking for him?"

I'm still holding her hand, I squeeze it tighter. "You don't need to worry about him anymore."

"I know. Even if he knows where I've gone, he wouldn't be able to get on the compound. I'll be safe there."

She still worries about him coming after her. Should I tell her he's gone somewhere he'll never return from? The problem with that, and why I haven't told her, is that it comes under the heading of club business. If she doesn't know, she can never slip up and tell anyone, even if questioned by the cops in the unlikely event that they connect us with his disappearance. Just her *knowing* he was dead could bring trouble to our door. If I'd told her while she was still in Phoenix, it would have changed her behaviour, even if she hadn't opened her mouth. Even now she's coming home with me, she's still better off not knowing the truth. So I give her the only thing that I can.

"You don't need to worry about him anymore," I repeat, stressing each word.

Her body stills, and she looks quickly at me. I keep my eyes on the road ahead, and give her nothing more, not a twitch, not a flicker of my eyes.

"Oh."

She knows nothing. But she suspects. She's grown up in the club and while we keep the women out of most shit, that someone is there one day and gone the next doesn't need to be explained. My own father was killed and buried under Road's track. *God damn his fucking soul.* Well, in his case, God has little to do with it, he'll be Satan's problem instead.

Proving she'll make a good old lady, she changes the subject. "Are we going to live in your suite, Drew?"

"For now. But I've been thinking ahead, babe. Shooter's waiting for you to come up with ideas of the sort of house that you want, and we'll have it built at the top of the compound." I purse my lips, wondering if she had other ideas. "I'm the prez, babe. I'm afraid I can't live in town."

"I know that." She turns and lances me with that megawatt smile. "I was just thinking how perfect it sounds. I'll be living among friends. I had the best childhood, Drew, playing with all the other kids. There were so many aunts and uncles, and I want that for my own children."

Did I say she'd make a perfect old lady? Fuck, yes. For the second time, I'm discreetly adjusting myself as my mind goes to what I'd have to do to put my baby inside her.

As we draw closer to the compound, she sits up straighter, seeming to check out the distinctive saguaro that signals we're getting close.

"Happy?"

"Ecstatic," she replies. "This feels so right." She bites her lip, then expands, "It was also right for me to go away Drew, to experience life. I've got all my yearning for something different in my rearview now. While I loved the compound when I was young, as I grew up, with Dad and all his club brothers, I had no freedom to explore and be me." She pauses, and chuckles. "I'd probably still be a virgin if I'd stayed."

I think she's probably right. With her close, I might have been tempted to go after her earlier, and Heart would have never seen her as grown up. Probably would have earned myself a beatdown for going after a member's kid.

I turn onto the track and drive up it, the gates open automatically at my approach. I nod toward Butcher, and park outside the auto-shop.

"Wait, I'll come round. Hey, Butch. Get Rascal down here to start moving Amy's shit."

A sharp nod is all I get back from the prospect as I go to the passenger side, helping her to step down.

"Ready?"

Her cheeks flush. "So ready."

With my arm around her, I walk up to the clubhouse, trying to keep the grin off my face, knowing she doesn't suspect.

"Surprise! Welcome home!"

A huge banner stretches over the bar welcoming her back, balloons seem to have bred in the five hours I've been gone and spawned numerous offspring. All the old ladies, members, and the kids she'd grown up with are here.

Her reaction shows she hadn't expected it as she stands stunned, needing my hand to push her inside. That they'd spent so much time preparing for her to come home shows how much she's loved.

But Amy being Amy turns to look behind her, peering around me. Then she turns back. "Who are we expecting?" she asks with a big grin.

"You, you fuckin' idiot." Hawk walks up and gives her a hug. That she allows him to shows how much she's improved over the past month. "Had to celebrate Prez bringing back his bitch."

Amy's chest inflates as she pokes her finger into his chest. "That's the last time you call me bitch, Eli. Or I'll tell everyone that I've seen you naked and playing with your dick in the bath."

Now it's my turn to bristle, until my VP says, "I was three, Amy. Three." He turns around to face the assembled crowd, all of whom are chortling. "Three. What kid doesn't play with his dick?"

"What man doesn't?" Lady calls out, and the women crack up.

Well, we're men. Got to admit Lady's got a point.

But as I watch them laughing, I notice Heart's not here, neither's Drummer nor Mouse. I expected them to be the first to greet her.

"Prez!" comes a loud shout. "We got problems."

As I turn to Amy to apologise, she prods me with her hand. "Go be Prez. Oh…" She pulls me back and lifts her mouth for a kiss. I don't disappoint her.

Putting two fingers to my mouth I whistle loudly. "Church. Now."

A few good-natured groans, but brothers make their way into our meeting room, taking their seats without delay.

I don't waste a moment wanting to get back to Amy as soon as I can. So as soon as everyone's settled, I kick things off. "What you got, Mouse?"

"Archangel's escaped from prison."

A stunned silence meets his words. *Oh. Fuck.*

"Knew we should have fuckin' killed him." Drummer's fist meets the wood. Murmurs of agreement suggest he's not the only one thinking it.

"Feds caught up with him first," Wraith reminds him. "We didn't have a chance."

"How the fuck did he get out?" I ask Mouse, trying to focus on the present and not re-examine the past.

"They were moving him to a different penitentiary, seems he was causing trouble in the one he was in. He obviously had help from the outside and the prison van was hijacked. Guards killed."

"Christ, he'll have everyone gunning for him," Hound observes.

"Wretched Soulz have put a price on his head," Heart says. He nods toward Mouse. "Word came in just before you arrived on the compound."

"Think he'll be coming our way?" It's Shooter who asks.

"Would he be that stupid?" Peg's shaking his head.

"He might be." I turn to Hawk, willing to listen to his analysis of the situation.

He doesn't disappoint. "One, he might see the compound as a place to hide out, and try and coerce us into letting him stay, or, he might have discovered it was us who left evidence for the feds which allowed them to convict him. In which case, he'll want revenge."

"What do you want to do, Prez?"

My fingers drum on the tabletop as I give serious consideration to our options. "I want a meet with Raptor." He's the prez of the local Wretched Soulz. "Archangel can pull together a lot of manpower, we need to be united on our approach."

"Of course, he might not be coming for us," Hound points out reasonably.

But he might. So, we need to be prepared for anything.

Archangel's bad news. Even after all these years, white supremacists are still around, and Archangel was the leader of a group call the Real Americans whose extreme racist and patriarchal views are luckily only shared by a few. My view is they are just people with violent tendencies who would put any label on their activities, just to have a justification for the killing, stealing and vandalism that is their way of life.

"Hound, look at our security, see if we can beef it up. Mouse, keep your ear out for any mutterings on the dark web."

"Lockdown?"

Shit. Today of all days. I've brought my old lady back to the compound, and now we're looking at this.

"My view?" When Wraith lifts his hand, I raise my chin. "Check security, but we go on as usual. Archangel must be lying low. Feds will be all over Tucson due to his previous dealings here. Like you said, Prez, let's combine our preparations with those of the Wretched Soulz."

"I'll get word out to the other chapters." I give a grateful nod at Hawk.

I lean back in my chair, and put my foot up against the table, my hand going to my chin. I don't need anyone to tell me, it's the thinking pose Drummer used to employ, but it seems natural to sit like this in the top seat. "Okay. Business as usual while we try and find out if there's any real threat. One word he's heading our direction, we'll revisit this discussion. Don't want to restrict our lives for absolutely nothing at all. But everyone be careful, two up when you ride out. Keep your fuckin' eyes open."

"Can I go and party now?" whines Blade.

Hawk rolls his eyes. "F.O.Gs," he says with disdain.

And with that the tension is broken. Even Drummer cracks a smile.

CHAPTER EIGHTEEN

Amy

As I watch Drew walk away, leading his men into church, I feel a burst of pride for him. He wears the hat of the prez so easily, and it's easy to see everyone respects him.

I'm neither surprised nor upset he's had to put the club first almost the moment we stepped foot on the compound. As the first lady I know what to expect, I've watched Sam handle the role with ease over the years, and know I'll do well enough if I just copy what she's always done. Mainly be there for my man, understand he's got responsibilities, and allow him to do them without complaint. Drew will make time for me, his old lady, but the club will always take priority. I haven't grown up in an MC not to know that.

"You're really back for good?" Zane, Drummer's younger son asks me. He's studying to be a civil engineer and we all suspect he'll end up working with Shooter in the Satan's Devils construction business. When he'd first told me the course he was on, I'd joked were there any impolite engineers, and he'd just given me a look and a wedgy when I'd stepped away. Boys, it seems, never grow up.

We shoot the shit for a while, then Olivia joins us, and Zane makes himself scarce muttering something about women's talk when I ask her about her wedding. Sam and Sophie, mother and future mother-in-law of the bride come over and join us. Then it's all about dresses, cakes, receptions. Turns out Sophie had a quickie marriage, and Sam wasn't given a ring at all, so they're both enjoying the thought of a good affair by proxy. But when I see Olivia rolling her eyes, I suspect she just wants to get it done.

"When you marrying Drew?" she asks me.

"When he formally asks me," I reply with a laugh. "I'll say yes, and just want that ring on my finger. I don't want any fuss."

"You think Heart and Marcia will let you get away with that?"

"They won't have much choice." I think my gaining my independence means I'm stronger to stand up for myself. Olivia has never been away from the compound.

Sam's eying us thoughtfully. "Is this not what you want, Ollie? A big wedding, with all the trimmings?"

Asked a direct question, she shrugs. "I'm already his old lady, I don't need a bit of paper to commit to Eli."

She wouldn't, she's been his and he hers all their lives. Born a couple of months apart, they've remained inseparable.

Sophie leans forward. "Look, how's this for an idea? A joint wedding?"

Olivia's eyes widen. "Now that's a thought. What do you think, Amy?"

I chuckle. "Drew hasn't asked me yet."

"Well hell," Sam sits back with a grin on her face. "Now that would be freaking amazing. The prez and VP getting married at the same time. Will take some organising though, reps from all the other chapters will have to be invited."

I hadn't thought about the politics of marrying the top man, to me Drew's Drew, not Wizard. I suppose I'd been naïve thinking we could just sneak down to city hall. Drew's not only president of this chapter, but of all the chapters of the Satan's Devils MC. Other clubs may see it as an insult if they weren't invited to a big bash to celebrate. While I'm not particularly shy, the idea of standing up and being the focus of attention is a scary one. I glance at Olivia, Sophie's suggestion which means I'd be sharing the limelight starts to sound very attractive.

"Ollie," I start slowly, "*if* Drew asks me, then I think it's a good idea if he's happy to go along with it."

Sam claps her hands. "There's no if about it, so I think we go ahead with the plan. I'm happy to help, Amy," she nudges me, "I'm your proxy mom. That's if Marc doesn't mind me helping out."

"What am I helping out with?" Marc comes across and sits down.

"Ollie and Amy's weddings. They've decided to tie the knot together."

"He hasn't asked me yet," I mouth to my stepmom, rolling my eyes.

Marc ignores me. "That sounds like a great idea." She looks around. "Becca, Darcy, come over here. We've got weddings to plan."

"Hey, and I'm what, chopped liver? I am the mother of the bloody bride," Sophie mock glares at Sam.

Sam grins back. "Left to you we'd be drinking tea and feasting on crumpets."

Sophie shrugs, then chuckles. "Cucumber sandwiches— with the crusts cut off of course—and tea cakes and crumpets.

Oh, let's see," she starts pulling at her fingers. "Sausage rolls, scotch eggs…"

"I like those," Olivia remarks.

Sophie winks at her daughter, then continues, "Toad in the Hole, Bubble and Squeak. Oh," she's trying to keep a straight face, "we could have Spotted Dick."

Sam's eyes widen in horror, and she turns her back on Wraith's wife, leaning pointedly toward me. "I'll be in charge of catering," she says firmly.

When I stop wiping the tears of laughter from my eyes, I wave at them to calm down. "Before you get carried away, we can't just decide to have a joint wedding on our own. I think Drew and Eli might want a say."

"I'll want a say in what?"

So caught up in the conversation, I hadn't realised church was over. I go bright red as I try to summon up an answer for Drew. I mean, I'm assuming he meant what he said and that he's going to ask me, but we're only just starting out now on our life together. He might have meant plan a wedding a year in the future. Maybe being an old lady and old man would turn out to be enough. Drummer hadn't tied the knot with Sam, and they couldn't be happier or more devoted.

Olivia saves me, saying breezily, "We were just discussing *my* wedding arrangements."

When Drew raises an eyebrow toward me, I know he isn't convinced. But it seems he's got something else on his mind. When he holds out his hand, I take it, and he pulls me up and directs me over toward the bar.

When we get there, he whistles loudly, attracting the attention of everyone, and of Pussy, the sweet butt who now keeps herself busy generally helping out and keeping the younger girls in line as she doesn't have much call for her sweet butt services nowadays. Woman must be sixty, but her figure's still fine, though her face might have her story etched within the lines.

Pussy approaches grinning widely. She bends down and comes up with a brown paper bag.

I forget to breathe, guessing what it is, ready to make the commitment to Drew. We might have been talking about weddings, but me wearing his rag, the Property of Wizard patch on the back feels far more significant. *He owns me.* It's all I've wanted since I was six.

The room falls silent.

Drew stares at me, finally giving me the words I've wanted to hear almost all my life. "Amy, will you be my old lady, ride through life by my side?"

My legs feel weak. My voice trembles as I reply, "Yes. I love you Drew."

He doesn't have to say it back, his love for me shines out through his eyes as he slides the leather cut out of its wrapping and holds it out for me to put my hands through the arm holes.

It fits perfectly, a waistcoat designed for the feminine form. I see my stepmom watching carefully as I slide it on, making me suspect she had a hand in choosing it. For a moment I stand stunned, breathing in the strong smell of new leather, then I launch myself toward him. Drew swings me up into his strong arms and my legs go up and around his waist. I raise my face and our lips meet. He thoroughly ravishes me, as I devour him in return. Lost completely in our own little world it takes someone's shout to bring us back to the here and now.

"Get a room!"

I feel self-conscious as Drew lets me down, but the joy surrounding us dissipates that feeling fast. It's not as if PDAs in the clubroom are unusual, or, when it's only adults, sexual acts brazenly performed.

"Amy." Dad approaches, stealing me from Drew and hugging me tightly. "This is all I ever wanted, you here, on the compound." His eyes glisten as he adds in a whisper, "Your mother would have been so proud." I know he's referring to Crystal, my birth mother not Marc.

But Marc's next to hug me and give me her congratulations too.

Everyone starts getting drinks and filling their plates with the food from the delayed buffet, when Drew whistles loudly again, following it by shouting, "Quiet!"

Gradually voices end conversations, and everyone turns to stare at him. I do too, especially when he sinks to his knees in front of me.

My hand covers my mouth when he starts to speak, "Amy, babe, I love you. You're wearing my property patch. What do you say to making it legal?"

"Are you asking me to marry you?" I gasp out, knowing that's what he's trying to say, but slightly uncertain.

"You're going to make me say it, aren't you?" He smirks. Then, as though like magic, a gorgeous diamond ring appears in his hand. "Will you marry me, Amy? Do me the honour of becoming my wife?"

There's only one answer. "Yes!"

"Double wedding!" Olivia shouts.

"What?" demands Hawk.

"What?" echoes Drew as he spins around.

Then I notice a silent conversation between the prez and his VP, a variety of raised eyebrows and chin lifts. After a seemingly successful conversation, Drew turns away and takes in the men and women he's responsible for.

"Double wedding," he announces to a deafening roar, stomping of feet, and the sound of fists hitting tables.

The noise continues when he turns back to me, his eyes

blazing with desire and emotion. Then, I'm over his shoulder in a fireman's lift, as he rasps, "Can't wait any longer to fuck you wearing just that cut."

"That's my daughter you're talking about!" yells Dad, but he doesn't sound upset.

"Hey, I haven't had a drink or anything to eat at my own party!" But really, I couldn't give a damn. Just want to show him I won't always be making it easy for him.

He pauses, but only for the brief moment he needs to shout over his shoulder, "Sam. Save some food for us, will you? And make it a decent amount. We'll need it."

The room erupts again, this time with lewd comments, hints and suggestions, and roars of laughter.

I'm giggling as he carries me out, letting me slide to my feet as soon as we get outside the clubhouse. I stare down at the gorgeous ring that he slid onto my finger and relish in the feel of the cut across my shoulders. I don't think anything he could do could make me love this man more.

As we walk he whispers into my ear, "Fuck, babe, you wearing my cut's got me so fuckin' hard I don't know if I can wait until we get to the suite. Might fuck you up against the wall.

"Drew!" I swat at him. "What if my dad were to walk out and see us?"

"Well, walk faster then."

To teach him a lesson I break into a run, turning so I'm moving backwards and tease him. "Think you can keep up, old man?"

Well it appears it's game on. I give a scream as he launches forward, and turn and flee, but as fast as I run, on his longer legs he's quicker, and soon catches me.

Pulling me back against him, he whispers into my ear, "You can't ever run away from me again."

Mirth over, I respond seriously, "Don't make me ever want to."

In an equally sober tone he replies, "Tore my own fuckin' heart out doing that to you, Amy. That look on your face? I never want to see that again." He places his hand over his Satan's Devils' patch on his cut. "I swear on my life, on my club, that I'll never do anything to hurt you like that again."

I turn and wrap my arms around him for a moment, just breathing him in. Then, lightening the moment, I raise my eyes. "I thought we were going to fuck?"

He barks a laugh, takes my hand and pulls me the few more steps it takes to bring us to the door of his suite, then we're inside and he's pushing me into the room used as a bedroom.

"Clothes off, now," he rasps, his chest heaving as though he's having difficulty breathing, and I suspect it's not caused by the short run. "Put your cut back on."

When I do, I stand still as he walks around me. His hand briefly lingers on my ass, then I sense him standing beside me as though reading the words written on the back.

"You're mine."

"I'm yours."

His circuitous route around me is reminiscent of the inspection of a Dom, the difference is I don't need to stay silent and I can ask him, "Like what you see?"

"Fuck yes." He slides his hand under my cut, resting his palm on the skin of my lower back. "You're no stranger to tats, babe. So, I want mine right here. Where I can see it when I'm fuckin' you."

"Alright," I agree. The idea of having his mark on me makes me shiver.

Now he's in front of me, trailing his fingers down my chest, reaching my lower stomach, and then beyond. "Fuck, you're wet for me, babe." He closes his eyes and grasps his cock through the denim, momentarily looking like he's in pain. "I can't fuckin' wait babe, I'll make it up to you later, but now I want it hard and fast. On your knees on the bed now."

Another shiver goes through me at his dominant tone. It's exactly how I want my man to be. As I obey him, he strips off his clothes in record time.

"I want to take you bare. Put my baby in you. Have you walk down the aisle knowing you're carrying my baby."

Our courtship hasn't been conventional, our decision to be together for life fast, and we've both agreed we want kids one day. He's not rushing me, his hands are gently caressing my backside, but his touch is sensual not sexual, he's not trying to get me into a state where I wouldn't care.

"You don't want to be one-upped by your VP," I tell him, partly worried it's the truth.

"Nah, ain't anyone here but us babe. And do you think I'd give a damn about that? This is us, no kind of competition. I seem to have been waiting for you forever, now I have you, I want you in every possible way that I can."

I feel the same about him, so my reply comes easily, "Yes. Take me bare."

No one's ever fucked me without a condom before, not even Flint. Whether or not it's my imagination, it feels different, a heat that I've never felt before.

There might not have been foreplay, but I'm more than ready for him. As he pushes inside, he groans then warns me, "I'm going to fuck my old lady now."

He does. His powerful thrust shoves me up the bed. I use my hands against the headboard to steady myself, which allows me to push back, meeting him and being an active partner. The thought that I might conceive as a result of this coupling is raising my arousal, bringing me close before even I expect it. He applies just enough pressure to my clit, and I scream as my muscles pulsate.

"I'm going to come, babe. Say the word and I'll pull out."

"Put your baby in me," I cry. "Please, Drew," I beg.

If I thought he'd been giving me all he's got, I was wrong as he starts hammering in. His power, his movement, his complete control over me has me coming again as he roars, and shouts, "Take it, take all of it."

Is it really possible to feel cum spurting out of his dick? I'm certain I can feel it as he floods my pussy. He stays inside, leaning over my back, as though keeping his cum in me as long as possible will maximise the chances of success.

Drew, me, and a possible baby. I grin as wide as a Cheshire Cat.

"Drew?"

"Yeah, babe."

"I'm not sure it worked. Can we do that again?"

"Sure can, babe," he replies, and I hear the smile in his voice. He pulls out and turns me, I notice his cock is still semi-hard, or maybe thickening again. He stares down at me. "Do you trust me, babe?"

"Of course, I do."

He leans over to the bedside table and opens a drawer. He pulls something out and shows it to me. "I mean, do you *trust* me?"

My heart rate speeds up as I see the fur-lined handcuffs he's holding. I swallow hard, trying to tamp down the wave of panic which floods through me. Drew frowns, his face tightens, but I know it's not because of me.

Suddenly I'm angry. Furious at what Flint took away from me. I take a deep breath then say, "Drew, I'm scared, but I trust you. I want to try this."

"You sure?"

I make myself remember how much of a turn on it is to give a man total control. The pleasure that's within my grasp if I can be brave.

"I'm sure."

"One word," he reminds me as he lays a key down within easy reach. "All it takes is one word."

For an answer I hold out my right hand, unsuccessfully trying to still the shaking. Drew takes it in his and cuffs it to the headboard. Then I hold out my left, and he does the same there. I test the restraints; the handcuffs rattle but are very secure.

"Close your eyes, Amy." The tone he uses makes my lids fall automatically.

I hear a sound as though he's fumbling in that drawer again. Only seconds later I feel something caressing my skin which feels like fur. It moves so softly over my nipples I can feel them hardening, I arch up into the touch when it changes… to a rough feeling, like I'm being scratched by claws. My body sinks back into the bed to avoid it.

Then as quickly as that started, the touch becomes gentle again.

Oh God. Now something's tickling me. I tense again as something feather like trails down my body.

He continues, I don't know which he'll be using as he mixes it up, one thing than another. I try to keep up with the sensations, my body feeling more alive than it has for months. I start to clench my thighs together as my arousal increases. I'm going crazy. I want him.

As he keeps his sensuous torture going, I start to become desperate.

"Fuck me, Drew."

He chuckles and I hear something hit the floor. Then he's

pushing my thighs apart, and then, he's there. Right where I want him.

This isn't fucking, this is making love. He's not rough, his pace slow and deliberate. I open my eyes to see him staring down intently.

"Love you to the moon and all the way back," he tells me, the intensity of his words matching the concentration in his eyes.

"I want to touch you."

Immediately after the words are out of my mouth, he's leaning to pick up the key, and two snicks tell me I'm free.

I pull his head down and he obliges me with his lips, our kiss deep, but gentle. And all the time his cock is moving slowly in and out of my body.

"Drew, oh God, Drew, I can't…"

"Don't hold back babe. Come for me."

I do, bowing forward and clasping him tightly. I feel him stop breathing, then take in a deep breath of air, then he loses rhythm and lets go with a deep groan.

"I can't describe how much I love you, Drew. I knew I was coming home, but home's not the compound. Home is you."

Another kiss, then he pulls out and rolls over. "Fuck, Amy. The feeling of coming inside you with nothing between us, I can't describe how it felt. One thing's for fuckin' certain. I'm not sure six kids will be enough, because you're either going to be pregnant or we're going to be trying."

"Drew!" I punch his arm lightly, chuffed he's remembered my childhood conversations about the number of children I once wanted.

"Come here." He pulls me into his arms and wraps them around me.

I relax against him, feeling completely safe and secure. Feeling, as I told him, that at last I'm home.

I allow him a moment before I say, "Drew, I'm hungry."

"Best get my woman fed then."

Night has fallen, stars pepper the sky as we walk back down to the clubhouse. As I breathe in the fresh air, tinged with a hint of pine blown down from the tree-covered mountains, it hits me again. *I'm home. At last, I've come home.*

CHAPTER NINETEEN

Amy

Flopping back on the chair I wipe my hand over my face. "I thought I was going to have some time to just chill and relax while I was taking a break between jobs. Didn't expect to be caught up in a whirlwind of wedding arrangements." I mock glare at Olivia.

I've been back three weeks. Three glorious weeks during which I've only confirmed what I thought all along, how wonderful it was going to be living with Drew and being his old lady. Of course it's not all clear sailing. Learning to live with a man means putting up with his little quirks, or at least, trying to address them. While he treats his cut with the reverence it deserves, and that's always placed carefully over the back of the chair, used towels are allowed to drop where they fall, and yesterday's clothes don't seem able to find their way to the hamper.

I, on the other hand, am a neat freak, and the sight of someone's dirty socks littering the floor annoys me. The first few times it happened, I found myself cleaning up after my man, then I decided to stop tiptoeing around him, and had asked him whether he wanted a housekeeper or a wife? I may have threatened if it was a housekeeper he preferred, then keeping his dick satisfied wouldn't be part of the job.

I grin as I remember the shocked look on his face, then the glance around as if he hadn't noticed how slovenly he was.

"Babe," he'd said. "Prospects come tidy that shit up."

"Not anymore," I'd reminded him. Nathan bursting in once at an inappropriate moment had been enough. "You're not a single man any longer."

Well, since our talk he has been trying. Luckily. It would be very hard to carry out my threat.

On his part, my tidiness means some of his shit goes missing as I put it away in places he doesn't expect. He doesn't get cross, just frustrated as he tries to work out the logic of how I like things stored.

So far, despite our differences, there hasn't been one cross word between us. I'm falling deeper in love with him every day. And the sex? Not disappointing or boring in any way. Just last night…

A clearing of a throat makes me open my eyes to see Olivia grinning. "I don't want to know what you're thinking about, do I? I guess it's got nothing to do with weddings. Or at least, not the ceremony itself."

My cheeks burn as I give myself away. I sit forward. "So where are we up to?"

Ollie chuckles, but allows the diversion. "Had a response from San Diego. Lost, Dart, Alex and Tyler are definite yeses, along with Pennywise, Niran and Salem. Oh, and Scribe— remember he replaced Grumbler as the sergeant-at-arms last year?"

My brow creases. I hadn't known, can't even remember

meeting the man, but then, I've been away for many years. "He retire?"

"Yes," she nods. "Ill-health."

"It will be good to see Tyler." I smile. I have a vague memory of him having seizures in the clubhouse as he had a serious condition as a child. It wasn't until I was older and I was studying nursing I'd understood that he'd suffered from sickle cell disease. Alex and he had moved to San Diego where Tyler was able to have a successful bone marrow transplant. He's a patched member in the California club now.

"Colorado's turning out in force. Pal, Jayden and their brood are coming of course, Ella and Faith, Beef and Steph. Demon, Violet and all the kids. I think four other members said yes. Oh, and Hellfire and Moira."

Hellfire must be close to eighty now, but he's still riding, or just enough so he can stay a member of the club. I suspect he'll fly down to attend the wedding.

"Utah?"

She consults her notes. "No response yet. And none from Vegas but I don't doubt they'll be showing."

"Martha wants to know numbers for catering as soon as possible. But she's happy enough with the menu we want."

"She is coming herself, isn't she?"

I raise and dip my head. "She's getting some temporary staff in."

Both of us wanted our wedding meal to be catered for by the Wheel Inn, the restaurant the club has run for thirty or so years. Martha's worked there for all that time, though she must be nearing seventy, she doesn't want to retire. She was promoted to manager when Sandy, Bullet's old lady, stepped down.

"Mind if I interrupt?" The speaker obviously takes it for

granted we won't, as he draws up a chair, turns it around and sits with his arms folded over the back.

"We were busy," Olivia points out to him.

Lady waves his hand dismissively. "Planning your weddings. That's what I wanted to speak to you about."

Olivia sighs and puts down her tablet. "What do you want to say?"

He nods at her tablet. "You've not given yourself long to get everything sorted."

"Like we don't know that, Lady." I roll my eyes. "But we're getting there. We'll go to City Hall, then have the reception at Satan's Angels." Using the strip club isn't ideal, but all other venues are booked, or reluctant to host bikers. I'd overheard Blade wondering if Dart's old lady Alex could still weave her way around a pole, but Wizard had clipped him around the head and told him he'd be wise not to make that suggestion to her in person.

"Why not hold it here?" Lady suggests. "There's a lot of food to be transported, the kitchen here has recently had a makeover with all new shit. Martha can bring stuff ready-made and reheat it if necessary, or do it from scratch here."

"That was our first idea," I speak patiently as though to a child. "But the clubhouse couldn't accommodate everyone we expect." I'd been tempted to use that as an excuse to limit the numbers of attendees, but Drew had shot me down. To deny anyone who wanted to see their national prez tie the knot would be highly disrespectful.

Lady's not perturbed. "It's going to be mid-March." It is. Ollie didn't want to wait until she was more than three months pregnant, not wanting to waddle up the aisle. If she is showing, her bump will only be small, and she'll still be able to fit into a shapely dress. The thought makes me place my hand on my stomach, wondering if I'm pregnant as yet. It certainly wouldn't be for lack of trying.

"We're aware of the time of year," Ollie starts, with a look and a miniscule shake of her head in my direction.

I interpret it as we've got a lot to do, and Lady is being distracting.

"Weather is more likely to be sunny than not, rain extremely unlikely, and temperatures will be in the seventies at least." Lady waves his arm in the general direction of the window. "Get some more picnic tables and have it out back."

I bang my palm against my forehead. We'd been so focused on finding an indoor venue, the idea of holding it outside hadn't occurred to us. Sounds stupid, but there it is. I raise my eyebrows toward Olivia who's looking thoughtful. "That could work, if Wizard agrees."

"But what would we do about an officiant?" I ask. "Wizard doesn't like strangers coming onto the compound, and anyone qualified might not want to be part of a biker wedding."

Lady's grin splits his face. He places his chin on his arms and enlightens us. "That's where I come in."

"You? You know someone who'd do it?"

His grin widens. "Yeah. You could say that."

"Who?" Ollie asks fast.

He keeps us waiting for a moment, then can't keep quiet anymore. "Me."

"You?" My eyes narrow.

"Been looking into it. Can get ordained and all the proper paperwork fast."

"But you're not religious? How the hell can you get ordained as a minister?"

Lady chuckles. "There's an organisation that supports any and all religions. Doesn't matter which deity or whether it's one or a number. All you need to do is say you follow some such creed or other, and they'll ordain you."

Olivia's trying not to laugh. "But you'd need to lie. You don't follow any religion."

"Actually, I live my life damn near the principles of one," Lady growls, in a voice warning us not to judge. Again I raise an eyebrow, and he continues, "Satanism."

Now both of us crack up and laugh. He's a Satan's Devil after all. But my laughter fades when I notice he's looking quite serious.

"I'm an atheist for a start," he tells us seriously. "Satanists don't worship anyone, least not the Devil. But they do have a number of rules that I'm quite comfortable with."

"Such as?" He's caught my interest.

"Show respect in someone's home, and if someone's in yours and doesn't show you the same respect in return, treat him without mercy." He shrugs. "Sounds fair enough to me. Then there's don't harm children and don't kill animals except for food or if you're attacked." He grins again. "Then there's the one against making sexual advances unless you're given the mating signal. I could go on. Thing is, Satanism actually makes a lot of sense to me, it's less invasive than any other 'religion', and doesn't involve sacrificing virgins or praying to gods. It's more about do unto others as you'd want done to you, and live and let live unless people cross you."

Hmm. Interesting. I make a mental note to look more into it later, but concentrate on the real issue for now. "So you could really marry us?"

His shoulders rise and fall. "Yes. As long as I fill in the forms."

Olivia's looking at me, her head tilted slightly to the side. I answer her unspoken question. "I like, no, I *love* the idea, Ollie, if Hawk and Drew go for it."

"It would be one more thing ticked off," Olivia agrees. "Venue and officiant."

Thank God. Or rather in this case, Satan. I've been beginning to regret agreeing to this double wedding.

"I'll get the ball rolling." Lady winks as he stands, and nods as he leaves us.

"Think we've made progress at last. I'm calling it a day now." I start to stand, my hand covering a yawn as I do.

"Yeah, okay," Olivia says distractedly, typing something on her tablet.

Back in the suite, I sit down and start pulling some plans toward me. So far I've not bothered to look for a local job. Not because I don't want one, but when I'm not planning the wedding with Olivia, I'm working with Shooter on his new project, building Drew and my house. Of course, that's still in the early stages, but floor plans have to be agreed for a start, and earlier I'd received Shooter's latest reworking.

"How's it looking, babe?" Drew enters, goes to the fridge and grabs a beer. He holds one out to me, I shake my head.

"Better," I tell him. "I like the layout of the bedrooms now, they're mostly the same size." If we are blessed with a family, I don't want the kids to have unequal rooms. Drew initially asked for seven bedrooms, we'd settled on four. I really hope he was joking when he said he'd settle for extending and adding on more when we need them.

Coming over, he takes a look. "I like that," he says. "And the bathroom adjacent to the master suite is huge. We can get a nice big shower in there."

"And a tub," I say fast.

"You women and your tubs," he chuckles. Then, his eyes meet mine, and his smile disappears, he suddenly looks very serious. I cock my eyebrow, a silent question, my gut suddenly rolling. "Need you to do something, babe."

Now I do verbalise the question. "What?"

Reaching over to the table, he opens his tablet and clicks a few keys. He starts to read something for a moment.

"Drew, what is it? You're worrying me."

There's a glint in his eye as he regards me. "Oh, you should be worried, babe." But the smirk he can't quite keep off his face starts to widen. "It's nice that ass play isn't a hard limit for you."

What. The. Fuck?

"And that bondage is a definite yes."

"Drew," I start, wondering how the hell he knows that. Then say louder and indignantly, "Drew!"

My old man, soon-to-be husband, is a computer hacker. He can go where most others can't, and apparently, where most with a smidgeon of decency wouldn't. There are only two ways he could have found out my limits. One, by asking Xander who wouldn't give away my secrets, and two by hacking into my private details at the club.

"You didn't!"

His lips press together unapologetically. "I looked into this BDSM stuff babe. There's a lot of sense in it. People fill in lists of what they definitely like, what they might be up to trying and what's an absolute no way, not ever. Both partners know what the other likes and wants, so there's no confusion."

I go red, both with embarrassment and anger. "That part of my life is over, Drew." I feel a tear well in my eye. "If you wanted to know details of what I used to get up to, you could have asked." Would I have told him? I don't know, maybe not everything. But the fact he's gone behind my back to find out hurts. There's also something he's missing. "Just because it's on the list doesn't mean I actually tried it."

"So, there could be things you'd like to try but never got

around to?" As the penny seems to drop, he leans forward, "Mind telling me where ass play falls?"

I stand and start pacing furiously. "If you want to know, the closest I ever got to that was when Flint abused me. So that's now off the list…"

He's there, in front of me, stopping my forward motion. His hands clasp either side of my face, holding fast. "And that's why I wanted to know. Why I want you to update the list."

"What? I'm not going back to a club…"

"Don't you think it's knowledge I should have? What turns you on, what turns you off? What we can try? What might trigger you? I told you, babe, this makes sense. Not just when you're playing with anonymous partners who don't know fuck about you, but to your husband who wants to give you what you want." He's staring at me as I'm trying to comprehend what he's saying.

I go to speak, but he hasn't finished.

"You're adventurous, sexually, and fuck, I love that. So am I. This list," he waves to where he'd put down his tablet, "well, it gives an unimaginative fucker like myself some fuckin' good ideas."

My mouth opens and shuts like a fish on dry land. My traitorous body starts to respond to the idea of Drew and I trying stuff out, maybe things that are new even to me. Oh God, yes please.

He's waiting for some response.

Surprisingly I feel shy when I tell him honestly, "I think I'd like that."

Now I'm in his arms, being held tightly. "I'll never push you into something you don't want to do, babe."

I've played in many clubs with many men, but there's never been one I wanted to experiment with as much as the man holding me now. "I love you," I tell him, pouring my heart into those three words.

"I love you too," he says back, then, nuzzling my ear adds, "Any chance you'd reconsider putting ass play back on your 'like to try' options?"

I bat his arm, while thinking, with time and with Drew, there will probably be a lot of things I'll be more than up to trying in the future. Ass play? Hmm.

CHAPTER TWENTY

Wizard

When I bang the gavel, everyone stops talking and heads all swing in my direction.

I get straight down to business. "Worked like a fuckin' charm." I nod toward Lady, giving him credit. "Amy came to me and posed it as a suggestion she and Olivia had come up with herself."

Hawk grins widely by my side. "Ollie may have said Lady put the idea in their heads, and did I mind?"

"And you said?" I prompt.

My VP's mouth turns up further. "I ummed and ahhed for a moment of course, then said it was her day so anything she wanted was fine by me."

I bark a laugh. "Sort of the same as I did, VP."

I can hear Drummer and Heart's sighs of relief from here.

"Thank fuck," says Mouse.

Hound's also looking relieved. "So the Satan's Devils' wedding of the century will be held here on the compound." And he's the one to give voice to show how grateful we are to the man responsible. "Don't know how the fuck you sold it to them, Lady, but thank you."

Lady shrugs. "Ain't a thing. Wasn't hard, as I can charm the pants off any man, getting two girls to see sense was easy."

Joker's levelling a hard stare at him. "You, me. Going to have words later, *Brother.*"

Uncontrite, Lady raises his hand and ruffles the hair of the man sitting beside him. He receives a punch in the stomach if the oomph from his mouth and the way he's now creased over the table is any indication.

"Hey, Lady. You now a minister?"

As the man in question's still trying to regain his breath, Joker answers for him, "He is. Paperwork came through yesterday. He's just got to clear it with the Tucson authorities but that should just be a rubber-stamping matter."

For a second, I stare at the brother who'll be marrying me to my old lady. His new certification means he can officiate over funerals as well. Hopefully we'll have more call for his services with matrimony, but it's good to have a brother who can do such things.

"Hey, Lady. Your new religion got any practices Prez and the VP should know about?" Marvel leans forward and stares down the table.

Lady, straightening, spares a glare at Joker that promises retribution later, and then turns his attention to Marvel. "Like what?"

"Like having to have all the wedding guests witness the consummation? You know," he goes on to spell it out as if we hadn't already cottoned on, "watch their first fuck as married couples?"

"Whether it does or does not," I call out, loudly, "that will not be happening here."

Lady's answer isn't very reassuring. "Satanism's easy, Brother. Basically it's whatever you want."

Blade's looking from Lady to Marvel, then to me, and finally Hawk. Unfortunately he's too far down the table for me to attempt to stop him with anything other than my death stare which still can't be quite as good as Drum's. It doesn't have the effect I wanted, as he opens his mouth. "So, you're saying, we could all agree we want to witness them fuckin' to make the weddings legal?"

Hawk speaks up from beside me. "You want to retain what use you have in those hands of yours, Brother?" His voice is deceptively even. But it changes as he snarls, "If you do, then you can shut the fuck up. I'm not fuckin' my ol' lady for your entertainment."

"Spoilsports," says Rock who I thought would be on my side. "We could have had bets on who'd last longest."

Hawk happens to catch my eye at that moment and damn me, for a second I wonder who'd win and then pushing down my competitive streak fast, I bang the gavel. "No fuckin' in public. No baptism in blood, urine or whatever else you've a mind to come up with."

"I'd have a twenty on Hawk," Marvel mutters to Rock out of the side of his mouth.

What the…?

"Oh, Prez, your face." Drummer's pointing and doubling up.

"Why the VP?" Wraith wonders aloud.

"Age, of course…"

"Shut. The. Fuck. Up." I bang the gavel a few more times. God, they're going to kill me. "I'll move a motion to ban F.O.G.s from this table if you don't zip your fuckin' mouths shut."

My lips twitch as Drummer makes a show of pinching his finger and thumb against his lips and making a zipping motion. In all the years he was sat at the head of this table, I would never have expected him to be so relaxed as to do that.

"Right," I start, my voice loud enough to cut through the laughter. "Let's get back to why it's necessary to have the wedding here, behind our gates." I turn to Mouse. "Any more chatter?"

"Suspiciously quiet, Prez," my brother-in-law respectfully replies. "You found anything?"

He's right. I've been trying to find what I can too. Something like this needs both our minds on it. "Apart from that initial whisper two weeks back, nothing."

We'd picked up a reference linking two things together. Satan's Devils and Archangel. But whether a promise or a threat, we couldn't be certain. We're treating it as the latter.

The double wedding for me and my VP is a massive occasion, and Satan's Devils will be coming in from all chapters, all Prezes and VPs as well as other senior officers will be present. It hadn't taken more than a minute for it to dawn on us that should anyone want to damage the club, a direct hit on all the top men at once would be hard to resist.

"I'm in discussion with the sergeant-at-arms and enforcers of the other chapters," Hound puts in. "They're bringing extra members to beef up our security. I want the whole perimeter monitored with eyes as well as cameras before, during and after the festivities."

"Mouse and I have discussed putting in more pressure sensors, further out from the current ones. We'll need early warning if Archangel's managed to pull together an army."

"They don't even have to be loyal to the cause," Peg puts in, grumpily. "Or to be paid. Many would jump at the chance to act violently, don't need anything other than the opportunity to smash a few heads."

"Won't be smashing heads if Archangel's coming for us." Throttle stares at his dad. "It will be war. What they'll want is us dead."

"That's if Archangel knows we betrayed him," Rock says.

"You want to take a chance he doesn't?" Throttle shifts his gaze across the table. "I don't, and I won't."

"We act as though he's coming for us," I tell them, decisively. "While the women are making their wedding plans, we'll put our own in place. I want this place buttoned up so tight getting into Fort Knox would be a fuckin' piece of cake compared to getting in here." It's not just my family I'm protecting, but the whole of the Satan's Devils MC.

"Prez." At his voice, I lift my chin toward Drummer. He's completely in control of himself and serious as his steel-grey eyes meet mine. "Anything you need, you got it."

I nod. I'd be stupid not to use him for advice. He'd led this club for as long as I've lived my life. He's got a wealth of experience that I can tap into.

I lift the gavel, but before I bring it down, I stress one last time, "Everything we can do will be done. Hopefully the wedding two weeks tomorrow will go without incident of any kind." I pause for a second before adding, "And no public fuckin'. Well, not from the brides and grooms. The rest of you can do what you want to."

"Orgy!"

My eyes go to the heavens as the gavel meets the wood dismissing the meeting, but the sound is drowned out by the laughter greeting Marvel's suggestion.

Another week passes. The girls are so tied up with getting dresses organised, necessitating complications such as some remote coordination as Jayden's little girls are going to be bridesmaids, and her sons ringbearers. Like most men, I leave the finer details to Amy, and she seems content when I tell her to just give me a time and I'll be there. I did put my foot down at having to wear a tuxedo, but raised it when she suggested if I did, ass play might be back in the cards.

I'm not sure what bribe Olivia offered, and if it was anything like mine, I wouldn't want to know, but Hawk's also agreed to dress up—just for the ceremony. Soon as rings are on fingers and vows exchanged, we'll be back in cuts and jeans once again.

Trucks roll up to the compound almost daily as we stock up with beer and supplies for the food Martha's cooking here. Each vehicle is checked carefully, going to the extent of doing sweeps underneath to make sure no explosives have been brought in. Supplier's trucks are allowed no further than the gates, the prospects brought in to carry it from there.

Each day passing, I grow more tense with all the to-and-fro of strangers going on, and the bright part of my day is going back to my suite and Amy waiting for me.

"You're having a lot of meetings. Is everything okay?" Amy looks up as I enter.

"I'm the prez," I explain, taking advantage that she's only lived at the compound little more than the month. "It's my life, I'm afraid." I step closer to her. "You look tired."

"I'll be glad when it's all over." She doesn't need to explain.

"Thank you, Amy. I appreciate you going along with it." I know both she and Olivia would have preferred a small affair. So would I, but it's a good way to reconnect with all the chapters.

"It's part of being a first lady." She turns in my arms and snuggles into my chest. "I'd do anything for you, Drew."

As I would for her. I squeeze my eyes shut as I cuddle her,

praying to whatever deity would listen that I'll be able to keep her safe.

The activity continues for the next week and a half. More trucks arrive, new picnic tables turn up in pieces and need to be assembled so some men are kept busy helping the prospects do just that. Others work under the direction of myself, Hawk, Mouse, Hound and Throttle to make sure our perimeter is secured.

"Wizard." Drummer's holding two beers as he enters my office.

I take the one he offers and nod him to a chair.

"So, it all kicks off tomorrow. You doing okay?" His eyes watch me searchingly.

He knows only too well what it's like to sit in my seat. "I worry I'm missing something."

"You probably are," he replies, not very comfortingly. As my eyes widen, he continues, "All you can do is depend on the good men around you, and that they'll react when something comes up that you haven't planned for. It's bound to happen, but how many vets have we got? Tens, probably dozens with the other chapters involved. They don't forget their training, Prez."

He's right. "It's a heavy load."

"Warned you about that, Wizard. Warned what you were getting into. Gave you every bit of advice and information that I could over the years." He places his beer bottle on the desk. "Never think that that president flash doesn't sit well with you, Drew. You worked for it, harder than any man I know. In here," he taps his head, "you've got what it takes. Saw from early on you were going to be my successor, and now I'm proud as hell working under you."

I go to open my mouth, to admit my fears that I've achieved too much too early, but he raises his hand.

"You're going to have doubts. You're going to second guess every decision. Fuck, give every thought a third, fourth or fifth go around. Then at the end you'll issue your instructions, and they'll be the right ones for the club, even if they have unforeseen consequences. If they do, you'll deal with them. If you weren't such a man, you wouldn't be right for the job. Don't you think I had doubts? Worries I hadn't thought of every last thing? If you acted like you knew everything, had it all at your fingertips, I'd be worried about you. Doubting means you never stop thinking, and can change your path fast if that's what shit needs."

Drummer never gave any sign of self-doubt. That he's now admitting it makes me feel easier about my own fears.

"Just want this fuckin' wedding over," I tell him. "There's such a big risk with Archangel on the loose, and no one being able to track him down."

"But, there's also no noise about people assembling," he reminds me. "You and Mouse have your ears to the ground. Fuck, Cad, Token and Keys do too. And the Utah guys, of course." He gives a quick grin and a shake of his head. "In my eyes we've the best fuckin' technical experts right on it. If there was a whisper of gangs coming together of the size needed to take the compound out, then one of you would have found something by now."

"Don't forget it was tech that took him down. He may have learned his lesson and is doing it by word of mouth."

Drummer nods. "And that's why you've got it covered by assembling our own fuckin' army." He stands. "Go get some rest, Prez. Leave it to Hound now. Peg's lending him a hand. You've got the two best fuckin' sergeant-at-arms in the business, so you go rest sound. Tomorrow, the other chapters will arrive and we'll go into defence mode with the plans that we can recite in our sleep. Day after you're marrying your ol' lady. All you got to do is dress up and say your vows, leave everything else to us. I'm not going to let you down, Wiz. I know I don't have rank anymore, but if something goes down while you're otherwise engaged, I'll get it handled." He gives me a sharp look. "Not stepping on your toes, Prez. Just lending a hand."

CHAPTER TWENTY-ONE

Wizard

The next day, I find I have a lot to be grateful to Drummer for. Visiting Prezes, VPs, officers and the members they bring along start to arrive from late morning onwards, and they all want a part of me. Those helping with security peel off with Hound, Peg and the other sergeant-at-arms, while those here just for the wedding want to socialise. Deciding I can't be in two places at once, I find I'm handing keeping the compound safe into the capable hands of Drummer, and he slips out of retirement and into his old role seamlessly.

Everyone defers to him out of respect for his previous rank, and when he says jump they still ask how high.

Amy's proving herself as a great old lady, though she's run ragged splitting her time between greeting newcomers, catching up with old friends, and making sure there are sufficient places for people to sleep.

Officers, we're making sure we've got beds for, members will be sleeping on cots or floors. Somehow, Sam and Amy have come up with a plan to house everyone, and so far the arrangements haven't caused complaints.

By early evening, everyone who's coming in has arrived, and the dinner, catered for by Martha, has been hijacked by being laughingly referred to as the rehearsal dinner. Lady cracks us up by appearing in the clubhouse wearing a black robe and Satanic mask. He makes Hawk, myself, Olivia, and Amy stand up and approach him, and takes us through all sorts of Satanic rights he says we'll be doing tomorrow.

At one point, the clubhouse fills with green smoke as he throws some concoction into a small fire in a cauldron. The coughing eventually dies down after the door and all the windows have been opened.

Then he and Joker do some sort of dance involving waving rubber chickens around, slapping each other with them. I notice Maya with her head in her hands, but her shoulders are shaking.

"Hey, Lady. Where's the fuckin' taking place? In here, or..?" shouts Marvel.

"I'm putting fifty on the prez!" yells someone, I think it's Shooter.

I preen for a moment, glad there's one person who's got faith in me, before coming to my senses fast. "There's going to be no fuckin!" I yell out.

"What's this about fuckin'?" I turn to greet Hellfire. He's still a striking figure for a man of his advanced years, his wife too, though she seems a lot shorter than I remember.

"Yeah," Amy tugs my arm and repeats, "What's all this about fuckin'?"

Olivia's by her side and glaring, as Hawk replies, "Believe me, you don't want to know."

"Prez? VP? Got a minute?"

Mouse is waving from across the room. I waste no time going to him, Hawk right there beside me.

Mouse indicates his office. Once inside, he fast lays out what he's picked up. While he talks, my hands clench. When he's finished, I stand, kick over a chair, and swear loudly. "That's it. The wedding is off."

"We can't just send everyone home," Hawk says reasonably. He indicates the stash on Mouse's desk, and, at my brother-in-law's nod, unusually for the VP, starts to roll a joint. A sign his voice might be calm, but he's just as worried as me. "Think Prez. If they're already assembling, then anyone riding could be picked off on the road."

Yeah. He's right. "Best they all stay here. But no wedding. I want all eyes focused on where a threat might come from."

"Know you're worried, Wiz, but all I've heard is people grouping together. Not even a mention of Archangel."

"But white supremacists, yeah?" At Mouse's nod of confirmation, I carry on with my thoughts. "Timing's too coincidental to ignore, and it's happening in Arizona?"

"Tomorrow," Mouse affirms.

I bow my head, then indicate Hawk. "Thoughts, VP?"

He rubs the side of his nose, then his lips press together. Finally he speaks, "We get Prezes, VPs and SAAs briefed tonight, they can start spreading the word. No excess drinking tonight or tomorrow, everyone stays sober, or those that haven't gone past that point yet. Everyone to be on their guard."

"I've already gotten the scanners working and the exclusion range for drones is in place. It's impossible to fly something in."

"We've got our own up?"

Mouse points to the screens. "Monitoring them now. Got Nathan and Butcher with their eyes glued to these and the other cameras in the control room. With the sensors and laser beams, and info back from the drones, nothing should be able to get close without us knowing." Thank fuck we've modernised our security over the years.

Hawk takes over again. "We'll get married as planned. Have the fuckin' reception, but do it in shifts so we've got as many men as possible armed and ready to take on whatever we might have coming for us."

I weigh my options. There's no benefit in cancelling the wedding now. Even sending people home tomorrow could be dangerous and leave me weakened without additional support here. If we're in Archangel's sights, I'm fucked whichever way I look at it. My only option is to keep everyone here and put up a united front.

I roll back my head and stare at the ceiling. This is all my fault. Should have been happy with Amy just as my old lady, or insisted we wait to tie the knot until we knew what trouble we were facing. Let Olivia have her way and just sneak off to the courthouse. But there's nothing to be gained by cancelling.

"I'll be here all night," says Mouse. "I'll keep my ear to the ground, see if there's anything more I can pick up.

"I'll stay…" I start to offer.

"Nah," he shakes his head, making his long hair fly around his face. "It's your wedding day eve. Yours too, Hawk. Go fuck your old ladies, and get some sleep. Rely on your brothers for once. First sniff of trouble, and I'll let you know."

How the fuck will I sleep? How the fuck do I keep this from Amy?

As we leave Mouse's office, ready to start gathering the top officers together, quietly and discreetly so the women aren't spooked, Hawk shows he's on the same wavelength. "Olivia's going to be able to tell something's up."

"I feel you, Brother," I tell him. "Just say it's pre-wedding nerves."

He shoots me a look, I shrug. Our women know us better than that.

Word quietly spreads around so soon the people we need are headed for our meeting room. Once inside, I let them in on what's going on, and what we fear is coming for us.

After I've had my say, it turns out my way of thinking which side is up is agreed on by everyone. The meeting with the prezes and their ranking men was surprisingly quick, and no one wanted to abandon ship and find safer havens. A warmth started to grow inside me as the reason for me being part of the Satan's Devils MC was demonstrated yet again. Doesn't matter what chapter we're from, the patch we all wear on our cuts unites us. God help Archangel if he thinks he can take us on. All he's got are men brought together by a common desire for mayhem and violence, what I've got is a loyal family at my back who'll stand shoulder to shoulder to protect each other and their way of life.

After our short meeting, Demon has the last word, though I doubt he expected it to ring out so loudly in the sudden lull in conversation. "Some things never fuckin' change, do they? We're always helping Tucson out."

His words break the tension. Truth be known, we help the other clubs just as much as they help us, but there was a time in the past when we had to ask for more than our fair share of support. After Beef initiates a final shout of, 'Ride Satan's Devils, Satan's Devils ride together,' the meeting breaks up.

I try to find Amy, but I can't see her around.

"If you're looking for your old lady, she's gone to bed." Hound's standing beside me. "You should go up too." As I open my mouth, he says, "Know you're the prez, but you'll have enough to deal with tomorrow. There's nothing to suggest they'll even be thinking of coming for us tonight, so you need to take the opportunity of having some downtime. We need you fresh and thinking straight in the morning."

"Should we have gotten the women out?" I ask him, wondering whether there's something I've missed.

"Leave them unprotected? Split our men to protect them?" Hound shakes his head. "We can circle the wagons better here, Wiz."

For a second, I wish Amy was still living in Phoenix. Was I selfish making her my old lady? Should I have left well alone and not interfered between her and Xander all those months back? No, I can't think like that because I am a selfish motherfucker. Danger coming for us or not, I want her here.

Hound's right. I've got to at least try to switch off and recharge my batteries. Tomorrow's going to be one fuck of a day, and not in the way I'd originally hoped. Now I'm just praying we'll all be alive at the end of it.

I clap my hand on his shoulder. There's no need for words.

Most of the women have gone by now. The sweet butts are around, doing what they can to keep visiting single men happy, at least they're smiling while they work, having a large pool to choose from tonight.

Now word about the danger heading for us has spread, as I make my way across the crowded clubhouse, instead of ribaldry about my forthcoming nuptials, men just offer me chin lifts, or words of encouragement. A few clasp my hand and tell me they've got my back. I can't help wondering if any who I bumped shoulders with may not be alive come tomorrow night. Or even, will I instead of being married by a Satanist, end up face to face with Satan?

I enter my suite, the prez's hat never having felt so heavy on my head up to now.

Not yet in bed, Amy's standing at the doors looking out at

the starlit sky, only a bedside light illuminating the room behind her. She turns as I close the door.

"What's going on, Drew?"

"We're getting married tomorrow."

"It's more than that. Are we in danger?"

"Amy, you know I can't tell you that." I lean my head back against the door. "We don't *know* anything. But we're taking precautions in case."

"Is it my fault?" she asks. "Should I never have agreed to have the wedding on the compound? Has bringing everyone here put us at risk?"

"Fuck no." I decide to tell her a little of the truth. "The compound is the easiest place to defend. Should there be any danger, that is."

The thoughts in my brain are bouncing this way and that, going between wanting to make my old lady happy and give her a day she'll never forget for all the right reasons, and trying to recall whether I've done all I can to keep all the men I'm responsible for safe. Not just my Tucson brothers, but those who wear Satan's Devils' cuts and who tonight are under my roof, together with the property they've brought with them.

I feel my shoulders slump under the weight and try to draw them back up. But watching her, I see her straighten her back, then she comes over. "Can I take this off, or are you going out again?"

"I'm staying here with you."

She checks, then at my nod of permission, removes my cut, taking as much care of it as I do myself. Then she removes my tee, but I stop her when she gets to my jeans.

"I'm leaving them on."

"In case you're needed?"

"In case," I agree.

She leads me to the bed. "Just hold me tonight, Drew. Tomorrow, let me know if there's something I need to do."

Fuck, but she's going to make a fucking good first lady. No demands to know what's going on, no fussing about anything at all. She's just giving me an oasis, a place of safety and calm, an escape from the chaos around me, and the turmoil in my head. Surprisingly, I sleep.

I'm shooed out of the suite almost immediately upon waking. The girls have got a fuck load of prep it would seem to get themselves and Jayden's kids ready. Amy will be heading up to Drummer's house as that's where they'll be dressing and having hair and nails sorted.

I go immediately to Mouse. He yawns when he sees me and stretches. "Nothing more."

I didn't even have to ask him.

I go back out into the clubroom.

"What time's the ceremony?" Red, still president in Vegas, calls out.

"Noon," I reply.

He nods and goes back to discussing things with his crew who are standing around him.

"Fuckin' hate this." Heart comes over. "Amy and Olivia's special day and it's being ruined."

"We'll do our best to make sure they enjoy it, a wedding to remember." Wraith comes across.

I just hope it's because their day was special, and not that it all went wrong.

Men wander in coming to fill their stomachs having been on guard duty during the night, others go out to take over. Everyone seems to know what they're doing.

"Just checking it's going ahead," Lady comes across to ask. His joking demeanour totally missing.

"We're doing this," I confirm. "I, er, don't rush it, Brother.

The girls deserve…"

"I know," he says. "I'll give them no cause for worry."

I'm rushed off my feet, making sure everyone's where they should be and all know what they should be doing. Most important of all, those who should witness our wedding organised with replacements for when they come back here at noon.

It seems no time has passed at all when a voice sounds from beside me. "Better get ready, Prez," Hawk advises. "It's eleven-thirty now. We need to get changed and be there before our brides turn up."

I allow myself a moment to remember why we're here. Bumping his arm with my fist, I ask, "We really doing this, Brother? Getting hitched?"

"We're really doing this." His smile is broad as he replies.

"Prez! Prez!" I'm halfway across the room when Mouse calls me back.

I'm at his side in a flash. "What you got?"

"A location. Flagstaff."

My eyes crease. *Flagstaff?*

Mouse talks to me like I'm a kid, saying each word carefully. "No idea of the target, but Flagstaff's fuckin' hours away. If they are assembling there, there's no way we'll be taking a hit."

It still takes a moment for it to sink in. Other men are faster and there are hollers and shouts. "We keep security tight," I tell Mouse, and Hound who's come up, my brain unable to process the threat may be removed. "Don't want to let down our guard."

"We won't, Brother," says Lost and Red together. "But some of the pressure's off and isn't it about time you went and got hitched?"

Well, thank fuck. As I realise the pressure has indeed lifted, my shoulders already feel lighter.

Hawk puts his hand on my back and pushes hard. I stumble forward, but turn around to him and bark a laugh. Me and my VP, getting married. Who'd have believed it?

We make quick work of stripping our clothes off and putting on those hated tuxes, Hawk's grimace matching mine. Then we're ready to go.

Outside, the yard has been decorated with a normal wedding arch. But there's not much else normal about it. Instead of white or pink roses, it's adorned all in black flowers interspersed with Harley badges and patches. Chairs, picnic tables and benches are a sea of black leather, with the women all wearing their property cuts, except for the youngsters from our chapter who are family but not otherwise associated with the club. Hawk and I go to stand at the altar, Hound's my best man, Throttle is Hawk's. Together we wait.

Joker says in a loud aside, "I don't think the brides are going to turn up."

I give him my middle finger.

Then Lady appears. Today he's not wearing a mask, but is dressed all in black with a black satin robe, his long hair tied back with a black velvet bow. His expression is serious as he carries a solemn looking tome, placing it on a lectern. I can't resist leaning in for a closer look. Well fuck me, it really is a Satanic bible. I crack a smile and nudge Hawk, who stares at it then laughs.

Then music starts playing.

I turn to see our brides.

Fuck me, but I've only got eyes for Amy. Both girls are in white, but that's about as much as I notice about Olivia, I can only focus on the woman who's mine. Her dress is short, just shy of indecently so. The colour might be virginal, but not the style. It suits her perfectly.

The ceremony itself passes in a blur. Lady takes his job seriously, taking us through our vows. We exchange rings, say our I dos, and then I'm married to Amy and Hawk's wedded to Olivia.

"Are you okay?" Amy asks, as we manage to get a moment to ourselves. My face is aching from all the smiling and my back is starting to sting from all the congratulatory slaps I've received.

I breathe out deeply. As the hours have passed, Mouse has kept checking, but the news channels are reporting that a government office was torched up in the north of Arizona, and Mouse had caught wind that the same voices he'd found arranging the meets were now taking credit for doing so. Seems we were worrying for nothing at all. The danger having receded has obviously made me happier, but I've still lingering thoughts of what could have happened had we been the target. Now with my old lady to protect, that beefed up security will become a permanent arrangement.

"I'm fine," I tell her at last.

Hawk approaches with his arm around Olivia. "We're going to blow this joint for a few." He catches my eye and winks.

Which seems like a fucking good idea. Maybe being deep inside my woman will help me relax.

"Think we'll do the same, brother." I grab hold of Amy's hand.

But as we start to walk away, it's Dollar who shouts out, "Someone starting a stopwatch?"

Hawk and I stop. I straighten my back, waiting.

"I'll have thirty on Wizard." That's fucking Beef.

"Fifty on Hawk." Bullet's a fucking traitor.

"Okay," says Rock. "Last one back obviously fucked the longest."

Hawk turns to me with his eyebrow raised. *Game on.* I grin back. Then, as we turn away, I have a better idea. I wait until we're out of sight. "When you've er finished, give me a call. We'll go back together."

"Get the last laugh." Hawk catches on and gives me a salute.

"What was that all about?" Amy asks, as I stand trying to work out how to get that dress off her.

"Who can fuck the longest, me or Hawk? Or who can get off first?" I realise I'm not quite certain what makes who the winner.

"What?" she spins around. "That's awful."

"Babe," I tell her, seriously, "it could have been worse. They wanted to watch."

She stares, frowns, then chuckles, then is outright laughing. Her hand covers her mouth. "Oh my God," she giggles, having difficulty getting out the words. "I can just imagine two pale white humping asses while the brothers stand around giving marks."

"And that's the last time you're ever going to have thoughts of Hawk's ass. Even if it is when he was three years old," I warn her.

I give up with the dress, simply bend her over the bed, whip it up and her panties down, rip my tuxedo pants off, and thrust my cock into her wet and ready cunt.

She's mine. In the eyes of the club, and in the eyes of the law.

Mine.

Forever.

My balls are drawing up, but I can tell she's not quite there yet. I slide one hand up and wrap it around her throat, she immediately tenses, and her muscles clamp on my cock.

"Drew," she gasps, "What…?"

"I read your limits list, remember?" I growl into her ear. Light choking was definitely on the plus side.

And fuck me, it works. She convulses and ends up coming first. I'm only seconds after, her clutching cunt meaning I've no chance to hold back.

As I lean over her trying to recover my breath, my brain seems to have one thing and one thing only on repeat.

Mine.

Forever.

Eventually I roll over onto my side, pulling her into my arms. Her body is trembling, and for a moment I'm worried, until a giggle escapes.

"Babe?" While I'm making my silent solemn vows to her, she's starting to laugh.

"Oh Drew, I'm just thinking how much I love you."

That's better, I think to myself.

"And how the first time I saw you in your bed you were wearing that Santa hat."

"It worked, didn't it?" I start chuckling with her.

As she turns her head for a kiss, I oblige. When we come up for air, she says, "I had no expectations when I came home for Christmas, never believed I'd find the love of my life on Christmas Day. I even feared I'd never want another cock near me."

"You won't ever have another cock near you, babe. Only mine. And I'll keep that Santa hat and wear it each Christmas."

She giggles again. "You do that, Drew."

"Just promise me one thing," I kiss her again, then continue, "it remains our secret."

I'm the prez of an outlaw MC for fuck's sake.

INK'S

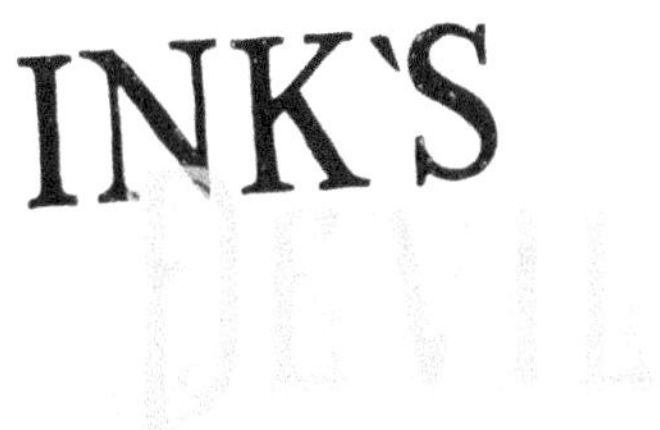

Ink

The tall girl with the blue hair intrigued me, I'd never been with anyone who could match my height. It was only going to be for one night, but it wasn't enough.

It's not forever, I'm not that kind of man.

She's a citizen and not someone to be pulled into our underworld.

Except, I didn't pull her in, she was already there.

She should be in jail, not me.

Beth

I saw Ink and wanted him. I couldn't let myself fall for him, so decided to enjoy it while it lasted.

My life was normal, uncomplicated, until my estranged brother dumped me in a mess. A fiasco which ended up with Ink taking the rap.

He wouldn't be in jail if he didn't care.

But whether he does or not doesn't matter if he's going to be there for the best part of his life.

It's all my fault

Devil's Dilemma (Colorado Chapter #4)
Coming Soon
Ink's Devil (Colorado Chapter #5)

Note 1:

Each book can be read as a standalone, but to get the best reading experience for the Satan's Devils, read the books in the order above.

Note 2:

While the Blood Brothers series is completely separate to the Satan's Devils series, there is some crossover. Turning Wheels continues the story of a minor character who appears in Second Changes, and some characters appear in both series.

OTHER WORKS BY MANDA MELLETT

<u>***Blood Brothers – A series about sexy dominant sheikhs and their bodyguards***</u>

Stolen Lives (#1) Nijad and Cara

Close Protection (#2) Jon and Mia

Second Chances (#3) Kadar and Zoe

Identity Crisis (#4) Sean and Vanessa

Dark Horses (#5) Jasim and Janna

Hard Choices (#6) Aiza

<u>Satan's Devils MC - Arizona Chapter</u>

Turning Wheels (Blood Brothers #3.5, Satan's Devils #1) Wraith and Sophie

Drummer's Beat (#2) Drummer and Sam

Slick Running (#3) Slick and Ella

Targeting Dart (#4) Dart and Alex

Heart Broken (#5) Heart and Marc

Peg's Stand (#6) Peg and Darcy

Rock Bottom (#7) Rock and Becca

Joker's Fool (#8) Joker and Lady

Mouse Trapped (#9) Mouse and Mariana

Blade's Edge (#10) Blade and Tash

Truck Stopped (#11) Truck & Allie

Satan's Devils MC - Colorado Chapter

Paladin's Hell (#1) Paladin and Jayden

Demon's Angel (#2) Demon and Violet

Devil's Due (#3) Beef and Steph

Devil's Dilemma (#4)

ACKNOWLEDGMENTS

This story came about because of you. That's right, you the reader.

When I wrote Truck Stopped, I let you into a glimpse of the future. So many readers enjoyed these 'flash forwards' and asked me to write a second generation series. At the time I said no. It was not in my plans, and would never be. Mainly because I like to get all my facts and background right, and how could I predict what the world would look like in twenty years' time? Obviously electric bikes would come to the fore, and I can include those, no problem. But what about things like phones? Would we all be using watches, or have a device implanted in our ears and we just think a name and contact with them?

Fanciful? Maybe. But the changes in my lifetime have been incredible. When I went to university, I took a computing course. The computer took up the space of a whole room and hadn't anything like the power and capability of the phone I carry around. Twenty years ago I would not have predicted I'd have a car that parked itself. In 2040 I suspect we'll be riding around in vehicles without having to touch any of the controls. To do justice to a book based in the future, I thought I needed to come up with a sci-fi world, and I wasn't prepared to do that.

No second generation books. No way.

But Amy had different ideas and became lodged in my head. It started with an image of a grown up woman racing home for Christmas to put the ornament that Heart had bought so many years ago onto the Christmas tree, just like she'd always done since she was three. It was that point I knew I was going to write her story. But I'd keep it short and just write a novella.

I have to admit to being a complete failure. I couldn't keep to my resolve not to write a second generation book. Although shorter than the books in my other series, Amy's Santa is too long to be called a novella. Lastly, well, if you've read the book, you'll know I've set it up for more in the series.

I've cheated with the world, and apart from electric bikes, haven't tried to predict the future, so I apologise for that, but hey, it looks like you're getting a new series. I must admit I love the F.O.G.s and can't wait to watch what they get up to.

Just one word about something I included in the book. Satanism is not devil worship, in fact it's not worship of any deity at all. I wanted Lady ordained as a minister, but couldn't see him as traditionally religious at all, so I did some research. As soon as I read about Satanism, it fitted him totally. It's not sinister at all in case you're worried. And, of course, as they're all Satan's Devils it was a no brainer once I looked into it.

So now the thank yous.

It's the first time I've worked with Wicked Cover Designs, and I hope, like me, you love the cover for Amy's Santa. Thank you Dar, I've enjoyed working with you.

Maggie, what can I say that hasn't already been said? Love

your professional approach, your responsiveness, and simply exchanging ideas and thoughts with you. You're everything I could hope to have in an editor. So glad I found you. Or was it the other way around?

Melanie has again done a stellar job on the proofreading. Producing books is not just sitting down writing, it's the process of publication too. To get the books into your hands (or onto your e-readers), ducks have to keep to their places in the row. Having a team of people who meet (or exceed) deadlines keeps everything running smoothly and my stress levels low. So, thank you Dar of Wicked Smart Designs, my new cover designer. My grateful thanks to Maggie, my editor, who is simply amazing to work, and to Melanie who has again done a stellar job on the proofreading. I really appreciate having such a professional and responsive team behind me.

Special mention must go to Danena, who once again tore an early version to shreds. Danena is great picking up on how people react in certain situations. Her observations really help shape the book. Love you, Danena, and can't thank you enough.

As normal I have to thank all my beta readers. Sheri, you always find something everyone else has missed. Alex, your input is invaluable. Same goes to all the team, Tami, Terra, Zoe, Nicole and of course, my husband, Steve.

I'd like to give special thanks to my PA, Tracy Wood. Tracy's had a hard time lately, but she's not stopped pimping me, keeping my page up to date and interactive, producing teasers and banners for Facebook etc etc. Words can't express how much I owe this woman who works tirelessly in the background for me.

I have left the most important to last, all you readers who take a chance on buying my books, and then telling me how much you enjoy reading them. My whole day can be boosted by one message, one comment or one review. You may have no idea how much it spurs me to write more.

The best way of telling me is to leave a review on whatever platform you read on, or anywhere you can review. I read and appreciate every review good or bad. Reviews help authors make sales, sales allow authors to pay editors, models and photographers, cover designers etc, and put food on the table.

What's next? Ink's Devil was to be my next book, but Amy had other ideas and leapfrogged over him. Don't worry, Ink's on his way and should be with you by the end of 2019.

As this is a Christmas book I should send my best seasonal greetings to everyone. However you celebrate (or not as the case may be), have a wonderful Christmas and best wishes for the New Year to you all. May the New Year bring everything you hope for.

Love

Manda

STAY IN TOUCH

Email: manda@mandamellet.com

Website: www.mandamellet.com

Sign up for my newsletter to hear about new releases in the Satan's Devils and Blood Brothers series.

Facebook reader group: https://www.facebook.com/groups/mandasbadboys/

facebook.com/mandamellet

twitter.com/manda_mellett

ABOUT THE AUTHOR

Manda's life's always seemed a bit weird, starting with a childhood that even today she's still trying to make sense of, then losing her parents in the late teens. Going from the tragic to the bizarre, who else could be unlucky enough to have had two car accidents, neither her fault, one involving a nun, and another involving a police woman?

There isn't enough space to list everything that's happened to Manda, or what she's learned from it. But by using the rich fabric of her personal life, psychology degree, varied work experiences, and amazing characters she's met, Manda is able to populate her books with believable in-depth characters and enjoys pitting them against situations which challenge them. Her books are full of suspense, twists and turns and the unexpected.

Manda lives in the beautiful countryside of Essex in the UK, the area's claim to fame being the Wilkin's Jam Factory at nearby Tiptree. She can usually find jars of jam which remind her of home wherever she goes. As well as writing books and reading, Manda loves walking her dogs and keeping fit. She lives with her husband of over 30 years, who, along with her son, is her greatest fan and supporter.

Manda is thankful that one of the more unusual, and at the time unpleasant, turns her life took, now enables her to spend her time writing. Confirming, in her view, every cloud has a silver lining.

Photo by Carmel Jane Photography

www.ingramcontent.com/pod-product-compliance
Lightning Source LLC
Chambersburg PA
CBHW070620170726
48291CB00003B/810